A STREET GIRL NAMED
DESIRE

DESIRE

A STREET GIRL NAMED
DESIRE

A NOVEL

TREASURE E. BLUE

ONE WORLD | BALLANTINE BOOKS | NEW YORK

A One World Books Trade Paperback Original

Copyright © 2007 by Treasure E. Blue

Published in the United States by One World Books,
an imprint of The Random House Publishing Group, a division
of Random House, Inc., New York.

ONE WORLD is a registered trademark and the One World
colophon is a trademark of Random House, Inc.

ISBN 978-0-345-49328-6

Library of Congress Cataloging-in-Publication Data

Blue, Treasure E.
A street girl named Desire : a novel / by Treasure E. Blue.
p. cm.
ISBN 978-0-345-49328-6 (pbk.)
1. African American women—New York (State)—New York—Fiction.
2. Women singers—Fiction. 3. Harlem (New York, N.Y.)—Fiction.
4. Street life—Fiction. I. Title.

PS3602.L85S77 2007
813'.6—dc22   2007017683

Printed in the United States of America

www.oneworldbooks.net

8   9   7

Text design by Laurie Jewell

This book is dedicated to my father, Robert Smalls Sr., who stood by me thick and thin through my search to find self. There were times when nearly everyone gave up on me and left me to the wolves, but you stood by your son knowing that one day he'd be able to stand on his own. Though we never really had a traditional father/son relationship in our past because of my vast inhibitions and turbulent lifestyle, you came to my rescue many times and were forced to learn the role of a father, subsequently forcing me to learn how to be a son. I love you, Dad.

Pain and suffering are prerequisites
for joy and happiness

—STEVEN B. SMALLS

PART ONE

This is the story of a girl who should have died the minute she was born, who was famous hours after she was born, who had to die and be born again countless times before she finally learned how to live. To most, she would simply be a story on the news that they could recall in casual conversation. She was that baby who had been born on that night in that way, to that mother who had let it happen. The sad part about it is, nobody ever really cared about this girl once she faded from the evening news and the morning papers. Nobody knew what happened to her after the media closed the chapter on her sensational story, after she ceased being the talk of all those people who just dismissed her as another sad sound bite on the evening news. She was just something to talk about to most people in her world. To others, she was just someone else to use up because they were trying to survive in the jungle they had all been placed in. And to some, she was someone to care about and save, a reason to love that became a reason to live. This is the story of what she came to be to herself.

CHAPTER ONE

February 1984. Underneath the elevated train tracks on 125th Street, outside the Metro-North station, a petite girl wearing a flimsy spandex skirt stood impatiently on the sidewalk, as scores of cars whisked by. Tourists did not come to this part of Harlem. This area, the east side of Harlem, was a haven for crack- and heroin-addicted whores, and transvestites looking to turn a few tricks. This night was cold, so bitterly cold that there wasn't a whore in sight. But there would always be an exception. One who would defy Mother Nature. One who would take the stringent cold and make the intolerable seem tolerable. One who would risk everything just for an opportunity to earn some loot to hit that glass dick. One who finally lost control because circumstances in her life had been beyond her control. One who descended into a depth of pain that now seemed impossible for her to dig her way out of.

Crack cocaine, the deadliest and most addictive drug known to man. A drug so powerful that under its spell, it caused some women to sell their own children or made a man get on his knees to suck another man's penis. A drug so insidious, it told your brain that you had to have it no matter the cost. Not even a wretchedly cold winter night could stop those on the prowl for the substance that provided them a temporary amnesia, a momentary euphoria, a desperate escape from the reality of their lives. This part of town was a jungle. Sad, hopeless and lonely people were the only hunters. Crack cocaine was their prey.

A few drug dealers also withstood the harsh elements. They did not have to hunt for their victims because their victims hunted for them. They lurked in harrowed darkness, rocking back and forth in their Timbos, waiting patiently in the cut to capitalize on someone's desperation.

On the stroll, seventeen-year-old Nika had a virtual monopoly on the competition. Not only did she carry the burden of the freezing cold, but also a fetus in its third trimester. Though she carried small, having sprouted the type of belly that made the old folks predict a girl, her pregnancy was still visible, discouraging several potential tricks. She hadn't turned a single trick in nearly two hours. Angry, cold and beasting for crack, tears falling heavily from her eyes at the thought of surviving another minute, another second without a blast. To make matters worse, a downpour of snow decreased the possibility of her getting her hands on what she wanted. Fighting back the tears, she eyed the dealers across the street and convinced herself she could pull off the impossible—get some vials on credit. Walking toward them, her mind raced as she pondered what new lie she could tell them. Gaining confidence with each stride, she put on her game face and began smiling gleefully.

One dealer seemed to read her mind. He stopped her dead in her tracks. "Don't even try it, bitch!"

His words cut through her like a machete. Her jaw twitched in anger, for these were the same bastards she had grown up with. The same bastards who had gotten her hooked on crack in the first place. The same bastards she had made rich with all the business she brought them. But there are no loyalties in a jungle. There is only the will to survive, at any and all costs. Everyone necessarily hardened so as not to become a victim. Heartlessness was the rule and not the exception. None of them wanted to serve her. They were used to throwing off the addicts who could not pay. Business was business. They left their hearts at home whenever they stepped out onto the streets.

From the dealers before her, Nika couldn't even be fronted a dime piece of crack. She cursed them silently and walked away.

As she trudged uptown in the six-inch accumulated snow, it was then that she began to feel the bloodcurdling chill invade her soul. It was also then that she felt a sharp burning in her stomach that forced her to keel over in gut-wrenching pain. Once the pain subsided, just as suddenly as it came, she staggered for about a block until she happened upon a potential trick walking in her direction. She quickly gained her composure and wiped the frozen tears from her puffy face. As quickly as hope arrived, it was just as quick to disappear. She rolled her eyes in disgust, recognizing the elderly gentleman standing before her.

"God can take away your troubles right this moment, Nika, if you are willing," he said in a soft voice while extending his hand.

The small, fragile man with soft reassuring eyes was Elijah Clark, founder and director of Visions, a neighborhood drug treatment center. A former addict himself, he spent many years sick and suffering on the mean streets of Harlem. After getting arrested, and nearly losing his mind, he kicked the habit in prison after he found God there.

"What did God ever do for me, Mr. Clark, huh?" Nika shouted. "Nothing! That's what. He never did shit for me. You hear me?"

Nika sucked her teeth and walked around him, not wanting to hear any of his preaching. But she wanted to make sure he heard hers. She looked back at him, screaming in a voice that made even a man who had seen it all recoil.

"He never did one fuckin thing for me since I was fuckin born!"

Elijah watched in silence as she screamed incoherently while walking off into the frozen darkness.

Defeated, Nika relented and walked toward her rented room on Lenox and 131st, when a tan Maxima crept up slowly behind her. The driver honked his horn and came to a stop. Her eyes glanced toward the vehicle as newfound hope overwhelmed her. She ran at almost breakneck speed, hopping in the passenger seat. Under normal circumstances she would have inspected the occupant a little closer to see if he was a potential threat, such as a vice cop, deranged freak or stickup kid. But this wasn't a normal night, so all bets were off, she thought as she stared wide-eyed at the man in front of her.

Smiling, she asked nervously, "Hey, honey, you looking for a date? 'Cause I . . . you know . . . ain't doing nothing, and I can take care of you."

The driver, a huge man who seemed stuffed into the moderately sized car, was surprised by her carefree spirit. He returned the smile, revealing crooked, buttery coated, yellowish teeth, as he leered lustfully at her petite, youthful body.

"Well, goddamn, girl," he said with excited pleasure in a thick, Southern drawl. "Now, that's exactly the type of whore I'm lookin for."

She smiled as she loosened her thin coat.

He examined her closer, frowning, "I be damned, girl, but you look like you have a child in ya."

"You ain't got to worry 'bout that, Daddy, because I can suck a mean dick, baby . . . I'll have you cumin in no time."

She quickly reached for his zipper. "You don't have to worry about me being pregnant, I promise you you gonna cum."

He shook his head, "Shit, baby, you ain't gots to worry, I loves to try me some of that pregnant pussy. From what I hear, that's the sweetest kind of pussy any ol way." Backing into an empty parking space, he smiled at her wickedly, smacking lips that were so purple they could have been stained by blueberries. "We can handle business right in the backseat."

The quicker the better, she thought, as she followed him to the rear. He immediately pulled down his trousers, and she followed suit, slipping out of her panties. As she awkwardly positioned herself for his entry, she caught a glimpse of his package. Her eyes widened as she stared in total disbelief at the size and girth of his penis—it was the size of a quarter horse's. Were she not in the throes of addiction, this would have been the moment where instinct would have kicked in and told her to protect herself. She needed the money for a hit so bad, but was she willing to risk injury to not only herself, but her baby, as well?

"Listen, baby, I don't think it's a good idea to put that thing up in me right now. How 'bout I suck you off and—"

"Fuck that head shit. I told you I wanted some pussy, so either that or you can get the fuck out." He quickly let her know he wasn't playing. He opened the rear door, exposing her to the frigid cold.

Once again thinking of the first blast, she nodded her head and eased back in her seat. Slowly, she closed her eyes, lifted her skirt and spread her thin legs. She winced immediately when she felt the head of his penis enter her. She bit down on her lip as he pressed forcefully, raw-dogging it, trying to put every inch of himself in her. As he plunged faster and faster, deeper and deeper, she begged him to slow down, but he could not hear her plea; he was in his own world, grunting, groaning, speaking in tongues, eyes rolling into the back of his head. He was unrelenting in his vicious assault of her vaginal canal. She could feel his dick banging against her cervix, making her uterus shift with each burning thrust.

"No . . . no more," she begged loudly, as she felt the ripping of her insides.

"Oh, shit . . . you maafuckin tight pussy bitch . . . oh, shit . . . right fuckin there . . . ahhhh . . . right there, bitch!" Gobs of spit dribbled freely from his bloated lips. She was powerless over the brute who forced her legs to spread wider and wider. Just as she thought she would pass out, the beast made an almost girlish squeal. He pounded her one last time and pulled out his dick, exploding sperm all over Nika's stomach and pussy hairs. Blood ran down her thighs. Breathing heavily, he jerked the remaining cum from his dick.

"Damn, sugar, that pussy was mad tight . . . Shit, if you want, we can . . ." He caught himself midsentence when he suddenly noticed his car seats were becoming saturated with thick bloody mucus.

"Bitch, you got fuckin blood all over my mama's seats! Get the fuck out . . . get out!"

"Okay," Nika responded meekly. "Just let me find my panties."

"Fuck your fuckin panties, get out my ride now!" he shouted. Looking in his flaming eyes, she knew better than to not comply with his order.

"All right," she agreed. "But give me my money first."

"Bitch, you should be paying me for fuckin up my car with your fuckin blood." He reached over and quickly opened the door for her to exit.

The thought of going home crackless enraged her. She looked him square in the eyes and demanded, "Motherfucker, I ain't going no place until you pay me my money."

He wrapped his huge hand around her small throat, trying to shove her out of the car. Her jones made her stronger than the man who had just overtaken her with his sex. "I ain't going anywhere until you give me my money!"

Seeing that she wasn't budging, he lifted one of his powerful legs and began kicking her without mercy. His foot thundered against her face and her hard stomach, but the pain made her more determined. It wasn't until he lifted his other leg, using both feet in seamless coordination, that he sent her body flying out the car like a rag doll. Lying in the snow, holding her stomach, she sobbed loudly. Blood and tears ran freely down her face. He watched her in silence as he exited out of the car on his side. Walking to the other side, he peeled off a twenty and let it drop on the ground near Nika.

Nika hurriedly approached the two dealers. Her spandex skirt had blood smeared on the front. Standing before them, she extended the bill out to them, clutching her belly as if she had to go to the bathroom.

"Give me two," she commanded, wiping snot from her nose. They all turned away. The shred of dignity they had left made them not want to contribute even further to the obvious insanity Nika had sunken into. They looked beyond her as if she weren't even there.

"Give me two," she repeated.

Finally, one dealer spoke. "Yo, Nika, why don't you call it a night, yo?"

Nika stared at him with confusion. "Yo, I ain't got no time for this shit, Chocolate, I been through too fuckin much tonight, give me two!"

"Not for nothing, yo, but you killing yourself out here, ma, and your fuckin baby."

Clutching her stomach tighter, she grew angry. "You can kill that worried shit. Now, give me two."

He shook his head, "Naw, fuck that. I ain't selling you no more. Bounce yo."

Nika pleaded, "What the fuck do you care. I ain't begging for credit. Give me two."

She wanted to leave but she knew no other dealers would be out. She fell to her knees and clutched his leg tightly and begged, "Don't do this to me. I . . . I just need these last two and I'm going in for the night."

The youngest dealer, about thirteen, interrupted, "Fuck that! I only got two left anyway, and it's cold as a bitch out here."

Chocolate shrugged. "Yo, you do you, nigga, I ain't selling her shit."

The youngun snatched the bill from Nika and shoved two vials in her hand.

Thirsting badly for the hit, she decided to enter the lobby of the closest abandoned tenement. She knew of one just around the corner. Another crackhead was already inside, scraping his stem when she entered. He asked her if she could spare a little piece of crack, but she ignored him and kept it moving toward the stairwell. It was dark and quiet on the second-floor landing. As she rummaged through her pocketbook, searching for her stem and lighter, a piercing sharp pain in her abdomen knocked her off her feet. She fell to her knees, into the puddle of water supplied by the stream of liquid leaking from between her legs. She gathered her composure and slammed both dime pieces at once.

Her eyes widened wickedly as she took a deep, deep pull from the pipe. The fire from the pipe illuminated the hallway with an amberish orange hue. The crackling from the pipe sizzled loudly as she exhaled. The drug raced through her body in an instant, causing her brain to register an orgasm-like elation throughout her body. All of her worries were suspended. A lightness filled her head. She had no thoughts, no memories. She was within a present and without a past at the same time.

As Nika stepped slowly down the stairs and out of the building, the warm, gooey liquid streamed more fluidly from under her skirt. Steam emitted from the liquid as it hit the freezing air. Oblivious to Mother Nature's wicked cold, she floated down the wary, dark street. She heard music, though she was not sure where it came from.

Oh, happy day . . . when Jesus washed . . . when . . . Jesus washed . . . he took my sins away . . .

Still in a blissful haze, she neared Lenox Avenue. A couple ambling past stopped dead in their tracks, staring wide-eyed with their mouths agape. It was a ghastly sight to see: a young woman dragging a newborn through the freezing snow by its umbilical cord.

Nika collapsed and lay in the snow, staring at the flakes that seemed to be racing to the ground. The snow surrounding her lonely body turned a rosy shade of pink. The color spread rapidly. Nika never felt pain when she was high. Nor fear. Nor loneliness. Her eyes descended slowly as the song continued, its volume fading away along with Nika's mind.

Oh, happy day . . . Oh, happy day . . .

⌐ ⌐ ⌐

Miss Hattie Mae Evans rarely moved beyond eyeshot of her kitchen window on the ground floor of the project building where she lived on Lenox Avenue. As a result, she was usually the first to know everything that happened in her neighborhood. On this night, just as she was closing the Bible she always read before bed, out of the corner of her eyes she saw a girl fall back into the snow, carefree, as if she expected to be caught by a lover's arms. Hattie Mae waited a few moments before she forced her sixty-five-year-old bones up out of her chair and headed for the hall closet. She laboriously put each foot into heavy black boots. On her way out the door, she grabbed the quilt off of the couch.

She cautiously approached the fallen girl, whose eyes were closed. She guessed that, despite the war scars riddling her face, the child was not more than eighteen. Staring down at the girl, Hattie Mae made no judgments about her except that whatever had led to this night was not the child's fault. She knew that no one would have willingly reached a point in their lives where they could lie unconscious, freezing to death and with a newly born baby dangling from between their legs. It was a sight that no human being who still possessed a heart could have ignored. It was a sight that made the elderly, childless, and stoic Hattie Mae want to weep without end. But she would have to do that later.

For now, she threw the blanket down next to the body. Bending down one leg at a time, not knowing if she would have the strength to get back up, she kneeled onto the ground. She placed one hand on the far side of the girl's body for balance. She used her other hand to lift the umbilical cord, placed it between her index finger and forefinger, then wrapped it tightly around her thumb. She sank her teeth into the cord, severing a connection between mother and child that would haunt them all for many years after this night.

CHAPTER TWO

A week passed before Nika awoke from her coma and found herself in a hospital bed. Groggily, she adjusted her eyes toward the ceiling. She had a long plastic tube implanted up her nostrils. As she looked around, she eyed the multitude of machines and coiled needles attached to her aching body. She closed her eyes, hoping it was just a demented dream. Slowly, she opened her eyes once again. She noticed a plastic bag with clear liquid dripping monotonously into a tube that was connected to her arm. She heard the beeping of the machines, then smelled foreign chemicals. A jolt of fear made her sit upright, inadvertently ripping the needles painfully out of her arms. One of the machines started ringing.

"Where's my baby?" she screamed. She looked around, pulling the tube from her nose. She was trying to get out of the bed when she fell with a thud onto the slippery, icy floor.

"Where's my baby . . . where's my baby?" she yelled, as she crawled toward the door.

The first to arrive was an older nurse, who yelled over her shoulder, "Get me some help in here now."

In a panic, Nika pleaded, "Where's my baby . . . where's my baby, please tell me what happened to my baby."

The nurse threw her arms around Nika in an attempt to calm her.

"Please, miss, tell me where my baby at . . . I'm sorry."

Two other black female nurses rushed into the room and immediately began assisting the first nurse in getting Nika back into the bed.

"No . . . let me go . . . let me goooo!" she moaned.

"Young lady," said the large, dark-skinned nurse. "You must calm down, you're in an extremely sick condition. You lost a lot of blood."

"I wanna know what's happening to my fucking child, and I want to know right now," announced Nika. She was angry and ready to fight. She had no memory of what had happened to bring her here. However, she did know that she had been pregnant before she got here. Her stomach was now back to its original size, though not nearly as taut as it used to be. The loose, saggy skin she sensed was evidence that she had, in fact, been pregnant. She had not dreamed it up. The fact that she didn't know what had happened in the interim—between being pregnant and now—was driving her crazy. The nurses did everything to calm her. All three of them held her arms and legs onto the bed.

"Bitches!" Nika shouted hysterically. "Stop telling me to calm down. I'll calm down when you tell me where the fuck my baby is at."

The older nurse inhaled deeply, attempting to supress her exasperation with the difficult patient. She could tell Nika was one who was easier to help when she was unconscious.

"Take y'all fuckin hands off of me," Nika screamed wildly. "If y'all don't tell me where my baby at, I'm gonna sue this fucked-up hospital."

The three employees restrained her forcefully as she continued to struggle. One of the nurses pleaded once again, "Please, young lady, you are making matters worse, you must calm down."

A demonic scowl crossed Nika's face, as she spit on the nurse closest to her. "How the fuck you like that calm, bitch! Tell me where the fuck my child is at."

The big, imposing nurse closed her eyes as the gob of mucus trickled gradually down her face. The room fell silent. The other two nurses loosened their hold on Nika and stepped away from her. Calmly, the nurse who had been accosted reached for a paper towel that was on a nearby windowsill. She snapped her fingers in the faces of the other two staff members. They gladly took their cue and immediately scurried out of the room, without so much as a second glance.

The nurse's unfearing response, and her authority, caught Nika off guard. Suddenly, the woman before her became a person who commanded respect. At a loss for words, Nika sheepishly muttered under her breath, "I'm . . . I'm sorry I spit at you, lady, but you know I'm right. I got every right to know where my baby at."

The nurse simply stared at the ceiling as she wiped the remaining spit from her face. She then inhaled deeply and spoke in a slow, measured tone. "So you want to know where, and what is wrong with your child? Is that the question you want to know, young lady?"

Shamefacedly, Nika nodded yes. The nurse took a half step toward her while taking off her glasses. Nika uneasily scooted back in her bed, fearing the worst. The nurse glared at Nika, and spoke through gritted teeth, "Well, let me answer that question by posing another: What the hell is wrong with you?"

She walked around to the foot of Nika's bed, picked up the chart and readjusted her glasses.

"Let's see, February 4, 11:41 P.M., one Jane Doe female, mid to late teens, and one newborn fetus, female, arrived via ambulance to emergency trauma center. Both victims diagnosed with acute hypothermia, mother and fetus suffered sufficient loss of blood and air to the brain. Baby Desire . . ."

The nurse looked up from the chart. "Oh, by the way, that's what the newspapers and the people around the country call your daughter."

After a brief pause, she continued, "Baby Desire, undetermined months premature, weighed in at one pound, six ounces, placed in humidification tent, in the neonatal intensive care ward, probable drug-related birth."

The words spilling from the nurses mouth overwhelmed Nika. Suddenly, visions flooded her mind: of wandering through the streets in search of crack, of being assaulted by a beastly man who had kicked her out of his vehicle, of taking a euphoric hit of crack to relieve her pain, of feeling something inside of her tumbling about in anguished trauma. She pondered the flood of memories, then lowered her eyes in shame.

The nurse looked up again. "Don't put your head down now, missy. I ain't nearly finished answering your questions."

The nurse stopped reading from the chart because she had seen cases such as this so often in the past twenty-three years at Harlem Hospital that she could describe the condition of a drug-addicted newborn from memory. "Mild to severe tremors; asymmetrically shaped arch in spine; abnormally small cranium; legs are barely the size of an adult's middle finger and feet are barely the size of the tip of an adult's thumb. She has a little breathing tube the size of a piece of spaghetti, so air can pump into her lungs, as she can't breathe on her own. While most newborn babies are crying for their milk, your baby is crying because she's fiending for a hit of crack. That sweet, beautiful, innocent child is suffering in the most horrible way because her mother wanted what she wanted when she wanted it."

For the first time, Nika looked at the nurse's hospital badge for a name: Nurse Dixon. Nurse Dixon threw the chart to the floor. She continued speaking, strained through her words.

"Now you show sudden goddamn concern for your child's health, demanding shit after nobody but you were the one to put her here."

Nika did not respond as the nurse continued to assault her with the truth.

"Tell me this one thing . . . what . . . gives you the right to show concern now? . . . TELL ME!" Nurse Dixon hollered. "And all that stuff about suing . . . you need to worry about those two police officers standing guard outside your door who are about to bring charges on you, so keep on."

Nurse Dixon stood there with her hands on her hips, awaiting a response from Nika. Her patient sat in the bed, holding the bedsheet tightly up against her chin as if it were a shield. It was the first time the nurse had truly looked at the scared and defenseless teenager. She could see remnants of Nika's innocence, now that she was unarmed by attitude. The child's eyes were soft and wide, begging for help in a way that her mouth wouldn't allow. What Nurse Dixon saw before her was a broken, misguided girl—a mere child curled up in a ball, trembling.

The nurse approached Nika slowly. She put her hand on Nika's shoulder and soothingly rocked her back and forth. Nika shivered as she reached out and pulled the nurse closer, spreading her arms around the woman's shoulders in a tight hug.

"I'm sorry . . . I'm sorry, I didn't mean to hurt my baby," Nika cried hysterically, as tears rolled silently down the nurse's face.

"If my baby die, I don't know what I'm gonna do," sobbed Nika. The weight of what she had done pressed down upon her chest like a freight train. All she could do to release the pressure was let it pour out in her tears.

Stroking her hair, the nurse assured her that God would make everything right.

"Dear God . . . ," Nurse Dixon began, and the rest of the words didn't matter as they fell over Nika and slowly began to help lift the weight.

They prayed together as Nika fell into a deep sleep.

* * *

Though Nika recovered rapidly in the week since she had awakened from her coma, the same could not be said about her daughter. When Nika saw Desire for the first time, the tiny child looked helpless in the incubator. The worst part was seeing the many tubes inserted in her. It brought tears to Nika's eyes each time she saw the sight. She prayed to God every night that if He saved Desire she would become the best mother she possibly could.

On their seventeenth day in the hospital, Nika and Desire had their first visitor—Miss Hattie Mae Evans, the woman who had saved their lives. Hattie Mae was a strong, religious woman who attended church several times a week without fail. Her life was typical of the black women who had struggled their whole lives, made it to this age, and now felt the need to help others carry their burdens. She had been born poor in the South, migrated to New York in her late teens, got a job as a housekeeper, married, and had a family. She lived off the modest pension check of her deceased husband, who had been a Pullman porter on the railroads. Her only son had died during the Vietnam War. Since then, she had committed her life to Jesus Christ.

Noticing a shadow in the doorway, Nika looked over to see a heavyset elderly woman carrying a bouquet of yellow carnations. The woman rocked from one leg to the other as she made her way closer to the bed.

"Nika, I'm Hattie Mae," she said, extending the arm that had a purse dangling from it.

Nika was pleased to finally have a visitor who wasn't employed by the hospital. She greeted Hattie Mae with a smile, then lost her hand inside of the elderly woman's oversized grip. Hattie Mae then placed the flowers in a cup that was on the food tray.

"These are for you and Desire," she said. "Ize been following y'alls progress on the news."

There was a long silence as Hattie slowly glanced around the room, while Nika stared at her hard—watching her look.

"Do you know how ya gots here?" Hattie Mae asked.

"In the hospital? Well—" Nika began before Hattie Mae interrupted her.

"Naw, anybody can get in a hospital." Hattie Mae seemed to lose patience. "I'm talking about dis predicament. How you get here in life? In such a short life. You livin too hard, chile."

Nika stared at the braids in Hattie Mae's hair, secretly admiring the neat separations between the six plaits. She looked at the elderly woman's face, noticing the smoothness of her brown skin, except for a few, sparing deep lines. It looked as if her flesh was folded over in those creases.

"Ya hear me?" Hattie Mae tapped the blanket to get Nika's attention. "Ya living too hard."

Nika wanted to respond, even if for nothing else but to keep her visitor around. There was no television or telephone in her room, so she had nothing to do. She appreciated the visit from Hattie Mae because it relieved her boredom.

"Ya living too hard," Hattie Mae repeated restlessly, wanting to make sure the young woman she had rescued heard her loud and clear.

Nika's lips got heavy every time she felt she had the answer to Hattie Mae's original question. Her mind darted from one moment to another, but she quickly dismissed each scenario as being "the one" that got her "here." She scratched her head. She was at a loss as to where to begin, so she didn't.

"You watch the news then visit the people in the hospital?" Nika asked quizzically. When the words came out of her mouth she was just as surprised as Hattie Mae. She didn't know what made her say it, but it had eased through her lips.

Hattie Mae stood up in a rush. She grabbed her coat and pocketbook and held them tight to her body.

"Chile, you betta learn to recognize the work of the Lord," she indignantly announced, and walked out the door.

        ⌐   ⌐   ⌐

Nika was surprised when Hattie Mae returned the next day. The old woman even brought another gift. This time, it was a small, finger-puppet-sized stuffed bear. She returned every day, bearing a present for Nika and Desire. To ensure Hattie Mae's visits, Nika quickly learned that she had to simply and directly answer her visitor's questions. Every time she began another long foray into the abyss of despair that had gotten her to the night in the snow, she looked at the woman before her and wondered how and why Hattie Mae stood to listen to such stories. But Hattie Mae was always undaunted by the tales.

Every day, Nika dug up a completely different story. One day she told Hattie Mae about foster care life. She explained that the foster parent she was placed with couldn't have cared less if she was there or not, so long as she received her checks and food stamps. She also mentioned that her foster mother had had a serious numbers habit. On another day, she told Hattie Mae about how being in the foster home made her desperate for attention;

there were simply too many kids in the home for her to receive the care she needed. She started stealing the toys that belonged to the other foster care kids in the house. She claimed it was there that she became a kleptomaniac and a natural liar. It didn't take Nika long to realize that the longer and better her stories, the longer Hattie Mae would stay. So she kept the stories coming, and the meetings between the women became a type of therapy for them both.

She talked about her foster mother's boyfriend, Uncle Skeeter, who'd had droopy eyes and a big fat potbelly. He had been married, but had stayed over at their apartment every Saturday night to get his groove on with her foster mother. She enjoyed his visits because every time he came over he would bring a brown bag filled with candy for all the kids. Nika said she got more candy whenever she sat on Skeeter's lap.

On another occasion, Nika confessed to Hattie Mae that she had been known as the fast little girl who was hot in the panties. She told her that she would let boys run trains on her on rooftop landings to feel wanted.

Hattie Mae didn't ask simple, obvious questions. *Where's your mother? Who's Desire's father? Where do you live?* She had her one question: "How did ya get here, in this moment?"

On one particular day that Hattie Mae visited, everything felt different. When she walked into the hospital room she didn't say a word. The only sound was from outside, the crackling of frost sealing itself to the window. Hattie Mae quietly took off her coat and sat in the chair next to Nika's bed. Instinctively, Nika looked off into the distance and began to speak:

"Sometimes I would go to the apartment of a friend who lived across the street. I would go over there and eat. Quite honestly, I didn't even really like her that much, because she was kinda slow. She looked kinda homely, you know . . . but I'll be damned if I didn't act like her best friend in front of her parents. On one of my hungry days, I went over to her apartment. She hadn't invited me or nothing. I just wanted something to eat. Her father answered the door as usual. He told me his wife and his daughter was out of town visiting some relatives. He let me in and made me a sandwich and gave me a glass of milk. He watched me eat it, the entire time."

Nika began speaking as if in a trance. Her eyes began to water as the memory flooded her. Hattie Mae braced for the ending that she could sense was coming. Nika continued.

"After I finished, I noticed he was still still looking at me, but this time in a way I knew. It was the same way the boys on the block used to act when they were trying to get the nerve up to ask me for some pussy and the same way Uncle Skeeter used to look at me when I walked past him in my underwears. To make a long story short, he told me he wanted to eat my pussy out. And I let him. I don't know why, I just did. He told me not to tell his wife, and especially not his daughter. He gave me a twenty-dollar bill. When he put that money in my hand, oh, my God, I was in shock, all I could do was stare at it. All of a sudden I started feeling real funny and my body started shaking. I didn't know what to think, how to feel, for a while. But then, I just figured something out. Or I guess I thought I did. Three things changed from that day on. One, I never, ever starved again. Two, I never fucked anyone for free again. And three, I never had an orgasm like that ever again."

Nika expected a response from Hattie Mae that she was never going to get. There was no scolding, no condemnation, no judgments, and no shock. No matter how elaborate the story, at the end of each visit, Miss Hattie Mae would simply ask the same question: "How ya get here in life? Tomorrow, I know you go'n tell me. So far, you tellin me about other people's problems and how you made them ya own."

Nika felt at ease talking to Hattie Mae. She didn't feel looked down upon. She didn't feel lonely anymore. It felt warm to know that someone would come and see her every day. It seemed she could depend on Miss Hattie Mae, but something wouldn't allow her to put all her cards on the table just yet. As much as Nika told Hattie Mae, there was a whole lot she never even mentioned.

       ❧ ❧ ❧

The worst story Nika could never face, let alone tell, began in 1970 in the Wagner Projects. Nika's mother, Sandy, had been seventeen when she got involved with an older neighborhood dude everyone called Ray-Ray. He was a mere 5′3″, but he held his own on the streets. He fancied himself a ladies man, but in all actuality he was a trick and young girls were his weakness. His primary sources of income were being a numbers bookie by day and a small-time pimp by night. If a person hit real big, he'd prefer to cut a man's throat than to pay him. One fifty-year-old man, who was unfortunate enough to hit the number twice in one week, accidentally fell off a roof a day before he was supposed to get paid off.

Ray-Ray's tactic for hooking whores was even worse—he'd get them hooked on drugs. His favorite target was teenaged girls—

the younger, the dumber, the better. He knew most young girls weren't diving into heavy drugs, but they considered weed harmless, because everyone did it. He used the herb as his devil in disguise.

One girl he was interested in was Sandy Mitchell. Sandy had a minimum-wage job as a cashier at the gas station on 125th and First Avenue. She was single-handedly raising her three-year-old daughter, Nika. When she met Ray-Ray, she was struggling to make ends meet. She thought Ray-Ray was sweet, because he'd give her daughter a dollar every time he saw her. Soon, he began visiting her in her small, one-bedroom apartment. He even assisted her in paying overdue bills. It was only a matter of time before she gave him her body, each time smoking a blunt before making love.

He took his time stringing Sandy out. He started first by lacing the weed with a little cocaine, then later on with heroin. Before long, Sandy began waking up dope sick, with flulike symptoms. One morning, she woke up in intense pain and complained to Ray-Ray about her illness.

He nonchalantly answered, "Oh, it must be the heroin that's making you feel like that."

She displayed a confused look. The fact that he could have been giving her more than herb had never crossed her mind.

He continued, "It's the heroin I mixed with the weed that's making you jones, baby."

Sandy was pissed off and wondering how he could have done such a thing without her knowledge. She jumped up in anger. "Ray-Ray . . . you been giving me fuckin heroin without me knowing about it?"

"Shit, I thought you knew. Fuck, I told you it was an Amsterdam blunt. That's how they get down in Europe."

"I thought you meant you got the weed from Amsterdam Avenue, not that you was lacing that shit with heroin."

Ray-Ray got out of bed and shrugged. "Shit, don't blame me if you ain't hip to what's up. Besides, you was the one asking me to bring the shit home every night."

He began to imitate her in a high voice. "Ray, don't forget to bring some of that shit we had last night. Ray, that smoke was good, roll me another one."

He threw his hands in the air, staring at her for emphasis.

Sandy shivered in pain. She tried to get out of the bed, but doubled over from the pain in her back, and fell to the floor hugging her cramping stomach. Ray-Ray helped her off the floor and back into the bed. He stared at her in disgust, then went into his pants pocket and pulled out a glassine bag.

"Here . . ." Ray-Ray passed the bag to Sandy, who threw it down on the bed.

She stared at it. "I know you ain't fuckin crazy. I'm not fuckin with this shit." She threw it back at him.

He shrugged. "Do you, then. I'm just tryna help you out. You said you feel fucked up. All you got to do to feel better is take a toot and all's good. Suit yourself."

He turned and went into the bathroom to take a shower.

Sandy fumed and tried to bury her head in the pillow, but she tossed and turned all the while. After a few uncomfortable seconds she sat up and looked at the small glassine bag on the bed and went for it. She sat back on the bed and opened the folded bag and used her pinky finger to scoop out some of the powder and sniffed it deeply. In a matter of seconds, the pain in her back, the chills and the nausea were gone. She laid onto the bed gently, letting the smooth, melodic high overwhelm her.

Ray-Ray closed the bathroom door, smiling wickedly to himself.

❧ ❧ ❧

It didn't take much after that for Ray-Ray to convince Sandy to sell her body to support her habit. He simply told her he didn't have any money because business was slow, but he knew how she could make some real fast. At the beginning, Sandy had it easy, because Ray-Ray would send the clients to her apartment.

As soon as Sandy began working for the small-time pimp, he started to abuse her physically. In his mind she was his property and he could do whatever he wanted with her, and he just happened to get off by beating the shit out of women. He would beat Sandy so brutally, anybody watching would have thought she was a man. He beat her with a closed fist, chair legs, two-by-fours, whatever he could get his hands on. During the abuse, he'd get a large hard-on while he watched Sandy whimper in submission. Afterward, he would make Sandy repeat that he was a better lover than any tall man she'd ever been with. It was then that he would turn gentle and compassionate, claiming that he only beat her because he loved her. In the same breath, he'd tell her he would kill her if she ever left him. If he couldn't have the pussy, no one would.

In no time at all, Sandy became a full-fledged junkie—mainlining heroin in her arms, and needing nearly a bundle a day to maintain her habit. It was around then that Ray-Ray was arrested on his third felony and had to do some hard time. This was both a blessing and a curse for Sandy. It freed her from Ray-Ray, but it also forced her to hit the streets and make shit happen on her own.

When she wasn't high, Sandy had plenty of time to think while strolling, looking for tricks. Her thoughts were always the same. She imagined getting off drugs. She wanted to get a real job and raise her daughter properly. She wanted to go back to the person she had been before she met Ray-Ray. Then the fear of withdrawal would set in. She didn't want to feel that pain wracking through her body. The numbing effect provided by the drug always won over her desire to quit. Every day, the same dream, though, because she would be reminded of it every time she looked into her daughter Nika's pure eyes. They were like opals that always seemed to be looking out, but you could never see in. Those eyes observed everything the one-bedroom apartment had to offer.

~ ~ ~

Ten-year-old Nika sat silently inside the dark, cramped closet for what seemed like the hundredth time that night. She wasn't afraid of the dark, like most kids her age; she was used to it. She knew by the sounds of the grunts, the squeaking of the bedsprings, that it was time to make her move. Ever so slowly she opened the closet door and slid on her belly as smooth as a snake. When she reached the foot of the bed, she peeked up and saw the john's white, hairy ass pump uncontrollably up and down on her mother. She had her timing down to a science. She reached her hand inside the man's pocket and pulled out his wallet. She thumbed through the wallet and skillfully pulled out large bills only. She was careful to place the wallet and trousers back in the exact same manner she found them. With the stealth of a ninja, she silently slid back into the closet just as the John reached his climax.

※　※　※

Sandy trained Nika well. Over time, they proved to be perfect partners in crime. Eventually, their good fortune ran out. The drugs and beatings from Ray-Ray had robbed Sandy of her youth and beauty. She had begun to look haggish. She was a muggy-mouthed dope fiend with rotting teeth. Multiple scars above her eyes gave her the permanent look of a seasoned boxer. This began to limit the number and quality of the tricks she was able to attract. Her habit got bigger, while her resources for supporting it shrank.

One night, wretched in pain and dope sick, Sandy thought about how she had spent the entire day trying to earn some money. After struggling all day she couldn't even borrow a dollar. As she staggered through her apartment door, Nika eagerly greeted her, searching her pockets for food. She hadn't eaten in three days and was beginning to lose her balance. "Mommy . . . ?" Nika asked in desperation. "Did you make any money?"

Sandy couldn't respond. She ran to the bathroom, but didn't make it to the toilet. She sat in a pool of despair, rimmed with her own vomit. Nika ran over and helped Sandy's trembling body onto the couch. Nika wiped the river of sweat from her mother's forehead.

"Please help me. God, please help me," Sandy cried as she

rocked back and forth in Nika's thin arms. Nika was desperate to help her mother, and knew what the solution could be.

"Mommy, you want me to go to the supermarket and steal something? We could get some food and some stuff to sell. We could get money, for the candy that makes you sing. The candy in the green bag. I could get it from the guy on the corner." She rocked her mother faster. "I remember how you showed me. Give him the money real fast in one hand, get the bag with the other. Fast."

Shaking her head, Sandy said, "No . . . no, baby, the store is closed."

"We could get on the train and tell people we are homeless. Last time we did that we made almost forty dollars."

Sandy thought about it for a second. "No, we did that at rush hour last time, it's . . . it's too late now."

Nika put her head down and accepted another hungry night. "All right, Ma."

Nika went into the bedroom and came back with a blanket. She wrapped it securely around her mother's rail-thin, shaking body. She walked into the kitchen and returned with two ice cubes. She stuck one into her mother's mouth. She slowly slid the other back and forth across her mother's forehead.

❧   ❧   ❧

Nika must have drifted off. When she opened her eyes there was someone standing in front of her that she didn't fully recognize. It was a woman. She had a blanket wrapped around her body. Her black hair was soaking wet, matted against her head. Her eyes, small and dark, were surrounded by a shade of yellow that matched her lone three teeth. Her eyes had large, dark circles around them as if she had been punched. Her lips were bloated and puffy, like balloons.

"Come here." Sandy curled her finger from beneath the blanket, motioning for her daughter to come closer. "It is time that you start earning some money for Mommy, for a change."

Sandy dragged Nika into the bathroom, and brought her out decorated in heels and lipstick.

CHAPTER THREE

It was several months before Desire was released from the hospital. By this time the story had long ceased being of interest to news reporters—and thus, politicians—but not to government agencies.

Prior to the custody hearing taking place on that day, Nika's lawyer had her criminal charges dropped. She was relieved not to have to worry about jail time. However, she did have to concern herself with the Administration for Children's Services. Once they started an investigation, they stayed on offenders like a plague.

Nika stood nervously before the judge in her custody case. Standing alongside her was her court-appointed lawyer. Nika gripped the Bible Hattie Mae had given her.

Judge Katie Ross, black, in her late forties, glanced intermittently at the defendant and the court papers in front of her. She was surprised by the young age of the defendant.

"Ms. Mitchell," the judge barked. "After reviewing your case and all the issues involved, I'm mandating you to an eighteen-month drug rehabilitation program, at which time a social worker will monitor your progress on a weekly basis. Now, in the matter of Desire Mitchell, the court will assign her to the custody of the foster care system."

Nika screamed loudly and covered her face with her hands.

"No . . . don't take my baby from me. I'm sorry for what I did. I won't smoke no crack no more. Please don't take my baby!"

Her lawyer attempted to calm her.

Nika yelled louder, "Get ya fuckin hand off of me, bitch. I'm not letting y'all take my baby!"

In an instant, a female court officer hurried over to restore peace.

"Ms. Mitchell. You must restrain yourself and allow me to finish," the judge said, pounding her gavel on the desk.

In a stern whisper, her lawyer said, "Nika, listen to me. If you ever want to see your daughter again, I suggest you calm down right now. Keep your mouth shut. Do you understand?"

The lawyer challenged Nika's malicious stare until Nika gave in to a more calmed expression.

The lawyer turned smoothly to the judge. "Your Honor, please forgive us for our brief moment of outburst. I'm sure you can understand a mother's feelings under such circumstances."

The judge stared at the counsel briefly, then at Nika. "Ms. Mitchell, right now you are acting on emotions, but in time you will see the reasoning of my decision. At this point and time, Ms. Mitchell, you must look at your present circumstances. You are homeless, unemployed, and addicted to an illegal substance. With all these things going against you, what could you possibly offer your daughter?"

Nika sadly eyed the floor.

"Ms. Mitchell," the judge said softly. "I have three children of my own. I cannot come close to knowing how it would feel to have my children taken away from me. However, I do know this . . . I know that if I weren't in the position to care for them, I would be happy and grateful to place my babies with someone who can do better than me."

Nika looked up, directly into the judge's eyes. Her experiences with Nurse Dixon and Hattie Mae had humbled her. Though initially they seemed to be the enemies, something inside of Nika allowed her to look past the possibility they were threats and understand that they could actually want what was best for her. She had not been expecting a lecture along with her sentence, but the judge had convinced her of something she hadn't wanted to see. She put her head down in devastation, letting the judge's words sink in.

"You have not lost your parental rights. You will be allowed to see your daughter on a supervisory basis, until you complete your rehabilitation program, get housing, and demonstrate to the court your transition into society," the judge announced.

Still uneasy and desperate, Nika pleaded, "Your Honor, ma'am, I understand everything you said and you are right. I'm gonna do everything I gotta do, but not knowing the people who gonna get my baby, I'm not sure if they gonna give my baby the attention she needs. My lawyer had warned me this might happen. So we filed papers to have somebody I know take temporary custody."

"Yes, I read the petition. However, that would apply only to the maternal grandparent only. And even still, for someone to be considered a candidate or a foster parent, they have to meet certain criteria. Unfortunately, the candidate was rejected because of age. At sixty-five, she is well past the foster parent maximum age, and that rules her out already."

The courtroom grew still. The judge shuffled the papers a few more times, then she noticed the name of the petitioner: Hattie Mae Evans. She stared at Nika for a moment.

"However . . . ," the judge's voice dragged, "howwweverrrr, I'm overruling the decision and will grant temporary custody to the petitioner."

Nika couldn't believe her ears.

CHAPTER FOUR

For the first seven months of her year-and-a-half-long stay, Nika had a hard time adapting to the Therapeutic Community she was placed in.

A typical TC is a long-term drug rehabilitation center in which the stay can last from twelve to thirty-six months. Similar to a boot camp, it is designed to break a person down and then rebuild him or her, both mentally and spiritually. Nika wanted to leave as soon as she arrived. Never in her life had she had to follow such strict orders and allow people to talk to her any old kind of way. On many days, she felt she could not take it any longer and wanted to leave, but always one thing stopped her—her baby. She knew she had to survive without so much as a glitch.

*. *. *.

Hattie Mae and Desire had bonded. At eighteen months old, Desire's health was no longer an issue. In addition to having Miss Hattie as a foster mother, Desire had Hattie Mae's church congregation behind her. Miss Hattie beamed with newfound pride and joy when she watched Desire get baptized. She praised the Lord for Desire's deliverance into God's kingdom and knew from that day on that He would take care of her.

Over the course of time, Nika hadn't missed a single supervised visit and became a model recovering addict inside her program. She obtained her GED, and her social worker was so impressed that she recommended unsupervised visits. In her mind, Nika started to become the person she had fantasized about being every time she had succumbed to the urge to hit the streets, and the crack pipe. With each new success, she felt her true self coming back. She saw herself being the mother that she knew she could be: caring, loving, attentive, and drug-free. The dream was starting to become a reality. But then Nika started slipping. Addiction, she would soon learn, was a lifelong cycle, a battle that she would fight each and every day of her life. This was the aspect of recovery no one could truly prepare her for. She would soon find herself overcome, despite all the progress she had made, by the urge to use again.

One night, at nearly 10 P.M., Nika was supposed to have Desire back home three hours earlier from her unsupervised visitation. Hattie Mae was going crazy with concern. Just as she picked up the phone to call the police, there was a knock on the door.

She didn't even bother to look through the peephole before ripping the door open. It was Nika, with Desire sound asleep in her stroller, hugging a little pink teddy bear. Hattie Mae pulled Desire from the stroller and hugged her tightly.

"I'm sorry," said Nika as she unpacked Desire's things. "We went to Coney Island. I didn't expect the train ride to be so long."

When Nika walked over to help Hattie Mae undress Desire, Hattie Mae smelled alcohol on her breath.

"Chile, tell me you ain't been drinking while you was out there with the baby? You know those people from the courts said you not suppose to use no nothing, especially around this here baby."

Nika tried to downplay the infraction.

"Hattie Mae, calm down, I ain't had nothing but a couple of coolers on the ride back from Coney Island. Dag, it ain't like I smoked crack or something."

"Still, anything can happen if you ain't right around the baby," Hattie Mae rebutted.

Nika sucked her teeth. "I ain't gonna let nothin happen to my baby, so you don't have to worry."

Hattie shook her head and chose not to argue any further.

"Anyway," said Nika, smiling as she kissed Desire's sleeping face, "I'm already running late, and, um, Miss Hattie, you think you can give me ten dollars to hop a cab so I won't be late and get in trouble?"

Hattie Mae went to her room and got the money for Nika. When she returned, Nika suddenly and unexpectedly gave Hattie Mae a kiss.

"Oh, yeah, I almost forgot." Nika reached in her pocket and

pulled out a cassette tape. "I made this tape for Desire so she could fall asleep at night. Can you make sure to get a tape player and play it for her?"

Not wanting to believe her strange sense of what was really going on, Hattie smiled as she watched Nika walk down the stairs.

≀   ≀   ≀

A week later, Hattie Mae heard a knock on the door at 3:46 in the morning. She turned on the lamp by her bed, quickly put on her robe, and went to the door. She adjusted her eyes as she looked through the peephole. "Who is it?" she asked in a tone much sterner than normal.

"It's me, Hattie Mae. Nika."

Surprised, Hattie took another look before unlocking the door. Nika stood wild-eyed, with a nervous smile across her face.

"Chile, what you doing here this time of morning?" Hattie Mae asked as she turned on the lights.

"Um," Nika began to utter, "they gave me my first overnight pass, and you know, I used it."

"If they gave you a pass, why you just gettin here this time of morning?"

Nika shrugged her shoulders, then responded, "Well, me and some friends from the program was having coffee at this shop, you know, and was talking and we lost, you know, track of time."

Nika wiped the pouring sweat from her forehead.

"Okay," Miss Hattie relented, "you go'n stay here tonight?"

Nika answered quickly. "Yeah, but I got to go to the store first and get me something, and I was wondering if you can lend me ten dollars?"

Miss Hattie asked, "What you want this time of night? Can't it wait till morning?"

"Well . . . ," said Nika, "I would, but my period just came down, and you know . . ."

Hattie Mae shook her head and then said that she understood. The Christian woman inside of her wanted to help Nika, but there was a feeling nagging her about what exactly she could be helping the child do. Hattie Mae wanted, needed, to believe that she had intervened and been able to save this young girl from the demons that had their grips on her soul. She needed to believe that it all wasn't for nothing, otherwise she could have left her and her child dying in the snow. She needed to believe that some good could change the world. It was this belief that kept her waking up every morning, and sitting in the church pews every Sunday. She decided to push the nagging voice aside, mute her insincts, and once again help the child she had rescued from the snow. She reached inside her purse and pulled out a small roll of money.

"I only have a twenty, so—"

Nika cut her off and quickly snatched the bill from her hand.

"I'll bring back ya change," Nika yelled on her way out the door.

Nika didn't come back that morning, and it was not her last early-morning intrusion. Nika began staying over at Hattie Mae's apartment every night, on the nights she came in at all. Over time, little things around the apartment—such as jewelry, money, frozen meats, and, yes, even her daughter's pampers and Similac—would disappear. And there came a point when Hattie Mae could no longer ignore the spirit inside of her that was trying to tell her what was really going on. Being the Christian woman that she was, Hattie Mae was willing to go to the end to help the young girl. Hattie was sure that one day Nika would have the willpower to beat the devil within her.

After two months, Hattie Mae's valiant efforts to save Nika's soul wore thin. She decided to confront Nika one day after she went to change Desire and found that she had no pampers to do it with. She was from a time and a place before pampers were even available, and she simply went and got the sturdiest pillow-case she could find. She ripped it until she was able to get a piece that was the perfect size to fashion a cloth diaper out of. Desire adjusted to the change like any child would—she was calmed that a need had finally been met and went to sleep. After carefully swaddling the child in blankets and laying her in the crib, Hattie Mae sat in the kitchen and began what was sure to be a long night of waiting for Nika to return. She eventually heard a knock on the door, well after four in the morning.

"What you still doing up?" Nika asked as soon as she saw Hattie Mae at the door, with all of the lights in the house on behind her. The telltale signs of crack use were there: Nika sweated and fidgeted without even knowing that she did so. Hattie Mae stared into the wide, wild, hopeless eyes of the child she had pulled out of the snow and from the brink of death. She fought back tears as she forced herself to do what needed to be done.

"Nika, it's time for you to leave this house and never come back." Hattie Mae stood strong in front of Nika, determined not to budge. Nika dismissed her with a roll of her eyes. She walked toward the kitchen to find something to eat, but Hattie Mae grabbed her arm and stopped her.

"No, you don't need to take anything else from this house. You done took more than enough. You need to leave. Now."

For so long, Nika had taken advantage of the fact that Hattie Mae would always be there, she couldn't immediately fathom the change. Despite the fact that she was high, she still respected Hattie Mae. She had the urge to push the old woman off of her, though in her current state she was probably too weak to do so. Hattie Mae's girth could have knocked her out cold. But Nika stood patiently, hoping that tonight she had just come home while Hattie Mae was in a phase that she only needed some sweet talk to come out of.

"I can't leave, Hattie Mae," Nika said. "You know I ain't got nowhere else to go. Damn . . . fine, I'll stop coming in late. If you want me to act like a kid, I will. I'll be home and in the bed by nine o'clock. Is that fine with you, Mama?" She was proud of her sarcastic sass, but Hattie Mae was unmoved.

"This ain't 'bout a bedtime," Hattie Mae bellowed. "This 'bout the fact that it's some people who don't want to be helped, no matter how hard folks try. I can't keep tryin no more. I'm starting to help you hold on to this devil and I ain't 'bout to do that. It's against my principles."

"Your principles gonna see me on the street?" Nika's true colors came out as she exploded. "Your principles gonna let you kick somebody out ain't got nowhere else to go? Is that your fuckin principles?"

Nika lost control. She jerked her arm out of Hattie Mae's grip and started toward the kitchen. Hattie Mae grabbed her again. Nika jerked her arm away again, this time even harder. Hattie Mae almost fell forward on the floor. This small slip did not deter Nika. She wasn't leaving without a fight.

"All right, you little devil," Hattie Mae huffed. "If you want to fight me, then let's fight. And you might even win, this time. But I got something you ain't got on your side. I got God on my side, and He might not win this time, but He might win the next. Or maybe the next. But me and you gonna fight in this house. Every time you darken that door, you better put on some boxin gloves before you knock. You ain't gonna keep throwing this child back and forth through all your mess. I'm not gonna 'low it. Not in my house."

Her words stopped Nika cold. Nika saw Hattie Mae as she had never seen her before. The old woman glared at her with her fight in her eyes. It was as if something inside of the old woman was stronger than she had let on. Nika became afraid, but she didn't want to leave.

"I ain't going," she said, starting to cry. Hattie Mae rushed to grab her by the shoulders.

"Then we gonna have to fight," she said, shaking Nika. "I want you out of my house. I don't want to see this spirit darken my door. I can't have this demon in my house. I can't do it no more!"

"I don't wanna fight, Hattie Mae," Nika cried. She tried to wriggle out of the strong, bold grip. "I don't wanna fight you."

Both women cried, and only one was sane. Hattie Mae finally spoke. "I don't wanna fight you either. You best leave on your own. I got your stuff in that bag by the door."

Nika glanced and saw a small brown grocery bag that she hadn't noticed on her way in. It proved Hattie Mae meant business, because she had obviously thought about this. It was no spur-of-the-moment decision. Nika knew the old woman would fight her if it came down to that. She couldn't bear the thought of raising a hand to Hattie Mae, just like she couldn't bear the thought of the strength inside Hattie Mae pummeling her into submission. Defeated, she started toward the door. The only thing she could do was avoid a physical fight, and instead hit Hattie Mae where she knew it would really hurt.

"Don't think you keeping my baby," she said as she grabbed the doorknob hard. "You forgot I'm the reason you got her in the first place. I'm go'n be the reason they take her!" She slammed the door so hard on her way out that several of Hattie Mae's framed family pictures shook off the wall. When Nika was gone and it was over, Hattie Mae noticed Nika had left her bag.

The fact that she was no longer welcome did not deter Nika from coming by at all times of the night, under the guise of seeing Desire. Each visit would end with Nika threatening to call ACS and have them take Desire away from Hattie Mae, who dreaded the thought and would always give Nika five or ten dollars just for her to go away.

*   *   *

The fiery reverend was drenched in sweat as he stood high and proud on the pulpit delivering his sermon, whipping the congregation into a rabid spiritual frenzy. Hattie Mae sat closed-eyed and smiling, praising Jesus for His favors and kindness as she clutched Desire in her arms. She was in a consecrated, sanctified holy bliss when she felt the tap on her shoulder. She opened her eyes, and there stood one of the ushers.

The usher bent down and whispered nervously into Hattie Mae's ear, "Sister Evans, your granddaughter done showed up again. She's standing in the foyer."

Only mildly annoyed, because at least Nika had come to church, Hattie Mae said, "Well, tell her to come in. She could stand to listen to God's word."

The usher put her head down and said, "Hattie Mae, I . . . I don't think that's such a good idea."

Hattie Mae gathered Nika must be so high that she was capable of making a scene. She sighed loudly and asked the usher to watch the baby. She hobbled toward the foyer doors, fully prepared to go through the motions of getting rid of Nika once again. She opened the door, and just as she thought, Nika stood in the corner of the foyer rocking back and forth as she waited. But something seemed different this time, something awfully different. Maybe it was Nika's sunken eyes and thin neck. Maybe it was the sneakers that she wore that looked three sizes too large and were obviously men's. But nothing was worse than the funk that emitted from her body. It clouded the foyer with a smell that was a combination of dried gutted fish and vomit. Hattie Mae could only shake her head in pity as she stared toward heaven for God's intervention.

"Nika," Hattie Mae pleaded, "you can't keep goin on like this. You got to get on your knees and ask God to take the taste for that drug out of your mouth, baby. You got to—"

"Hattie Mae, please," Nika yelled in frustration. "I ain't tryna hear that right now." Her voice was so hoarse, she sounded like a man. "I just come here to borrow some money 'cause I'm sick. I don't feel like hearing no preaching."

Hattie Mae just looked at her as Nika's dead red eyes stared back. She shook her head.

"No, chile, I ain't givin you no more money. I told you, I can't keep helping you kill yo'self."

"All right, then, we gonna see what happens when I call ACS to come get Desire from you. You gonna see how lonely and miserable it's gonna be without her."

Unmoved, and tired of Nika's idle threats, Hattie Mae challenged her, for what she hoped and prayed would be the last time.

"I don't care what you say. I'm still not giving no more money!"

Nika looked in Hattie Mae's eyes and knew she meant it, the same way she had meant it the night she kicked Nika out of the house. Nika broke down in tears and begged as she tried to hug her. "Please, Hattie Mae, please . . . just give me ten—I mean . . . um . . . twenty dollars, and this be my last time, I promise you."

Hattie Mae felt Nika's cold and crusted hands dig through her bra. She grabbed Nika's hand, and Nika was cold busted. In a panic, Nika continued in search of the stash. The fight that had been avoided the night Hattie Mae threw her out seemed certain to happen here and now. They struggled violently until Hattie Mae's Sunday dress and brassiere ripped wide open.

Nika screamed, "Just give me the motherfucking money!"

Exposed breast and all, Hattie Mae lifted up her huge arm and slapped Nika senseless across her face and screamed even louder, "I rebuke you, Satan, in the name of Jesus!"

Nika landed on the ground and looked up and saw Hattie

Mae's exposed bare breast as some of the sisters rushed over to cover her up. Hattie Mae looked down upon Nika and then at the money gripped in her own hand.

"If this money caused you to do what you just did, you can have it." She threw the money on the floor. Nika scurried quickly to pick it up.

"But remember this," Hattie Mae continued. "God bear my witness, don't you come back around here no mo unless you get yo'self together, 'cause this the very last time I'm giving you something."

At that moment, and for the first time in a long time, Nika was ashamed. When she dragged herself up off the floor, the ominous silence was deafening. Whether out of disgust or pity, the hundreds of eyes that beamed on the poor wretched soul before them burned through her. Suddenly, the silence was interrupted by a shrill cry—Desire. Nika watched the sister hand her baby to Hattie Mae, who shushed and cooed her, rocking her softly in her arms. Fighting back tears, Nika slowly and cautiously approached the bundle held in Hattie Mae's protective arms. Nika extended her arms to Desire as she looked at Hattie Mae. Hattie Mae handed over Desire as Nika trembled with outstretched arms. She pressed her cheek to Desire's and softly began to sing:

"Trouble in my way, I have to cry sometime, so much trouble, I have to cry sometime, but I know that Jesus . . . He will fix it, my sweet Jesus, He will fix it after while . . ."

The reverend began singing the song softly, and the rest of the congregation followed suit. Nika handed Desire back to Hattie Mae. She wiped the remaining tears from her eyes. She took a deep breath and headed toward the door. She wasn't going to be the "trouble in her daughter's way." But the demon inside of her wasn't content to let the one who had rebuked her and separated them go without punishment. The demon inside of her was spiteful, even to the one who was responsible for her and her child being alive in the first place. She walked out of the church, determined that if she was going to have to continue to suffer, then she wanted Hattie Mae to join her. She needed to turn on Hattie Mae to satisfy the demon inside, the misery that wanted company. A few days after Nika walked out of the church, ACS came to Hattie Mae's house and ripped Desire out of her arms.

CHAPTER FIVE

By the time Desire Mitchell reached thirteen she had become a professional foster child, having been placed in over thirty foster or group homes. For the most part, all of her caretakers considered Desire troublesome and incorrigible. Her assets were her resourcefulness and her street smarts. Despite the abuse and neglect she endured in foster care over the years, she had learned to adapt to hostile environments. It hardened her. No matter how much she was beaten by her foster parents, she would never give them the satisfaction of shedding a tear in front of their faces. There were only so many times they could beat her before she became numb.

She became a master manipulator, thief, and con artist,

learning to use her wits and fists to deal with whatever circumstances challenged her. And if need be, and always as a last resort, she would aim to kill. Desire had learned the art of spit razors—spitting out an Oxford razor that she kept stored in her mouth at all times. Her hidden secret could slash anyone who posed a threat. Desire even learned to eat and sleep with a razor in her mouth, and no one ever knew it.

She soon found herself living with the Corleys, a family straight out of a bad fairy tale. The environment Hattie Mae could have given Desire, despite her age, seemed foreign in the surroundings that Desire came to hate. There was Mother Corley, a bitter, wicked woman in her forties. She was always angry because of a lack of money. Money was the only reason she had taken in Desire. The cash stipends and food stamps allotted to her monthly added to income she desperately needed just to get by. She had twin daughters, Layla and Kayla, spoiled rotten fifteen-year-olds who despised Desire from day one for moving into their apartment and taking away one of their bedrooms. Desire was just one of many kids on rotation through their apartment. At first, the foster kids had been new playmates and potential siblings. But they always left almost as quickly as they had come, only to be replaced by new faces taking over the extra bedroom. The twins couldn't even remember all the names and faces. Desire was just another name and face that Mother Corley made clear was simply an extra resource to keep money coming in, certainly nobody that would be invited to make a real home there. When Desire moved in, Kayla and Layla treated her as if she weren't even there, because they knew one day soon she wouldn't be.

Mother Corley let Desire know from the jump that she wasn't shit and not to expect shit from her. If she wasn't there to eat when food was placed on the table, then she went without a meal. If she wasn't in the house by 11 P.M., she wouldn't be let in. The last thing that she made clear was that if she ever caught Desire stealing or putting her black hands on one of the twins, she would beat her ass.

Despite all the rigorous demands and constant nitpicking, Desire was happy; at least there she knew who the enemies were and where they stood. Desire wasn't afraid of them, by any means. She allowed them to talk all the shit that they wanted and let them have their way. She didn't want to go back to the state-run facility, where she would be monitored all the time, just like being in jail.

In the evening, Desire came and went as she pleased, though she mostly stayed in. The only thing that Desire cared about was the cassette tape that she still held on to, the one with her mother's voice on it. She had never known her mother that well to begin with. She had been literally torn from her minutes after birth, and the separation had only gotten wider over time. When Nika had disappeared for the last time, Desire was too young to have committed her face to memory. The only connection she had to her mother were moments of hearing her voice streaming from a cassette recorder. She treasured these moments in the privacy of her room. Desire played the tape every single night just as she went to bed, and guarded it with her life. One of the reasons Desire stayed in at night was because she was tired from all of the mischief she got into by day. She rarely attended school and would occupy most of her day with the other truants and runaways at the underground arcade room on 42nd Street. It was there that she spent most of her time, but one day, when she ventured beyond the arcade, she met a twelve-year-old Brooklyn runaway, Tiah, whom she would take under her wing.

Desire met Tiah one day when, prowling the Fulton Street Mall in Brooklyn with a couple of the other gang members, she laid eyes on an unattended shopping bag full of shoes. Even though the girls who were the possible owners stood nearby gossiping and laughing among themselves, it was an opportunity Desire couldn't pass by. She waited until all four of the girls in the pack had turned their backs, then she raced toward the bag like a jungle cat. She snatched it up in one move. She heard somebody shout, "Yo, that bitch running away with yo bag!" but she didn't look back to see who had said it. Adrenaline rushed through her body as she ran faster, certain that the pack of girls was behind her. Her own gang had been oblivious to the fact that she had even made a move. She didn't know where they were and didn't have a second to think about it. The wind hit her in the face as she weaved in between the thick crowd of shoppers in the mall like they were parts of an obstacle course. She may have been able to save herself by dropping the shopping bag, but as she ran she thought of the amount of money she could get for what was inside. That amount would get her one step closer to escaping the Corley house and possibly getting her own place. The dream of that place kept her running.

Unknown to her, a girl had noticed someone running through the crowd as if her life depended on it. The same girl saw the pack of heavier girls who struggled to keep up. This girl was bored and lonely, happy to have something exciting to look at to take her mind off the fact that she had to figure out somewhere to sleep that night. This girl wore clothes she had been recycling for days, and her hands tightly held the straps of the book bag on her back. It contained everything she owned in the world, which was not much. This girl had stepped away from the sidewalk and into the street to get a better look at the action. This girl had noticed the pack closing in on the runner, and had strained her neck to get an even better look. This girl didn't notice that the runner was headed her way. This girl was Tiah.

Desire slammed into Tiah, knocking both of them down. A couple of shoe boxes spilled from the bag, but Desire didn't let it go. She lay sprawled on the sidewalk, dazed and out of breath. Having fallen, she had disappeared into the crowd that went about shopping. The pack had slowed down, wondering in what direction the robber had gone. Tiah had not been running like crazy, so she was able to get herself together seconds before Desire, who was slowly coming to and trying to figure out her next move. Tiah saw the pack of girls stop and look around. She shoved Desire, who first looked at her like she was about to kill her. Desire spit a razor out of her mouth, ready to slash the girl's throat, certain that this was somebody who was ready to beat her to a pulp over a bag of shoes. But she had spit the razor too far, nearer to her enemy's hands than her own. As she scrambled to grab the razor off the street, Tiah flicked it away and grabbed Desire's hand. Desire was thrown off guard. The girl hadn't snatched up her weapon to use it against her. Her instincts told her to relax.

"Don't stand up," the girl warned her. "They lookin for you. You gotta crawl."

Tiah then started to slither through the crowd as people finally began to stop and notice. Desire blindly followed. The pack didn't notice the people pointing and laughing at two black girls, one dragging a shopping bag full of shoes that were one by one spilling onto the street, girls who scooted on their bellies on the dirty cement. Tiah led Desire behind a car whose owner had parked illegally with the hazards flashing. The pack was too busy going after the people who were picking up the fallen shoes like they had just struck gold to notice Tiah and Desire slip into a clothing store, where they waited together, for what seemed like hours, inside a locked fitting room.

ਲ਼   ਲ਼   ਲ਼

Living with two sisters had created a need in Desire to have one. At the Corley's there was no one to talk to or interact with. She came through the door, took off her coat, went to her room and daydreamed. She would hear Layla and Kayla listening to the latest R&B songs, watching funny television shows and sharing all the gossip from school. She always wanted to join them, but knew she wasn't welcome. In Tiah, she saw the realization of the dream to have a partner, a sidekick, a die-hard companion who could play the same role as a twin sister. Like Desire, Tiah was in the streets running away from a home that made her miserable. In the streets, a mentor is often necessary to survive. She was young, fresh, green and at a loss as to how to survive in the jungle that had created her predicament. She needed Desire, and Desire needed her.

Forty-second Street, or the Deuce as some called it, was where Desire joined the brazen Midtown Pickpocket Exchange, a highly organized band of thieves who robbed tourists. Within minutes after getting the cards or checkbooks, hijacked by a skillfully practiced hand, the victim's identity would be lifted and placed on a bogus state ID card. By the time the victims realized they'd been hoodwinked, each and every credit card that was missing would be maxed out to the limit. Though Desire was younger than the rest of the gang, they saw in her a determination to be down and a willingness to learn any hustle or grind to the smallest detail. When Desire was permitted to join the crew, Tiah naturally went with her. The two were like a package deal. What gave Desire the most pleasure was stealing, plain and simple. Whether straight boosting or prowling with the wolves, Desire was queen bee in this domain.

Contrary to popular belief, a booster was the type of thief who required some degree of technical savvy in addition to sharp instincts. He or she might have to pop or demagnetize security alarms, or ink tags, all the while playing the role that they belonged in the store. The boosters who rolled in packs used the wolf technique, initially begun by a group of grimey Brooklyn cats who made a name for themselves in the news and the streets with their guerilla-like tactics. They would roll sometimes fifty deep in a pack and bum-rush an entire store, ripping items from the shelves, emptying the store in a matter of seconds, like a swarm of locusts. Desire was down for almost anything, but since she was used to doing dirt by her lonesome, she became a natural solo booster. She did, however, teach Tiah the game, so her young protégé wouldn't have to starve on the streets.

"The stuff that's gonna be worth the most ain't gonna have the labels blastin loud and clear," she told Tiah one day. They had taken the train to 34th Street to scout out Macy's Department Store. Desire had no plans to try to boost from Macy's, at least not then; the crowd was always too thick and the security was always too tight. On her own, Desire could have probably made it out with a small stash that would bring her a lot of money on the streets. But with Tiah by her side, she didn't want to take the risk that a mistake would be made. So she simply guided her protégé along the expensive shoe, purse and perfume aisles and pointed out the things she should be looking to boost.

"Anything that say Chanel, Gucci, Prada, Louis Vuitton . . . all that's gonna be worth something on the street. Like we can sell it for just a small fraction of what the price really is and make a lot of money."

Tiah looked amazed at all the genuine items whose knockoffs she had only seen. She marveled at how much sturdier and more expensive they appeared. Even the perfume seemed to smell stronger. In the first-floor handbag section, she looked at the price tag hanging from one large, white leather Coach bag with a hard brown buckle. She bucked her eyes at the amount.

"Two hundred and ninety-nine dollars!" she yelled. Desire shushed her immediately.

"You can't never do that," she warned. "Don't never act like you surprised at the prices."

"But I can get this for forty dollars in Chinatown," Tiah stammered.

"Naw," Desire corrected, "you can't get *this.*" She pulled the bag down from its prop in the middle aisle display. It was securely bolted to the panel by a hidden cord. A blond saleswoman looked over at them suspiciously. Desire pretended not to see her as she opened the bag wide for Tiah to look inside. Desire was elated to have someone to talk to who actually wanted to listen to what she had to say. She pointed at the small leather square sewn into the inside of the purse. Tiah looked at it and began to read slowly, as some of the words were hard for her: "This is a Coach bag. It was handcrafted in China from natural cowhide leather. The var . . . ia . . . tions in the grain are cha . . . rac . . . ter . . . istic of natural full-grain leather. It's su . . . pe . . . ri . . . or crafts . . . man . . . ship and attention to detail reflect our com . . . mit . . . ment to en . . . dur . . . ing qua . . . li . . . ty." Tiah stopped.

"Keep reading," Desire told her. Tiah looked surprised.

"But it's just a really long number," Tiah said.

"See, that's how you can tell what's real and what's fake," Desire told her. "That really long number is what you gotta be looking for. Them bags in Chinatown ain't got this number on the inside. That's called a registration number, and all this expensive shit we can't afford, now, you best believe it got one. Some of 'em might look real, but they gonna tear up way before this one will. This one won't never tear up. This one one day might be worth even more than what it's already worth. You know, if you save it for a real, real long time, then somebody might find it and want it even more 'cause they ain't making 'em no more."

"But what's so special about it?" Tiah asked. "It look like the same bag—"

Desire interrupted her. "Technically, it is. But see this number, that's what make the difference between the rich and the poor. Rich people buy the bags with the numbers. We buy the bags with just the look. But some of us got some style and sense. I don't want to carry no broke-ass fake bag. I want to carry the real thing. I want to carry the bag that the rich folks know is real."

"What's the difference?" Tiah didn't understand what Desire was trying to say. But Desire had already made up her mind to be patient. She had already learned the things about the world that nobody had taught Tiah yet.

"The difference is what it mean to everybody else, not you," Desire said. "This bag with the number mean rich. That shit without the numbers mean fake and you just a wannabe if you carrying it. You really ain't shit, you just pretending to be. I ain't tryin to be no pretender."

Tiah shook her head, soaking in all Desire was telling her. The blond saleslady had appeared behind them. She cleared her throat loudly and folded her arms.

"Excuse me, can I help you two with something?" She didn't even bother to smile at the two street girls, who she had been trained to watch if they drifted into her section.

Desire simply looked at the saleslady and smiled.

"Not yet," she said, and grabbed Tiah by the hand to lead her out of Macy's. "You have a nice day," she called back to the saleslady.

≈   ≈   ≈

Desire didn't have the rich people stuff yet, but that didn't mean she didn't want what she did have. At the Corley's, Desire had never bothered to unpack her belongings, instead opting to be mobile and ready to go at a moment's notice. All her worldly possessions were contained in a cheap cardboard suitcase. Most of it were things she had stolen: a couple of bags, items of clothing and cassette tapes of her favorite singers. Her prized possession, though, was the cassette tape that she kept stashed safely inside rolled-up tube socks, along with a few hundred dollars she had saved. Desire would stay away for a day or two. She did it several times and was never missed. When she walked into her room one evening, after being gone for the whole night before, she knew immediately that someone had tampered with her things. Something just didn't feel right in the room, like even the energy had been misplaced. She noticed a slight wrinkle on her bed that had not been there when she had left. Almost nothing in the room belonged to her anyway. The bed, a small chair, bookshelves with no books and a dresser drawer with no clothes were all just props in Mother Corley's act, cover-ups to her real agenda: to fool the social workers into believing that she really cared about making a home for the kids she took in. Desire didn't give a fuck about anything in the room but what was in her suitcase—most of all, the cassette tape. Instinctively, she ran to her suitcase and unzipped it in a panic. Her hands searched the corners for the socks. Unable to find them, she dumped everything on the floor, sifting through each piece. Desire stood up and began searching the room. She looked in the trash can, and that's when she saw it.

"What the fuck?" she muttered as her eyes finally rested on what was left of her cassette tape. She bent down and pulled out a tangled mess of tape that was unreeled, the plastic snapped in half. Desire stared at it with dread as her jaw began to twitch wildly. A single tear fell from her eye, and others were coming fast behind it. She wished Tiah were there so they could bum-rush the two bitches she knew had done it. Just as she began to plot the revenge that she and Tiah might carry out on the evil twins, she noticed a shadow by her door. She heard footsteps running softly, and then a door quietly snapped shut. A demonic scowl overtook Desire's face. She took off down the hall and burst into her foster sisters' room. She held up the ruined tape with one hand.

"Who the fuck touched my shit?"

Both girls were on their beds, with magazines open in front of them. Kayla frowned and said, "What stuff?"

"You fuckin heard me," Desire yelled as she approached the twin with authority. "Which one of y'all bitches did this shit to my tape?"

"How you gonna come bustin in our room accusing us of stuff, Desire? Nobody touched your shit," Layla lied.

Desire continued to press. "I ain't playing with y'all . . . who went through my shit?"

Kayla sucked her teeth and said, "I don't care if you playing or not, but we ain't touch your stuff."

"What?" Desire said as she opened her arm. "Y'all afraid to tell the truth to a little old girl like me? What . . . y'all afraid or something?"

Layla stepped in Desire's face and said, "You can talk all the smack you want, I ain't afraid of nothing, slim."

Desire shook her head and snickered and said, "Just as I thought, y'all bitches are pussy—ain't got no heart!"

Desire chumped them both, then pretended to be leaving.

Kayla yelled, "Yeah, bitch, we went through your shit, now what the fuck you gonna do about it? This is our house and everything that's up in here is ours." She turned to her sister and said sarcastically, "All she worried about really is her lil bit of money she probably sold her ass for." She reached in her pocket and pulled out the tube sock with the money in it and threw it toward her. "So take the shit and get out."

Desire paid the money no mind. "I don't give a fuck about the money! Just tell me why'd y'all do this to my shit."

The twins had never seen this mean streak in Desire. They wanted to dismiss her, but something told them somebody should at least try to offer an explanation. Desire looked like she was ready to explode if something didn't calm her down. Layla was the twin who didn't want to take the risk.

"Aiight, we were just curious to know what was on that tape. We ain't heard nothing but a lady singing some church song, and that's when the tape player started eating the tape and it got bunched up."

"Fuck her, Layla, you don't have to explain shit to her. So fuck you, fuck the tape and fuck that dope fiendin ass bitch on the tape who was singing!"

Desire snapped, and jumped on Kayla with lightning-quick speed. She whaled on her with no mercy, slapping her until she fell to the ground.

"You fucking bitch," Desire yelled as she stomped the twin relentlessly.

Kayla curled into a fetal position. She protected her head, and Layla, who was stunned to see the frail little girl tear into her sister like a wild beast, grabbed Desire from behind to stop her from further assaulting Kayla. Desire countered in one precise move. Instinctively, she expertly spit the razor from her mouth and into her hand. It went down so quick the poor twin didn't even see it coming. Desire caught her in the arm with the razor. In blind fury, she looked at Kayla and was ready to put in work on her face, when all of a sudden she felt a harsh blow to her head. The last thing Desire remembered was seeing stars after Mother Corley dealt a sickening crack to Desire's head. She delivered one more hit for good measure, landing Desire in the hospital.

≈ ≈ ≈

Desire suffered a contusion to the brain and a broken arm. She was a ward of the state, and was supposed to be protected as such. Knowing this made Mother Corley nervous. She suddenly changed into the perfect image of the "nice" foster mother, bringing McDonald's, a brand-new outfit from the Gap, and plenty of sweets to Desire's hospital room. Desire had no intention of telling the authorities who Mother Corley really was. She had been through this so many times before and had taken far worse beatings from the best of them. But there was no reason not to let the fat bitch sweat a little, she thought.

"So, Desire, you know if those people start coming 'round, snooping, they go'n put you back in the system. I hear them places is just like prison. They lock you in your room and everything. That ain't no place for a young lady to be. Don't I let you do what you want to do? Do I ever say anything when you stay out all times of night?" Mother Corley asked all of this in a whisper, as she looked over her shoulder toward the young patient in the bed next to Desire's. "Now, all you got to tell them is that you fell down the stairs, and that will be that. So you better—"

She was interrupted by a nurse who entered the room.

"Oh, hi," said the nurse, with a smile. "I'll be over in a moment to take her vital signs. I'll take the other patient's first, so you have to step out for a second if you don't mind."

Mother Corley smiled and nodded as she walked away, satisfied that she had put up enough of a front for an authority. How a foster child could have ended up with her was evidence of the system that didn't care. To Mother Corley, Desire had simply become a paid bill, more food in the refrigerator, extra benefits that a woman who didn't have many other choices could use a child for. She barely loved herself or the twin girls she had been left alone to raise. There was no way she could love Desire. Someone who needed serious help had been put in charge of helping another. It was an arrangement that would never work.

Mother Corley's smile disappeared as she slyly turned. So low that no one else in the room could hear, she reminded Desire one last time, "You being discharged tomorrow, so remember what I said, lil heifer. I'm the only one who want yo black ass."

Desire just stared at her, not saying a word. She let the words sink in and didn't even try to think of what an alternative would or could be. She was stuck here, in this predicament, and had nowhere else to go. She had no choices. After the nurse finished taking the other patient's vital signs, she approached Desire's bed with a mobile blood-pressure stand. Her face was warm and open, even though the girl in front of her was obviously untrusting. But this nurse was used to working with these types of cases. She could almost guess, without trying, what possible circumstances could have landed this child here. She smiled at Desire and said, "Hello, young lady. I'm Nurse Dixon. What is your name?"

Desire simply stared at the ceiling, opting not to answer. She hated authority figures anyway, so the less said the better.

The nurse awaited an answer, but there was none. Unfazed, she continued smiling and said, "Don't feel like talking much? I understand." She reached for her chart and said, "Let's see, Desire Mitchell . . ." As if struck by a bolt of lightning, she looked at Desire and then again at the chart. She searched the chart for Desire's date of birth, and sure enough, in black and white, February 4, 1984, a day she would not forget. Her mind raced back to that day many years past when she had come to work to find that a child who had been rescued from certain death in freezing East Harlem snow was now fighting for her life in the neonatal crisis ward.

Quickly getting over the initial shock, Nurse Dixon put the thermometer in Desire's mouth. She also checked her blood pressure. She was nervous about what she knew in her gut of the identity of her latest patient, but she needed to continue to do her job. She asked Desire to sit up so she could wrap her arm with the pad. The flimsy hospital gown shifted and exposed a horrid scar on the patient's back. When Nurse Dixon caught a glimpse of it, she gasped. The conclusion as to the origin of the scar was undeniable.

Desire knew that the secret was out. She knew exactly what professionals were trained to look for as evidence of child abuse. Desire could not think of being torn from one hell, one that she had come to at least know, into another that was potentially worse. She pleaded as if her life depended on it.

"She didn't do this to me; these are old . . ."

Nurse Dixon's arms were folded. She looked unconvinced. Desire continued to beg.

"Please don't tell nobody, or they gonna send me to a group home again."

Nurse Dixon was speechless as she stared into Desire's terror-filled eyes. She broke her professional composure and threw her arms around Desire. She was torn apart by the fact that a patient who had been born in such horrendous circumstances had returned to the hospital in arguably an even worse situation. Nurse Dixon could not help but think that it would have been better if Desire had not made it, that the child's fight to save her own life was not worth the pain she continued to get in life. All she could do was give Desire a warm hug to calm her down. Desire could not hug her back.

"You poor child," Nurse Dixon whispered as she embraced Desire. All she could think was "Why?" but she couldn't say it. She had to regain her composure in order to do her job. "Do you have any other injuries like this?"

Desire did not answer. She wanted to show and tell, but she was afraid to. However, Nurse Dixon was just as insistent with Desire as she had been with Nika years before. She wanted answers, and was not going to leave the room without them. It was a tug-of-war, but Nurse Dixon convinced Desire to show her the other wounds. Slowly, Desire disrobed. Nurse Dixon could not believe her eyes. Desire's body was a map of abuse. Nurse Dixon stared in total horror upon the multitude of purplish-black dead flesh from past beatings.

The nurse had seen it all before, but never like this. For a child that suffered at birth unwittingly and without fault of her own, only to suffer unimaginable pain that no child should have to bear, all because she fell through the cracks of human bureaucracy. In all the cases that she'd seen in her thirty-plus years, nothing, even this day, had had such a profound effect on her as the case with Nika and Desire Mitchell years ago.

Nurse Dixon was on fire.

"I know who you are," she told Desire. "I was the nurse who tended to you when you were born. I remember your mother, like she was just here yesterday."

The words felt strange coming from Nurse Dixon's mouth. For Desire, they hit even harder. It felt as if a searing piece of metal had pierced her insides. This was followed by an overwhelmingly warm and exciting feeling. But Desire did not want to show even an inkling of interest. She had been disappointed way too many times by people in her life pretending to care about her. She simply listened. She wanted badly to ask her how her mother had looked, why her mother had left her, and where her mother was now. But she couldn't bring herself to know any more.

Nurse Dixon didn't press Desire that day, but she looked her in her eyes and promised her that she no longer need worry about being placed in a group home.

"What, you gonna adopt me or something?" Desire asked.

Nurse Dixon smiled cunningly and answered, "No, but if God's willing, I know someone else who will." Seeing Desire's confused expression, Nurse Dixon assured her that she had everything under control.

۳   ۳   ۳

The next day, Mother Corley was at the hospital early. She rushed Desire to get dressed.

"Hurry up, I ain't got all day. I already missed a day of work and I ain't missing another."

Just as Desire had finished getting dressed, Nurse Dixon entered the room, along with another woman. The nurse had a serious and concerned expression on her face. Desire quickly sized up the strange woman, relieved to know she wasn't from any of the social welfare agencies. She didn't have one of those stiff, fake smiles like the others. This woman beamed from the inside out as she stared at Desire.

Mother Corley looked at the papers in the nurse's hand. "Are those her discharge papers? I have to get to work."

"No, ma'am," Nurse Dixon announced. "Desire will not be leaving with you today."

Mother Corley shook her head angrily. "Oh, no, I ain't missing another day of work 'cause of this child."

"Ms. Corley, that is the least of your worries," Nurse Dixon said. Everyone in the room was quiet and tense. Desire could sense that things were about to drastically change.

Mother Corley stood speechless. She turned her attention and anger toward Desire.

"You ungrateful little heifer. After all I did for you, you betray me?" The outburst showed her true colors. Nurse Dixon decided to get down to business after that.

"This is a paper relinquishing your custody of Desire, and the other one is a temporary order of protection to stay away from her until you appear before a judge," announced Nurse Dixon.

Mother Corley fumed as she read the papers. Her ruse was up.

She did not even have a shred of integrity left to ask for forgiveness.

"Fine . . . keep her ass," she spat. "She ain't worth having anyway. Who gonna want your thieving, black ass now?"

Nurse Dixon smiled. "By the way, I'd like to introduce you to Ms. Hattie Mae Evans . . . Desire's legal guardian."

For a moment, all the women in the room were still. Then Hattie Mae could no longer contain herself as she laid eyes on the child whose life she had saved. She had given up all hope of ever holding Desire in her arms again, yet here she was, right before her. Hattie Mae walked over to Desire slowly. She looked at the bandage on Desire's head and the cast on her arm. She took a deep breath, then lifted the back of Desire's shirt. She stared at Desire's wounds, then closed her eyes to hold back her tears. She didn't want to imagine what had happened to Desire.

"She had that before she came to live with me, huh," Mother Corley huffed. She was desperate for a way out, but there was none. Nobody responded to her as Desire allowed herself to unstiffen in the strange woman's arms.

CHAPTER SIX

Time had created an unfamiliar foreignness between the elderly woman and the child whose life she had saved. As Desire adjusted to her new environment, she and Hattie Mae seemed like strangers. Desire, still apprehensive, refused to unpack her things even though she had her own room. Miss Hattie stayed out of her way and didn't impose questions upon Desire. For her, it was simply enough to know that the girl now, again, had a loving, caring and safe place to live. She did try to constantly reassure Desire that this was her home and that she was welcome to anything in it. Desire would simply reply, "Yes, ma'am," with a wide smile. Hattie Mae did not know if the girl actually believed it yet. But she was determined to prove to Desire that she was for real.

One time, in the middle of the night, Hattie Mae was awakened by a slight noise coming from the kitchen. She got up to inspect. As she flicked on the kitchen light, Desire quickly closed the refrigerator door. She was holding something behind her back. She hadn't told Hattie Mae about how she was denied food—not just at Mother Corley's, but other foster homes as well. Hattie Mae saw the scared and guilty look in Desire's eyes as she tried to hide what she thought was thievery. Hattie Mae needed to let her know it was not just okay to eat here, but to not be ashamed of the need.

Hattie Mae smiled and said, "Have as much as you want, just wash out whatever you use." She scrunched her face and continued, "Grandma Hattie don't like no roaches." She winked and returned to her room.

There were other incidents such as this, where Desire resorted to behavior she had used to survive and found that Hattie Mae did not scold her for her actions. Desire spent many hours locked behind the door of her bedroom, and she never had to worry about Mother Corley questioning her about her need to be alone. She did not express much joy when Hattie Mae would bring her little presents: books, nice hair clips and bows and even pretty blouses and sturdy shoes. Sometimes, they both would merely stare at the television for hours, watching channel after channel. Desire never requested to watch anything special, though Hattie Mae always took the time to ask. Desire had not grown up knowing that she had the power of choice, and Hattie Mae simply let her come to that realization in her own time. However, the peace and calm in the house slowly earned Hattie Mae a quiet respect from Desire. Desire did not know that this was the beginning of love.

Months after she had arrived, Desire became comfortable enough to ask about her mother. One night, out of the blue, over a plate of spaghetti, Desire simply asked, "Is it true that I was born in the street and that you saved me and my mother from freezing to death?"

Hattie Mae was speechless. She couldn't find the words to tell Desire the truth. She didn't know if she should lie or not. Furthermore, she was shocked that Desire even knew this information. But then Desire reached into her pocket and pulled out a wrinkled and yellowed newspaper article. She threw it on the table in the midst of their dinner. The headline read: "Mother, Fetus Near Frozen to Death on Harlem Streets." She had found it earlier tucked inside one of the many Bibles Hattie Mae kept scattered throughout the house.

Hattie Mae stared at the article, then took a long gulp of the sweet iced tea she had made for dinner. She did not have to read the article to know what it said. She had read the words many, many times, committed them to memory on the long nights she had had to pray herself out of worrying about Desire. Desire continued to glare at her, forcing Hattie Mae to finally speak.

"Well, I guess it is 'bout time you learn your history, chile," she said, rising to clear the table and rake their plates.

"Is this my history?" Desire pleaded. "This where I came from? This how I was born?"

Hattie Mae gripped the edge of the kitchen sink for the

strength she would need to explain the truth, and for the strength Desire would need to hear it.

"Desire," she began, "yo mama loved you very, very much. Yo mama was a good girl who got caught up in bad things. She was in a terrible predicament. She had the devil inside of her and he wasn't leaving."

She turned to find Desire's head bowed. She went back to the table and took Desire's face in her hands.

"But that don't mean she didn't love you, chile," Hattie Mae told Desire. "That don't mean she didn't care. She tried to keep you, but them drugs just had her too tight. She had to give you up. And she gave you up to me. And then when I wouldn't 'low her to keep on killin herself, she got mad at me for trying to do what was best for her 'cause she didn't think it was best. She had the state take you away from me, but she ain't do it to hurt you. She did it to hurt me. But don't none of that matter now, 'cause God is good. The Savior always gonna win in the end. It took him some time, but he got you back to where you need to be."

Everything in Desire wanted to be tough and strong. But this news was too much. How could her mother have really loved her if she had done the things that made Desire come into the world to nearly die in the freezing snow? How could her mother give her up if she had really wanted her? And how could her mother truly want her if she had torn her away from a good home and started the cycle of broken ones she had suffered through? She wanted to ask these questions of Hattie Mae, but couldn't find the words. She was blank as she tried to hold it together and soak in the news.

"We just gotta pray for her, chile," Hattie Mae continued. "We gotta pray that she out there taking care of herself, that she gonna be all right, that one day she gonna wake up and realize what she losing now by being out in them streets. All that ain't got nothing to do with you. She gotta do that for herself."

Suddenly, Desire ran from the table. Hattie Mae was startled as Desire's chair toppled over. Seconds later, she heard Desire's door slam and loud music coming from the other side. Hattie Mae decided to just let Desire be that night, as she had on so many others.

～ ～ ～

Two months passed after Desire learned the truth of where she had come from. Desire was settled in at Hattie Mae's and enrolled in her first year of high school. Hattie Mae's only request of Desire was that she attend church with her every Sunday and go to school without fail. Desire agreed, but also asked to make a request of her own.

"Of course, chile, anything yo grandma can do. What is it?" Hattie Mae said.

Desire went to her room and immediately came back out and reminded her, "Now, remember, Hattie Mae—I mean Grandma—you promised me." Hattie Mae looked at Desire with a wide smile and nodded. Desire turned toward her room door and yelled, "Tiah, you can come out now."

Suddenly, the young girl that Desire had befriended from 42nd Street appeared. She walked timidly into the kitchen. She and Desire had continued to wild out in the streets, but now Desire faced the fact that it could be time to stop all that. She felt safe enough that she could try to change things in her life. Desire's absence from the streets had affected Tiah terribly, since the girl had no one else to truly care about her. She had several older brothers but they were more concerned about the streets than her. For weeks, they had been meeting secretly. As Desire slowly pulled herself out of the gang's mischief, Tiah had become more desperate. She had begun asking Desire to sneak her into Hattie Mae's apartment in the middle of the night so she could have somewhere to sleep. She always left before dawn. It had been Desire's idea to see if Hattie Mae would let her stay permanently.

All smiles, Desire said, "Grandma, this is my friend Tiah. She ain't got nowhere to go."

Hattie Mae was stunned as she stared at the girl in front of her. Tiah's shoes were battered and her clothes looked too small. Her hair had been sloppily done. Tiah shook so nervously, a whisper could have blown her over. Hattie Mae said nothing then. She needed to think about what she wanted to do. She simply grabbed Tiah's hand and brought both girls into her wide arms.

"You want something to eat?" she asked Tiah, as the frightened girls pressed into her chest exhaled.

ɛ   ɛ   ɛ

Tiah was also a ward of the state, with no guardian in the picture. Part of the reason for that was because the authorities couldn't find her. Tiah had disappeared from the face of the earth as far as most of her state caretakers knew. Minimal effort was put forth to find her, because most social workers' case files overwhelmed them. They had chalked Tiah up to just another set of numbers that needed to be entered into a database. There were codes for everything, even missing children. They knew that she would turn up again, someday, and become an active case again. Until that day, they had to write her off and go on to the other piles of folders that had overtaken their desks. Hattie Mae was determined that this child would not be a case closed.

Hattie Mae knew that it was God's will to place Tiah in her life, just like it had been His will to bring Desire to her. She knew that her age was an issue and reached out once again to her old friend Judge Ross for a favor. The women had not forgotten the horrible incident that they both had been a part of correcting. They had not forgotten the role they played in truly rescuing Desire from what would have been certain death had she stayed with Nika when she was a baby. And once again, Judge Ross expedited the case and granted Hattie Mae total guardianship of another true unfortunate—Tiah. That same day, Desire asked and was granted that her name be changed legally from Desire Mitchell to Desire Evans. Tiah could not believe what was happening. Everything had happened so fast, it was as if she were dreaming. One day her world revolved around running from authorities, stealing to keep money in her pocket and finding a place to crash for the night and then transformed into having a foster mother and foster sister, going back to school and having a stable place to live. Almost overnight, her confidence began to build, and she had a positive outlook for the first time since she could remember. She had met a girl who had promised simply to teach her how to steal to survive, and now that girl had given her a home. She was attached to Desire like a puppy attached to its new owner.

As Desire lay in bed on the eve of becoming an Evans, she repeated the name over and over again in her mind. Suddenly, she heard a silent whimper coming from Tiah's bed.

Desire sat up and asked, "Tiah, you all right?"

Tiah didn't answer, so Desire rose from her bed and approached her and asked again, "Tiah, you okay? Why you crying?"

Wiping her eyes, Tiah said she was okay. Desire sat down next to her on her bed and said, "Tiah, if you ain't happy here right now, it's all right, but trust me, you gonna get used to it . . ."

Tiah wiped her eyes again and said, "Naw, it's nothing like that, I guess I'm crying 'cause I'm happy."

Desire stared at her and smiled. Tiah continued, "Desire, you was the only one that showed me love out there on them streets." Tiah strained for the words. "And then . . . then . . . when you got a home, you ain't forget about me, you came and got me, and now I got a home, a real home with a real foster mother and. . . ."

Tiah tried to fight back the tears, but she lost.

"Now I have a real, real foster sister in you, Desire . . ." Tiah broke down. "I . . . I don't ever know how to thank you . . ."

Tears fell from Desire's eyes as she hugged Tiah, telling her she didn't have to say any more.

"I love you, Desire, you my real foster sister," Tiah cried.

Desire raised Tiah's wet chin, squared her face toward Tiah's eyes and said, "Listen to me, we ain't foster sisters, we *sisters*. You hear me? Sisters, and we always gonna be together."

Through her tears, Tiah looked into Desire's eyes and asked, "For real, Desire?"

"For real!" Desire nodded as they embraced.

PART TWO

This is the point in the story when most people want to kid themselves into believing that the happy ending has arrived. This is the point in the story where it should have ended. But it didn't. This is no neat happy ending, for the story continued, because the forces that created them had not gone anywhere. The girl had been pulled out of the streets, but the streets were still there. And the streets did not like to give up the ones that it had claimed as their own. The bustling, historical and sometimes beautiful Harlem streets that were finally starting to attract tourism and businesses and middle-class people were not ready to give up on the task of creating chaos, sadness and confusion. Change didn't happen as fast as the rest of the world wanted to believe it could. The people, places and unfortunate conditions that had created the tragedy that was the girl's birth were still there—only they became more hidden. In new buildings being erected in vacant lots that had been havens for crack addicts, behind sparkling new facades that were meant to attract renters with higher incomes, on streets where new businesses were springing up faster than the people who lived around them could make the money to shop inside of them. These streets were brand-new to some, but old to many. No matter how much the look of the streets and the price to stay on them changed, there were those who would never forget what the streets had been and done to them. There were memories on those streets that newcomers did not see and papers did not report. There was sadness and anger on these streets that had made people want to tear them off the Island of Manhattan. And the taste of the streets was a hard one for those they had conquered to spit out.

CHAPTER SEVEN

Thanks to Hattie Mae, Desire and Tiah were active members of the youth Bible study classes, which met weekly, and they had given up on running with pickpocket and boosting gangs. They had lost the urge to mingle with boys who tried to convince them to have sex and girls who were too insecure to not be jealous of every other female who crossed their paths. The world Hattie Mae created for them was like a new one. In addition to Bible study classes, Desire and Tiah both joined the junior choir. They grew to love singing the gospel and both had magnificent voices. Every week, on Sunday the church would rotate between the adult gospel choir and the junior group. Desire developed such a passion for singing that it took over her soul. She decided then and there that it was possible she could become a singer.

The knowledge of the circumstances of her birth had faded somewhat from her memory. She had decided not to let her past get her down. She worked hard to learn singing techniques even though she had a natural talent. She dreamed of being lead singer of not only the junior choir, but the adult choir as well. However, something, or someone, always stood in her way. That someone was a girl named Chanel, who was the same age as Desire. Desire knew she could sing better than Chanel but felt that because Chanel's uncle was a deacon in the church, Chanel was given preferential treatment. Chanel had it all: voice, cute looks and she had been a singer for most of her young life. Even her name was associated with everything Desire had dreamed of being: rich, respected and prized. Tiah paid the girl no mind. But whenever Desire looked at Chanel, who was given the most attention and praise of all the young singers, she felt an uncontrollable flood of envy. In her mind, Chanel became an obstacle to her success, just like the horrible foster homes and mean streets had been. Desire knew that almost everything she had gotten in her life before Hattie Mae, she'd had to fight for. And she was ready to fight for the same praise and recognition that was showered on Chanel each week. If she was given just one chance at lead, Desire would prove to everyone that she deserved it. And she planned on doing just that.

Setting her plans in motion, she recruited Carvelas Vera, a virtuoso pianist who played for the entire congregation. Carvelas was also in the choir and attended Desire's school. From the moment they had officially met at the first choir practice Desire and

Tiah had attended, Carvelas had a crush on her. Desire didn't pay the small, funny-looking boy with the quiet presence any mind. He was nothing like the suited-up, loudmouthed and aggressive boys on the streets, the ones who normally caught Desire's attention. Carvelas was different. He talked to her with respect. His eyes didn't seem to bore holes through her clothes. He didn't treat her like she should bow down to him. Although Desire didn't think they could ever be any more than friends, she decided to at least allow a friendship. It was Tiah who had first pointed out that Carvelas might have other things on his mind. One night in choir practice, she passed Desire a note scribbled onto an old church program.

"Carvelas keep looking over here at you," it said. Desire muffled a giggle as she read it. She looked over at Carvelas, and sure enough, he quickly turned his eyes away as soon as she looked.

"I don't know what he looking over here for," she wrote back to Tiah, being careful to be as inconspicuous as possible so that no one would notice.

"He looking over here 'cause he want to do it to you!" was what Tiah wrote, before placing the program in Desire's lap as soon as the director turned his back. Desire laughed out loud. Tiah giggled, and everyone looked over at them.

"What y'all laughing at?" Chanel demanded to know. She didn't like the fact that she was not the center of their attention, as she was about to begin practicing her latest solo.

"None of your nosy business," Desire snapped back. Carvelas looked intrigued by Desire's fiery reply. He put his head down and pretended to be shuffling the music score in front of him.

"Well, y'all need to be paying attention," Chanel commanded.

She was a prima donna who thought she had the right, even over the director of the choir, to correct them.

"You don't need to be telling us what to do." Desire stood up and the program fell from her lap. Tiah quickly picked it up so no one would find it. Desire and Chanel stared each other down, both of them with hands on their widening hips.

"You just mad 'cause we ain't falling all over the floor over you, like the rest of these stupid folks," Desire said.

"Who you callin stupid?" one of the other high-school-aged choir girls asked.

"You, all of y'all," Chanel said, wanting everyone to turn on the new enemy who had turned on her.

"You the one that's stupid," Desire said. Tiah grabbed her by the hand and tried to pull her back into her seat, but Desire was not going to budge. The choir director finally became aware of the insurrection. He walked in front of the podium where Chanel had been preparing to show off once again.

"Is there a problem, ladies?" he asked.

"Not yet," Desire said. She sat back in her seat and avoided the glare of Chanel and the others. She became even more determined in that moment to do what she knew she needed to do. And the first thing that needed to be done was a private conversation with Carvelas. It happened while everybody was packing up, ready to burst out of the church and onto the streets.

"Hey," she said to him, innocently, as he packed away his music.

"Hey," he said back, avoiding her eyes.

"I hope you don't think I'm crazy 'cause I was snapping at Chanel," Desire said.

"Well, Chanel can kind of get on your nerves," he confessed. They both laughed.

"And she can't even really sing that great," Desire said. Tiah came running into the church to let Desire know Hattie Mae was outside waiting for them. Hattie Mae wanted to take the girls to Sylvia's soul food restaurant for dinner.

"Tell Grandma I'll be just a minute," Desire said. She needed to set her scheme in motion, but she wasn't about to miss out on some macaroni and cheese and fried chicken from Sylvia's.

"You know how she get when she ready to go," Tiah warned.

"I know Hattie Mae," Desire said. "Known her longer than you have. She'll wait." Desire turned back to Carvelas as Tiah left them alone.

"You really don't think she can sing?" Carvelas asked. He was grateful to be getting some attention. What would make Desire hold up dinner just to talk to him? Desire knew her tactic of making him feel special was working.

"I ain't saying she can't sing," Desire continued. "I'm just saying some of us can sing too, so why she gotta get all the attention?"

"Well, you know her uncle a deacon . . ."

"Exactly! That's the only reason. Carvelas, you think it's fair that she always get a solo just 'cause she can run to her uncle and complain?"

Carvelas was not one to choose sides. He liked to keep peace with everyone.

"Naw, I guess it ain't fair. But can't nobody do nothing about it."

"You think?" Desire asked. She noticed another church program resting on top of his piano. She opened the LV bag she had stolen when she was boosting, and pulled out a pen. Carvelas looked over her shoulder as she began writing her phone number on the program. She handed it to Carvelas. He was speechless. His heart began to flutter and he could feel his palms getting sweaty. He wanted to turn a cartwheel down the church aisle, but he had to hold on to his manhood. So he just shook his head.

"You want me to call you?" he asked, and he couldn't hold back a slight grin.

"Yeah," Desire said. She started to walk away from him. "I gotta go to dinner with Tiah and Grandma. Call me later on tonight."

"Yeah, okay," Carvelas said, and let himself smile as wide as he could once Desire had turned her back.

ื่ ื่ ื่

Sunday's service at Bethel A.M.E. Church was packed to capacity. The junior choir was scheduled to sing that day. It was standing room only, shoulder to shoulder as the members cooled their bodies with their hand fans. Of course, Hattie Mae sat front and center to watch her girls sing God's praises. Desire was nervous as she peered at all the people in the church, but her mind was set: she was about to show everybody who the real diva was. The moment had arrived for the deacon to introduce the choir to the congregation. As the band began to play, Desire watched Chanel step from the choir and down to the microphone. Desire looked over at Carvelas. He caught her eye and nodded, then gestured toward the microphone that he had on his piano. She was ready.

Desire eyed the microphone that Chanel would be using. Tiah

stared at it too. The volume was turned down lower than normal on the microphone, and only three people in the room knew it. As Chanel began singing her song, she immediately noticed the problem. Always graceful, she continued singing with a smile as she got through her first verse. Suddenly, and to the choir's surprise, Desire stepped out of the choir and toward the microphone on Carvelas's piano. The audience simply turned their eyes to Desire, believing that this was just another surprise the young singers had in store for them. Carvelas continued playing, pretending nothing was strange about Desire using his microphone. He played his heart out for Desire. Just as Chanel was about to belt out the second verse, she heard Desire's powerful voice filtering through the speakers.

The congregation rose to their feet, clapping in unison as Desire sang the song. The choir director was thrown off balance and into shock for a moment, but he saw the crowd's response and continued leading the choir. The choir looked confused, but the director turned his back to the audience and shrugged his shoulders.

"Keep on going," he desperately mouthed to the choir, ready to finish the song just so he could get to the bottom of the change of plans he had not been made privy to. Tiah continued to sing innocently as the director stared at her and shrugged her shoulders and started to rock back and forth to the rhythm of the song. Chanel was furious. She was thrown off, and started to sing out of key. Her out-of-key notes hit the ears of everyone in the church hard. People stared at her, but not for a good reason. She tried to get back on key, but had lost it. She was messing up the song, just as Desire was making it sound better than it had in practice.

Though angry, Chanel sang along with a fake smile. She slowly eased back into the fold of the rest of the choir, and Desire became the only soloist among them.

Desire was transcended. It was as if all the years of pain and suffering were coming out in song. Hattie Mae was in tears as she rose to her feet and praised the Lord. Carvelas played the piano as he never had before, determined to satisfy his dream girl. Desire was not nervous or scared. She had sang the song so many times and in so many different ways that she could have sung it in her sleep. Everyone else disappeared as she sank into her own world. By the end of the song, Desire had everyone on their feet, clapping, praising and worshipping the Lord in a frenzy. When Desire came out of her spiritual high and opened her eyes, she realized what she had done. She watched everyone applauding and crying out to the Lord. Even the choir director looked satisfied, relieved that what had first looked like a disaster had actually become the choir's best performance in recent memory. No longer upset, because Desire had made him look better, he nodded his head in approval and got ready to receive all the compliments that were sure to follow this Sunday's performance from the junior choir. Desire turned and looked at her sister, Tiah, who was also clapping and smiling, and then at Carvelas, who winked at her, then at Hattie Mae, who she knew was so proud of her. But the last face she saw was Chanel's, with the defeated girl's evil and wicked eyes staring at her.

༂ ༂ ༂

Desire knew Chanel would not take being upstaged at church lying down. Desire and Chanel were like nature's perfect enemies.

For two people who were so different and who couldn't stand being in the same room together, they amazingly followed the same path. They were both in the 11th grade, were the top two in the graduating class, could throw down like their lives depended on it and wouldn't back down to anyone.

But Chanel did have an edge on Desire in two areas: looks and dress. Desire had never been the dressy type. She was more of a tomboy and preferred to wear sweats, hoodies and baggy jeans. Her only interest in fashion had been the dollar amount she could get for the clothes she boosted. Chanel, however, was a fashionista who stayed laced in all the latest clothing. She was the center of attention wherever she went. The competition between Desire and Chanel would always spill outside the classroom and into the hall or the neighborhood. Though they hated each other's guts, they never came to blows—until one day.

It was during lunchtime in the cafeteria, Desire was sitting with Tiah and the rest of her clique. Chanel and her clique sat at a table behind them, and Chanel started talking shit.

"Hey, Renee," Chanel said loud enough for everyone to hear, "I was watching this old movie last night called . . . Damn, I forgot the name of it."

She snapped her fingers.

"Oh, yeah, it was called *A Street Hoe Named Desire.*"

The girls at Chanel's table all started cracking up laughing. What nobody knew about Chanel was her mother was an alcoholic and her father was a perpetually unemployed man who walked in and out of their lives. In fits of alcoholic rage, Chanel's mother took her father's absence out on her. And she would badger Chanel with degrading insults in an effort to make herself feel better. The only breaks Chanel found from this verbal abuse happened at church, and during the rare weeks when her father reappeared and made her mother calmer. But once he left, the ridicule Chanel's mother poured upon her started again—comments ranging from telling her that she wasn't never gonna be shit to warnings about her pretty little ass popping up pregnant. Ridicule was a tactic used to hurt Chanel, and she had learned to use it to hurt others.

Tiah looked at Desire, who seemed to not have heard what Chanel had said. She asked, "Yo, Dee, you know that bitch Chanel is talking about you?"

Desire seemed aloof and disinterested. "Yeah, I know."

Disgusted, Tiah said, "And you ain't gonna check that bitch?"

"Chill out, yo," Desire whispered. "You can't let a bitch like Chanel know what buttons to push," Desire continued. "That only gives her more power to use against you. Just wait and listen and use whatever she says against her."

"Yo," Chanel said to her homegirls, "that bitch hair so short, she curls her hair with Rice-A-Roni."

The whole cafeteria busted out laughing. Their reaction spurred Chanel on.

"The bitch hair so nappy, she have to take Excedrin every time she comb her hair."

Chanel had everybody in the cafeteria on their knees with laughter. Her assault continued and Desire was the center of attention. Carvelas didn't have the same lunch period as the girls, and suddenly Desire wished he were here. He'd have her back the same way he had that day in church. She was sure of it. Tiah stared at Desire, who still remained calm, not saying a word. She knew Desire damn sure wasn't afraid to scrap, because she'd seen back in the 42nd Street days how Desire got down. She used to rob and beat down hoes twice her size. So Tiah knew she would wax the floor with a chick like Chanel. But still, she couldn't take anybody dissing her sister.

Tiah stood up, stepped toward Chanel's table and yelled, "Fuck you, you stink-ass bitch! If I hear my sister's name come out your mouth again, I'm gonna close that shit. Now fuck around if you want!"

Everyone went "Oooooh," instigating the situation even further. Desire closed her eyes, shook her head and stood up.

Chanel chuckled loudly, stood up, rolled her head and eyes, then spelled,

"D-E-S-I-R and a motherfucking E. Bitch. Now, what the fuck you gonna do about it, lil hoe?"

Tiah rushed toward Chanel, but Desire grabbed her by the arm and whispered, "Chill out, baby girl. Ya sister got this bitch."

Tiah looked at the glint in Desire's eyes. She knew Desire had something in store for Chanel, so she smiled and backed away.

Desire slowly approached Chanel and her crew.

"So I'm a bitch, Chanel?" she asked.

Unfazed, Chanel stepped in her face and said, "You heard me. I ain't stutter! You a bald-headed, bummy bitch."

Desire just chuckled.

Chanel stared at her and asked, "What you laughing at?"

Shaking her head, Desire said, "I heard you say those same tired jokes just last week when you was talking about . . ."

Desire's head turned toward Chanel's homegirls and smiled, then said, "Oh, never mind."

The girls that Chanel was with stared at each other. Both of them had short, nappy hair, the kind that all the kids had learned to make fun of. Long waves that hung down a girl's back was what the boys admired, and so what all the girls wanted. Nobody had taught them to think otherwise. They both caught a complex, right then—wondering which one of them Chanel had talked about.

All eyes were now on Chanel. She blurted out, "Y'all gonna believe her? Y'all know I don't talk about none of y'all behind your backs—now, do I?"

One of her homegirls said, "I don't know, 'cause you did tell me just yesterday that Jasmine needed a perm something bad."

Jasmine's eyes lit up and stared at Chanel.

"You been talking about me behind my back, Chanel?" she asked.

Chanel sucked her teeth and said, "What, you stupid enough to believe her?"

Angry, Jasmine countered, "Who you calling stupid, you stupid bitch?"

"If I'm a bitch, slap a bitch, bitch!" Chanel shouted as she squared up to her.

"Naw," said Jasmine, "you hit me first, and you'll see what happens."

"No, hit me first," Chanel said.

They went a few more times, until Desire stepped between them, presumably to end the beef.

She looked at them both as they stared each other down. Desire extended a hand to each girl. She looked at Jasmine and said,

"Here's what you do: slap my hand and I'll relay the slap to Chanel, if you want."

Jasmine slapped her hand. Then Desire slapped Chanel, and all hell broke loose. Chanel and Jasmine started throwing down like Ali and Frasier. The gym teacher, who was in charge of this lunchroom period, rushed over to stop the commotion, but he was too late. He blew his whistle, but Chanel and Jasmine were already knuckling too hard to notice. A crowd had built up around the girls within seconds. Desire and Tiah walked away, giggling their asses off as they gave each other a pound.

CHAPTER EIGHT

After school, Desire and Tiah hit the block. The Harlem streets were alive with shoppers, vendors, other kids their age and people coming home from work. Somehow, the energy and excitement of the streets was less threatening now that both girls had a place to escape from it. They were too caught up in their gossip to pay much mind to the homeless people rambling down the street, talking to themselves and asking for change. They walked past the images of lonely and desperate people staring out of windows, wanting to be with people but too caught up in their misery to do so. They walked past the gangs of boys wilding out after school, trying to lure the two girls into their folds, eyeing them as potential sex partners. Desire and Tiah would just keep on walking, offering only a slight "Sup?" to their admirers. But they also walked past blocks of people sitting on cars with the stereos blasting, dancing in the streets. Or a Hispanic vendor here and there selling flavored ice cups. There were packs of children in uniforms leaving school as well, being led by caring and concerned parents. It had been hard for them to notice what was good about the streets when they had lived most of their lives caught up in the bad. The time after school when they walked home was their time to keep their bearings on all that they had come from.

They were about to step in their building when they noticed a crowd of guys watching someone get a beat down. Scenes like this were typical, and depending on their mood, the girls would either walk past or try to get a glimpse of the action without getting too involved. Today, they weren't in a hurry. Hattie Mae never questioned them when they were a little late coming in from school. She always just assumed they were out being girls. She didn't worry about them as much anymore. But today, there was something about the action that made them have to get into it.

"Hold up, Tiah, I think that's Carvelas fighting!" Desire shouted once they got closer to the chaos.

Tiah squinted her eyes and said with surprise, "Carvelas? You think so?"

Desire said, "Yeah, I think so, come with me."

They walked toward the melee and discovered that, sure enough, it was Carvelas, fighting valiantly against a local troublemaker named Lyfe. Lyfe was tall, lanky, and had a mean scowl. He had a reputation as a big gun on the block. He ran with a pack of other troublemakers, who considered him their leader. He was used to getting whatever he wanted from his followers: cigarettes, blunts, takeout from the corner restaurants, even sex from the girls who followed up behind them all. Desire and Tiah had mostly avoided him up to this point. But not today. Desire pushed her way into the brawl and said to Lyfe, "Leave him alone, nigga."

Lyfe didn't know Desire or Tiah, so he assumed they were just average Janes. He huffed, "What you say, lil bitch?"

Calmly, Desire said, "You heard me."

He could punk the average person out with a simple stare, but not Desire. She read right through him and knew he was a faker or he wouldn't be fighting a boy like Carvelas, who was clearly smaller than him.

Bloodied and bruised, Carvelas stepped in front of Desire. She couldn't believe how he looked and wondered what on earth would land Carvelas, of all people, into the middle of a brawl. He was normally so quiet and peaceful. He panted, "Desire, I ain't afraid of him. I got it."

"I know," said Desire. "You showed him what's up."

She took Carvelas by his arm and attempted to walk away. The crowd around them made their objections known, as they protested loudly that the fight was ending. Desire heard laughs and taunts aimed at Carvelas: "pussy," "scared little nigga" and even "he got a bitch fighting his battles for him." Lyfe stepped in front of them and said, "Bitch, where you think you going?"

Desire looked at him and said, "Yo, check this out, I ain't gonna be too many more bitches, nigga. Now, if I ever see you touch him again, you gonna—"

Lyfe cut her off and jumped in her face. He said, "You gonna do what?"

Desire answered point-blank, "You gonna get your back dirty." She then smiled.

Lyfe looked around and said, "Who the fuck this bit—"

Before he could get the words out, Desire and Tiah were on him, as Carvelas held Lyfe's crew back. Chaos erupted on the street while Desire kicked Lyfe all over his body. Tiah sat on his chest and held him down so Desire could do her damage. Desire was like a wolf. The old, familiar urge to fight had been reawakened and renewed. As she pummeled Lyfe, she beat down the Corleys, the other foster families, the pack of bitches who had chased her down the street the day she met Tiah. She was even fighting the mother who had abandoned her. Even Tiah was shocked at Desire's ferocity. Desire barely knew Carvelas, and here she was fighting for him like he was Hattie Mae.

An NYPD squad car squealed its siren. This caught all of their attention, except Desire's. Carvelas had to stop her, grab her hand and lead her away from the approaching car. Lyfe's crew ran in one direction. Carvelas, Desire and Tiah ran in the other direction—but not before Desire kicked Lyfe in the nuts one more time for good measure.

They finally reached a corner where they were out of sight and danger. They all stood with their hands on their knees, trying to catch their breath. Carvelas looked around them for any sign of Lyfe and his crew. When he was sure the coast was clear, he started leading them back to his building in a roundabout way.

"What was that all about?" Desire asked Carvelas.

"That nigga wanted my sneaks," Carvelas answered, pointing to the pair of sparkling new burgundy and white Jordans.

"How he think he can just take your sneaks?" Tiah asked.

"You know how that nigga is," Desire said. "He act like the whole world owe his ass something. Stupid-ass motherfucka."

Carvelas was too caught up in how he had seen Desire throw Lyfe off. He became even more intrigued with her, and certain that they were friends. She was one fierce bitch. He was a little bit ashamed and embarrassed, though, that a female had had to fight his battle for him.

"They all threw me down to the ground," Carvelas tried to explain. "Nigga was too pussy to fight me one-on-one, man-to-man."

"You ain't gotta explain that to me, Carvelas," Desire said. "I know all about that nigga. You watch. He gonna get his one day. Shit, I might just be the one who serve that sorry-ass motherfucka for good."

She and Tiah slapped up high-fives, while Carvelas just laughed. They were able to get to Hattie Mae's without the cops or Lyfe's crew sneaking back on them. However, Desire's battle with Lyfe would sneak up on her one day when she least expected it.

CHAPTER NINE

Desire had never had a real boyfriend. The only pictures of romantic relationships she got were from the television and the streets. In her mind, they all were based upon nothing but drama. She saw men as dogs who just wanted to sex you and then dump you. The only thing they had ever seemed good for was providing backup in a fight, and she had changed her life, so she didn't need anybody to have her back as much anymore. However, over time, her relationship with Carvelas began to mimic something like a girlfriend/boyfriend thing. Something that had started in church as what was, in retrospect, a silly little scheme had blossomed into a tight friendship. Though it was clear that Tiah was Desire's main sidekick, Carvelas followed behind as a close second. They often walked to school together and met each other in the hallways. They talked on the phone whenever Carvelas could actually catch Desire, although he was too shy to call as much as he really wanted to. He had his pride. But his pride broke down when he needed to ask someone to the prom. Desire was the only woman he wanted on his arm. One day, Carvelas met her in the hallways, not to talk or walk her to class, but to hand her a letter.

"What's this about?" she asked him, shocked. It was the first letter she had ever received in her life.

"Just read it," Carvelas commanded. He disappeared in the mob of loud students, leaving Desire standing there with her mouth open. She ripped the letter open as soon as she made it to algebra class. Luckily, she sat way in the back, and nobody ever really paid attention anyway. She was overtaken by Carvelas's words as she read.

Desire,

Well, I guess you should know by now that I got some feelings for you that's more than friendship. I don't know what they are, but I guess I just really wanna get to know you better. I mean, more than just hanging out in the hallways and after school. And I know what you thinking. I ain't trying to get down with you like that. That's not what I'm about. Plus, I know Sister Evans don't go for that no way. But I really like you. I respect you. I ain't trying to do nothing but be somebody in your life that you can count on. You seem so strong, and I like that. Maybe you don't need nobody to count on. I don't know. I just know I'd like to try to be something in your

life. That's all. Whatever you want me to shape up to be is
fine with me. That day I saw you sing, I don't know, I just
felt something for you. I was playing. You was singing. It was
like we was a team. I just want to explore that a little more. I
don't usually talk like this and I hope this don't throw you off.
I ain't trying to ruin our friendship. I totally understand if
you ain't feeling me like that. It's not gonna change the way I
feel about you. I was wondering if we could start getting to
know each other better at the prom. My people know who you
are. They gonna hook me up with the dough to get us a limo
and everything. We can step out in style. I want to ask you to
be my date.

Desire was overtaken. She had finally heard from the horse's
mouth that Carvelas did, just as Tiah had said, want to "do it to
her." Not now, but this was how it started, Desire knew. What
she liked about his letter was that there was one in the first place.
Carvelas proved with it that he was different. But then again, she
had already known that. He didn't want to jump over the steps no
other dudes were ever interested in. He wanted to treat her right
first. There was something the algebra class was supposed to be
doing, but Desire wasn't interested. She ignored the problem Mr.
Garcia had put on the board for them to do and wrote out her
own problem with Carvelas in the notebook in front of her.

Carvelas,
  You know I feel for you too, boo. You my buddy, my
backup, in church and on the streets. We got a lot of music to
make together, I'm sure. I guess I just don't know about every-

thing else you talking about. I'm not into hitting the sheets. That's not my style. And you're being nice about it now, but how I know that's not all you want? I don't know, I guess I just don't trust nobody. Ain't been too many people in my life to trust. I don't think I want to take the chance that you're one of them. I just like things the way they are now.

She knew enough to make Carvelas wait for her answer, which really wasn't an answer, just more questions. She met Carvelas at his locker after school and gave him the letter. She walked away before he could ask her if she wanted him to join her on the way home. She didn't even tell Tiah what was going on, nor Hattie Mae. The next morning, Carvelas was standing at Desire's locker when she arrived at school, with a letter of his own. As she had done, he walked away as soon as he gave it to her. She answered him, again, after school. For days, she and Carvelas wrote, communicating without spoken words, fighting out their feelings on the page.

Desire,

Well, I guess I should have known that it wouldn't be easy. That's really what I like about you. You tough, you protect yourself. You give everybody a hard time so they can't get close to you. I know you won't believe me, but I used to be the exact same way. I don't know why. I had a lot of bullshit happen when I grew up. Fights, drugs, my cousins dragged me into things I didn't really want to get dragged into. They called me stupid for going to school and wanting to work on

*my music. I thought I was supposed to be out here pushing
everything away that was good for me, jumping into everything that wasn't. But then, I don't know, one day I just woke
up. Believe it or not, it was your grandmother who pushed me
there. You was still away, hadn't started coming to church yet.
She heard me practicing one day after choir practice, when I
thought everybody else was gone. She was still there, cleaning
up, dusting off the Bibles, tidying up the pastor's office. And
she came in, and damn, I remember it like it was yesterday.
She told me, "Boy, you can play your little butt off." I was
shocked cause I didn't know nobody was listening. She pulled
out the hymnal and made me play some songs. It was cold
outside, really a blizzard, and neither one of us was in a rush
to get back out there. So we waited it out with my music, and
I played for her all night. That was, I don't know, kind of like
a turning point for me, a couple of years ago. But I don't have
to tell you about your own grandmother. You already know. I
guess I want to talk about you. Or me and you. What's up,
Desire? Why you think I'm not worth the risk?*

Carvelas,

   *Read closer. I actually ain't never say you wasn't worth the
risk. I'm just saying I have to take a chance to find out. And I
don't know if I feel like doing that right now. Things are all
right in my life. I'm singing in the choir, I'm handling my
business in school, everything is gravy at home. I'm even
thinking about trying to be a singer, like going to college to
study it and having a manager while I'm there. Me and Tiah*

talking about making a group. Getting some other girls to-gether to sing and dance. I like my life, and for a long time I didn't. I just don't want to fuck up what I already got going on. I'm not surprised by anything you said about Hattie Mae. That's her ass all right. She really do love people more than she love herself. For a long time, I didn't love her. I didn't know I could. I guess it was the same thing with her as it is with you. You know, that trust thing. That whole not wanting to get hurt. But I don't know, I guess over time she convinced me. Maybe you can too.

Desire,

We ain't got that much time. The prom is in a couple of weeks. I gotta get, you know, suited up. And so do you. It's been a lot of time already. You've known me for a long time. Damn, you had my back in a fight. You can fight with me but you can't love with me? Women . . .

Carvelas,

Oh, you love me now? Or I'm supposed to love you? Or are we supposed to make love? Okay, I'm sorry, I'm making fun of you, and I don't want to do that. I like hearing your feelings. I got feelings of my own. I'm just not ready to share 'em yet. The one thing I will say is that I been through some shit in my life. I had a lot of times when nobody was there to have my back, not even my grandma. I love her to death, but I know I gotta make my own way eventually. She ain't gonna be here forever. And I ain't got no reason to believe you'll be. I gotta look out for number one. Guess it's that protection thing. I ain't never gonna lose it. Might as well tell you bout me. Bout Desire. This girl you think you can love. I ain't never had a mother. A lot of what you may have heard about me in church is really a lie. Grandma ain't really my grandma. She got me and Tiah cause we both didn't have nowhere to go. Can you believe that? Me and Tiah was both broke, homeless, foster home after foster home. How you think it feel when your own damn mama don't want you? If your mama can leave you, anybody can. Grandma could meet her somebody and get her a new life and leave me too. How I'm supposed to know? How I'm supposed to tell? I just like it better keeping people at a distance. I got Tiah and Grandma on the inside. That's enough for me.

Desire,

    The things you telling me still ain't changing the way I feel about you. All that shit is your past. Sister Evans is your grandma. Believe it, she is. Just cause y'all ain't connected by birth don't mean it ain't true. I got shit in my own past to worry about. My daddy ain't want me. He didn't want shit to do with me. Never has, and I finally figured out he never will. But I found me some ways to get over that. I got my music. I member one time I was in this restaurant with my mother and her friends. It was up on Sugar Hill. This piano music was playing in the background. It sounded like a million little bells ringing together like they was dancing. And when the waiter came to our table I asked him what the music was. He said it was somebody named Monk. And I knew he had to be black cause they only played black music. And I was like, shit, a black man making a piano sound like that. And when I'm in church, I'm playing the gospel. But I'm playing jazz, blues, all that. I'm gonna play all that one day. Desire, you can sing. You can sing your ass off. You gotta focus on that now. You gotta let the past go. All that hurt you got is in the past. Focus on the present. Think about the future, with me maybe.

Carvelas,

You're asking me to do a lot. When you ain't walked in my shoes, you can't really understand where I feel like I need to go. But I guess you convinced me that you at least really want to go to the prom! I don't see the big deal myself. I mean, I ain't interested in getting all dressed up just to profile in front of people. Fuck that. I profile every day, on my own, and I ain't gotta spend money to do it. But I guess Hattie Mae would like to see me go. I guess I could do it for her. So yeah, we can go to the prom together. But wait until I buy my dress before you buy your suit. I ain't going with you unless we match.

⌞ ⌞ ⌞

Despite the temporary agreement they had come to, Desire still had mixed feelings about Carvelas. She confessed what was going on to Tiah one night as they sat out on the stoop while Hattie Mae busied herself inside.

"So you really gonna go to the prom with little ole Carvelas?" Tiah asked.

"Shit, he asked," Desire said. "I ain't never been on a date before. And Grandma will let me go 'cause she likes Carvelas a whole lot. She the one got him playing in church."

"How you know that?" Tiah asked.

"He told me," Desire answered, looking away and imagining Carvelas walking up the street.

"Hold on, bitch!" Tiah shouted. "When you and Carvelas been talking alone? I'm with you damned near all the time. How come I ain't see none of this? You been sneaking out of school to kick it with him?"

"Calm yourself, chick," Desire answered. "Since you insist on knowing everything about my life, I'll just tell you we been writing a lot of notes. That's all."

"Oh, snap! Writing notes . . . that's what you do before you start sexing."

"We ain't sexing and we ain't gonna sex. I only like him as a friend. I don't know, I really just don't see Carvelas like that. He like my play brother, you know."

"Well, who do you see like that, then?"

Desire was very peculiar when it came to what interested her. She wanted anything that she couldn't have, and one such person was Tony Evers. The 6′1″, handsome, All-City basketball wizard, who was Chanel's boyfriend.

"I wouldn't mind getting Tony alone! Chanel don't deserve nobody that fine."

Tiah looked shocked by Desire's response. They had both

talked about Tony, but she didn't know it was that serious for De-sire.

"Hell, take that bitch's man if you don't want Carvelas," Tiah advised.

Desire still wasn't sure if she wanted to take it there with Carvelas. Tony seemed to be a much more mysterious prospect.

"That just might be what I do," Desire said, wondering how she could without hurting Carvelas.

ɞ   ɞ   ɞ

It was a hot, muggy morning and more than 150 students were waiting to go into the auditorium to get prom tickets. Carvelas had given her the money to pick them up. As Desire stood in line, she watched Chanel's boyfriend, Tony, approach. He had on a brand-new warm-up suit and some sparkling new Jordans. His wavy hair was perfectly faded. At every step other boys extended their hands to give him a pound. Desire turned her back as he approached. When he got to her she was surprised to hear his deep, spine-tingling voice call her name. She turned around and said, "Yeah, what's up?"

He smiled, showing a perfect set of pearly white teeth. "Yeah, what's up? Your last name is Evans, right?"

"And?" Desire was nervous, but played it cool. This was the first time they had ever spoken to each other.

"Well," he continued, "my last name is Evers, so that means I'm right behind you." He smiled again.

Desire had a weakness for ballplayers. She loved their attitudes and swaggers. She also liked the attention that they got, as well as how they were respected by everyone. Desire was all about respect, getting it and keeping it. It would help to have somebody on her arm who had it to the degree that Tony did. The line moved slowly. Everybody wanted to make sure they would be suited just right. Desire and Tony spoke for the full hour and a half it took to get their tickets. Tapping his tickets against his mouth, Tony asked, "You gonna be at the prom?"

It was on. Nothing was going to stop Desire from going to the prom. However, she needed to lay down a few ground rules with Carvelas.

"But I got some stipulations first," she said. "One, pick me up at my house at seven sharp. Two, make sure you bring my corsage. And three, give me a hundred-fifty dollars so I can get my hair and nails done." Desire extended her hand to him like he just walked around with that type of money. She may as well let him know early that she expected to be taken care of if things were to go any further. She had feelings for Carvelas as a friend, but the hustler mentality she had had to employ for so long had trained her to use anybody to get what she wanted. She wanted Tony, she already had Carvelas. It was like instinct for her to use Carvelas to get what she wanted from Tony. She had no plans of really hurting him. Not to mention, Carvelas was getting what he wanted as well. She *was* going to prom with him.

"Okay, I got some stipulations too."

Desire twisted her face. She shifted her weight onto her other foot and folded her arms as she waited for him to continue.

"I just want me and you to walk in together arm in arm." He waited to see her reaction.

"What else?" she said.

"And for you to give me the first and last dances." He smiled with relief when she looked at him and said, "No doubt."

❦   ❦   ❦

Desire had her hair cornrowed down her back by the Africans on 125th and her nails done by the Koreans right across the street. She and Tiah headed to Macy's to look at gowns. The conversation with Hattie Mae about Desire attending the prom with Carvelas had gone well. The part about buying a gown had not.

"I'm so happy you got you a little date," Hattie Mae had exclaimed after Desire told her the news. They'd quickly run down the list of what she would need: a prom gown, shoes, and bag to match and earrings. Then Hattie Mae had marched to a closet that was full of so much junk from the past that they usually had to lean against it to close it. She had almost opened it before changing her mind. "I don't want all that junk tumbling out on me. I'ma hafta get my sewing machine later . . ."

"Grandma, get a sewing machine for what?" Desire had asked. Tiah had just sat silent and confused.

"I'm making yo dress, chile," Hattie Mae had answered.

❦   ❦   ❦

Though they didn't really want to do it, they felt like they had no choice, Desire and Tiah decided to resort to boosting a prom gown. They didn't want to hurt Hattie Mae's feelings. But she had begun describing the gown she was going to make for Desire, and there was no way Desire was going to have her grand entrance ruined by walking into prom in a homely gown made by her grandmother. Desire was only into fashion because of the money it had made her in the past, not for her own glamour, but she had an agenda for prom night. She couldn't look like anything but the flyest girl in the room if she was to get Tony Evers's attention.

On 34th Street, Desire and Tiah admired all the fashion mannequins in Macy's windows. Desire stopped suddenly when she saw a dress that would make her curves pop out once she slipped it over her body. The dress's red color made her think of fire. It was a floor-length gown with a train that glided in back like a red carpet, almost as if whoever wore it was a star on their way to an awards ceremony. The front of the dress was a low-cut V-neck, with just enough support to boost her small breasts. It was sexy and provocative yet still tasteful. That was the image she was hoping to project. Tiah nodded her approval. This sleek and ultrasexy dress was by Christian Lacroix, and probably cost well over a thousand dollars. Desire and Tiah formulated a plan before setting out on their mission.

They entered into Macy's revolving door. Both girls knew their roles well. If caught, the other was supposed to pull the nearest fire alarm to clear out the place. Slowly but surely, the old instincts were starting to come back to Desire. The thought of boosting a gown was more appealing than the thought of describing exactly what she wanted to Hattie Mae, and all of them making it together. Having a family project. In a weird way, Desire wanted to know if she still "had it." Something inside of her didn't trust the security and comfort she had, not yet. She wanted to know that she could still access her skills when necessary.

She and Tiah entered the evening gown section of the store

and found that there were no more gowns like the one she wanted. Not wanting to draw attention to themselves, they didn't bother to ask the saleslady where some more gowns might be. Desire wanted the dress she wanted. None of the others moved her the way that one did. They were about to leave the store, when, finding themselves in an uncrowded section of handbags near the Madison Street exit, Desire suddenly had an idea. She consulted with Tiah on what she was going to do.

"I need a distraction," was what Desire said. She thought quickly, then snatched Tiah's purse off of her arm. Tiah looked astonished.

"For now, your bag has been stolen," Desire whispered to her. "I need you to get each and every person in this section looking for it."

Tiah followed orders without question. They both could be drama queens when they needed to be. Tiah spotted one salesgirl who was adjusting gowns nearby. She immediately went into theatrics, running as far away from Desire as she could.

"My bag is missing! Somebody got my bag," Tiah shouted. Everyone who had been browsing turned their attention toward Tiah. She continued shouting as the salesgirl left her customers.

"When did you last have it?" the salesgirl asked Tiah. Tiah's goal was to get everyone as far away as possible from Desire. The customers who had been shopping previously began to whisper among themselves.

"It's a big brown bag. Black straps," Tiah said. "Look around, everybody!"

Everyone in the section began looking into the folds of the long gowns hanging from the racks. Another saleswoman walked over to Tiah and the salesgirl who was helping her. She went to get security, while Tiah led the salesgirl to the fitting room. The coast was clear for Desire to make her move.

Quickly, she slipped into the large window that was dressed with the beautiful gown. The security guard responsible for that section had joined everyone in searching for Tiah's bag. Desire heard Tiah shouting from across several aisles, "Somebody has to look . . . the person could be gone by now!"

Desire worked quickly. It was hard for her to squeeze behind the partition that barricaded the window off from the rest of the store. She slithered in between, however, and though she had to work fast, she needed to do it without panicking. There was no sense in displaying her thievery for all of Seventh Avenue to see. She carefully but swiftly disrobed the mannequin so no one looking from the outside would become suspicious. The dress was a combination of light silk and even lighter chiffon. Once Desire got it off the mannequin, she rolled it up and threw it into the large Macy's shopping bag that was merely part of her disguise. She continued to hear Tiah's shouts, so had no reason to believe that she wasn't covered. She checked the roll of fabric for the feeling of a hard square that could be a store alarm. But she had inside knowledge from one of the pickpocket gang members. Loss Prevention rarely bothered to alarm-tag display items. One, most people weren't bold enough to attempt to loot store-window items. Two, the precaution would certainly ruin the beauty of the display.

Desire peered out of the barricade and into the store. The commotion Tiah had created was winding down. No one was suspicious that Tiah could have been lying, but everyone had gotten bored with the drama. Tiah pretended to break into tears as the two saleswomen and a security guard tried to explain to her the procedure for reporting a bag as stolen.

"But I just got paid and I had all my money in that bag," Tiah whined, as she watched Desire wriggle from behind the display-window barricade. She waited for Desire to walk out of the revolving doors, onto Seventh Avenue, before she composed herself. She continued listening to the instructions before she began to walk hopelessly away. It was necessary for them to get out of the area now. Tiah interrupted the security guard. "I'll handle it," she assured them, and she hurried toward the revolving doors to catch up with Desire.

Without speaking, the girls ran to the D subway stop on the corner to catch the express train to Harlem. As they sat on the train, Desire thought about her scheme, and how easily it had worked. She began to imagine what else she could take, and what she could do with the money. She brushed away the thoughts, though, thinking how much better off she was now—in school, with Carvelas and Tiah and, most importantly, Hattie Mae. But the seeds had been planted for her to slip right back into the life she had escaped.

CHAPTER TEN

Desire and Carvelas pulled up in front of prom in a limousine. Desire stared out into the crowd through the tinted window as her fellow classmates hovered around, waiting and watching everyone who arrived. This had been a tradition for many years in Harlem. A high school affair took on the debauchery of a player's ball when it came to the clothes. Those that came to the prom looking busted and broke would never live it down for the rest of their young adult lives. Kodak didn't lie. But all whose wears were tight got a pass from being talked about. If they were dressed fly, they got a ghetto status as someone to be reckoned with. Desire wanted that status.

The chauffeur opened the car door, and Desire stepped

out of the vehicle. She took a deep breath. She felt naked and out of place as everyone stared at her. Carvelas clutched her hand as they entered the party. The latest song from Blackstreet was blasting from the DJ's speakers. The closer she and Carvelas got to the gymnasium door, the more she wished that she were invisible. Desire was baffled when all the young boys from her school that never spoke to her before looked like they now had something to say. Then it hit her. When they spoke, they did not look her in the face—they all were looking at her breasts. The dress made good on its promise to bolster her cleavage, and everyone took notice. Desire had never exposed her body because she was always rail thin and preferred to dress in baggy clothing. Her body's growth spurt had happened so fast that she barely had time to adjust. With newfound confidence, she purposely began poking out her chest for all eyes to see.

Carvelas asked Desire if she wanted to go get some refreshments. Desire wanted to make the night special for Carvelas, so she decided to be as agreeable as possible.

"Okay, boo," she told him.

As they walked toward the food line, they ran right into Chanel and Tony. Chanel's dress was fly—tight, short and black—but it was not nearly as dramatic as Desire's ensemble. It took Chanel a moment to recognize Desire. Tony's eyes bucked, and he looked like he was salivating. It was as if his girlfriend wasn't even standing there. Like everyone else who knew her, Chanel and Tony related Desire to a tomboy who wasn't very feminine. She'd stood out in the crowd of girls who had their hair perfectly coifed and were dressed in outrageous outfits. Tonight, Desire had proved even her worst enemy wrong.

As the evening wound down, Chanel began to fume. It had become obvious that Desire was the object of Tony's attention. Although Desire had come with Carvelas, they both had their own socializing to do within the partygoers. Each and every time Tony spotted Desire alone, he made his way toward her while Carvelas's back was turned. Tony kept finding excuses to leave Chanel's side, and each time she went to look for him, he was in heavy conversation with Desire.

"Why every time I turn around you all up in that bitch face?" screamed Chanel once she was able to get her man back and alone.

"Why you keep sweating me?"

" 'Cause you playing me! We suppose to be together and all you doing is sniffing up her ass all night and dissing me in front of my friends. So you better make up your mind right now who you want to be with," Chanel threatened.

"You're right, Chanel. Here's five dollars, take a cab home."

Chanel stood stunned as she watched him walk away. The DJ announced that it was time for the last dance. Carvelas slipped him a twenty to play Lenny Williams. But when Carvelas went to get Desire, he saw her in the arms of someone else.

Time seemed suspended as Desire danced in the warm, strong arms of the most popular guy in school. Desire smiled wickedly as she watched Chanel storm out of the prom. She put her head back down, closed her eyes and savored the moment. Abruptly, in the middle of the song, Desire pulled away from Tony. She felt the excitement of trumping her enemy making the blood pump through her veins. She had secretly admired Tony for the longest time, and here she was, getting the last dance with him at the prom. She needed to pull back to get her bearings. True enough, Chanel was gone. What she didn't know was, so was Carvelas.

Desire beamed as she walked off the dance floor thinking of how she must have crushed Chanel. Desire went searching for Carvelas, but he was not in the gym. She went outside to see if the limousine was still there. When she opened the door she saw him sitting alone, with his head down.

"What, you mad 'cause I was dancing with Tony?" Desire sucked her teeth. "I just did that to make Chanel mad, I didn't want him."

"So you gave him the last dance and ruined my night just so you could get back at Chanel?"

"I tell you what: if you got somewhere for us to go, I let you get some," Desire responded. She had no intention of really sleeping with Carvelas. She only said what she thought would make him feel better. Desire felt bad about hurting him, but she knew she needed to look out for number one first. Anything and anybody else came second. She was already three steps ahead, thinking of how she was going to get out of fucking Carvelas, when he let her know she didn't have to.

Carvelas shook his head and frowned, "I don't want no sex from you, Desire, because you feel you owe me. I told you already, I respect you more than that. All I wanted was to have the last dance. Take us home, man."

The driver responded, heading down the avenue as his charges sat in awkward silence. Desire decided to speak as they neared her building.

"Carvelas, I really didn't mean nothing—"

He put up his hand to shut her up. Desire was shocked by the gesture. Carvelas normally catered to her every whim, even if it was only to speak. She felt rejected. Carvelas must be like all the other cats who just wanted to pump her and dump her. When niggas don't get what they want, they change. When the limo pulled up in front of the building, Desire knew she wouldn't be needing a ride home after telling Carvelas off. So she let it rip.

"Fuck you, then!" she shouted with her hand on the door. "Fine, be a pussy nigga like that."

She waited for Carvelas to snap back at her, but he didn't. He looked hurt, and simply shook his head.

"Don't call me anymore," Desire said. "We can't be down like that if you can't just chill over a stupid mistake."

"Go in the house, Desire," Carvelas said. "I don't want to see you anymore either."

"Fine, then," Desire shouted, running away in the six-inch heels she had bought behind Hattie Mae's back.

Inside, Hattie Mae had waited up. Tiah had gone to bed, resigning herself to getting the details in the morning. At first, Hattie Mae looked overjoyed to see Desire walk through the door like a stunning princess. Then she noticed the shoes.

"Now, I know we agreed that you could wear that dress your friend loaned you, but chile, I don't know 'bout them shoes . . ."

Desire wasn't in the mood to talk.

"Nothing wrong with my shoes."

Hattie Mae's mouth stayed open as Desire shoved past her. Watching her from behind, Hattie Mae couldn't help but think how much Desire moved like her mother had. For two people who had never known each other, they were almost the spitting image of each other. Suddenly, the feeling she had when Desire's mother had begun to steal from her years before came back. Out of the blue. She followed Desire into her bedroom. Desire was attempting to undress quietly, so as not to wake Tiah.

"How was the prom?" Hattie Mae asked. She was eager to get in on a little of the girls' lives. They were both growing up, fast. She wanted a connection that was stronger than one they had, which seemed to be hanging on by a thread just because they all continued to go to church together.

"It was all right," Desire muttered.

"Just all right?" Hattie Mae asked. She watched Desire carefully put the six-inch heels into a sturdy box. Just as Hattie Mae was thinking how much they looked like "hooker shoes," she remembered that Desire had supposedly borrowed the shoes as well, supposedly from the friend's mother. The box looked brand-new. What type of mother would loan her daughter's friend a pair of expensive, brand-new shoes?

"How did Carvelas act?" she asked. She tried to think of a question that might be exciting for Desire. "Did he give you a good-night kiss?"

Having slipped on a nightgown and tumbled into bed, Desire didn't seem to be in the mood to talk. "No. I don't like Carvelas like that. We went as friends, that's it." She spit the words out with so much attitude, Hattie Mae felt like she had been stabbed. What was going on? It was as if Desire's entire personality had changed in the last couple of weeks. Hattie Mae didn't want to think the worst. Growing pains, she told herself.

"I'll tell you about it tomorrow, okay?" Desire said, and mustered the smile that she knew Hattie Mae lived for. Hattie Mae nodded, and turned off the bedroom light.

"Don't forget to talk to the Father tonight," she said, before closing the door.

❧   ❧   ❧

Tony's interest in Desire was more than fleeting. He knew he had Chanel in his back pocket, eating out of the palm of his hand. He didn't even bother to explain to her where he was on the nights that he was sniffing behind Desire. He showed up at her door one evening dressed in a freshly pressed Karl Kani shirt and crisp black slacks. Hattie Mae was not impressed. It was almost as if she could smell the dog inside him.

"I'll go get Desire," she said after she let him in.

"Thank you very much, ma'am," Tony answered, then sat down on the couch. Tiah came from the kitchen and tried to hide her amazement that *the* Tony Evers was actually sitting in her living room.

" 'Sup, Tony?" she asked, admiring his outfit. She had rollers in her hair and was embarrassed. She hadn't expected a man to be early to pick up someone for a date.

"Hello . . . Tiah, right?" They heard Hattie Mae huff from inside the kitchen.

"Yeah, it's Tiah."

Desire emerged from her bedroom dressed like a goddess. Tony's eyes bucked when he saw her outfit. Desire normally wore her hair in a sloppy ponytail. But tonight she had curled her shoulder-length tresses into dozens of ringlets. After prom night, she had figured she couldn't go wrong with red. She had gone to

Modell's on 125th Street and found a red body dress, with holes in the sides hugging her tight waist. Hattie Mae came from out of the kitchen and her mouth shot open.

"Where you think you goin?" she asked. Desire tried to keep her cool, wanting Tony to believe that she could do whatever she pleased.

"Uh . . . I'm taking Desire out to dinner," Tony offered.

"Not in that," Hattie Mae said. "Now, you go back in there and put some real clothes on. Otherwise, we can all sit at that table in there and eat what I done fixed."

"Grandma, you seen this outfit before," Desire lied. Her eyes pleaded with Hattie Mae to not embarrass her in front of the most popular guy in school. Tiah sat uncomfortably on the edge of the couch, near Tony. Hattie Mae noticed how handsome the young man was. He *was* dressed nicely, and Hattie Mae had respected the fact that he had called her "ma'am." She decided to let Desire get away with something—this time.

"We'll be back before ten," Desire said, grabbing Tony's hand and leading him toward the door. Before they left, however, she dropped his hand and walked over to give Hattie Mae a huge kiss. "If you're asleep when I get back, I'll come wake you up."

"Okay, baby," Hattie Mae said. After Desire and Tony left, she and Tiah headed to the kitchen to eat.

≈   ≈   ≈

It turned out Tony was taking Desire not to some fancy restaurant for dinner, as his outfit suggested, but to the apartment of one of his older friends, who had graduated and now sold drugs. The apartment was near 131st and Lenox, and the inside hallways of the building were littered with cigar ash, cigarette butts, and paint that had chipped off the walls. They could smell weed reeking through the hallways on their entire walk up to the third floor. As soon as they entered the apartment, they were in the kitchen, where a pregnant girl sat at a table with a huge pile of weed in the center. Desire had never seen so much weed in her life. The pile had to have been at least two feet high. The pregnant girl quickly snatched up small portions of the pile and stuffed them into little plastic baggies of various sizes. She took one look at Desire and rolled her eyes. All the other guys were trying to control their stares, since it was obvious that Desire was Tony's date. Rap music blasted from the stereo, so no one was able to talk. Tony slapped hands with the few guys standing up in the room. One of them was already passing a blunt, and Tony and Desire were next in the rotation. Desire had not smoked weed in years, ever since she had decided to turn her life around, but she decided to loosen up a little bit tonight. She was certain that this was just a pit stop to get her a little high before Tony took her to dinner. She had a couple pulls of the blunt to relax.

After the blunt was finished, Tony led Desire down a long hallway into a small living room, where another group of guys sat around smoking blunts and playing Nintendo. They looked up long enough to undress Desire with their eyes. One of the guys even stopped playing so he could mutter, "Damn . . ." Everyone in the room simply exchanged head nods. Desire sat down uncomfortably next to Tony, wondering just how long they were going to be here. Above the music and video games, she could hear the apartment door opening and closing as customers stopped by. Tony sat blunted out on the sofa, enthralled in the other guys' video game and ignoring Desire completely.

"You trying to get in?" one dude asked Tony when it became clear he had lost a game.

"Naw," Tony answered. "Well, I'm not trying to get in *this* game, if you know what I mean."

The guys in the room chuckled as if Desire weren't even there. She just smiled uncomfortably as Tony grabbed her hand. Then he began rubbing the skin that was exposed through the holes in her outfit. His hands did feel good against her skin.

Suddenly, he said, "Let's go in the back."

Desire agreed. She did not like the crowd that was in the apartment. It reminded her too much of cats she had run with in the Midtown Pickpocket Exchange. She was past all that now.

Tony led her down another hallway in the L-shaped apartment. There was a tiny room in the back with a twin-sized bed. The room was lit by a red light. Posters of singers from *Fresh* magazine dotted the walls. Desire noticed the bed looked like it had been slept in and made up hastily. Within seconds, Tony was grinding a very hard penis against her and grabbing her ass.

"Wait a minute, Tony," Desire said as she fought his tongue, which was rolling around in her mouth. "I thought we was going to dinner?"

"We gonna go to dinner," Tony said. "Let's have some dessert first."

He lifted Desire up and placed her on the bed. All of his weight crushed down upon her, making it hard for her to speak.

"Tony, I ain't say I was gonna go out with you so I could fuck you," she said.

"I ain't sayin we gotta fuck," Tony said. He was out of control. He was the star of the basketball team, and had the strength to prove it. He was well over six feet tall. Desire tried to push him off of her, but failed.

"Why you wanna fight me?" Tony asked. "You know you want this dick . . . I seen the way you been looking at me from the first day we met."

Desire relaxed a little and let Tony's kisses overtake her body. Suddenly, she could tell that the music had been turned up on the other side of the door. She then noticed a used condom tied into a knot and thrown in a corner. It was hard for her to enjoy Tony's kisses as he made his way down to her breasts when she was wondering just how many other girls had been in this bed, and whether or not Tony had been with them. Tony continued to suck her breasts and rub his hands along her thighs. Desire was so high that she forgot about the other people in the apartment, and she let him pull her dress up so that he could wrap her legs around him.

"There you go . . ." Tony muttered, as he became even more excited. The tiny bed began to squeak as he pressed himself up against her with all his might, taking his hands and rubbing her between her legs. Desire was uncomfortable, but she let him keep going because it felt good.

Despite all of her experience on the street, Desire had none when it came to sex. She had never let any of the guys in the gang get near her. Other than some occasional kissing and bumping and grinding with a couple cats over the years, she was fairly inexperienced for most girls her age. Tony could sense that and it was exactly what he liked. He got tired of chasing after skuzzy hoes and not knowing where the pussy had been. He couldn't wait to get deep inside Desire.

Desire hadn't been expecting for him to move her panties to the side and touch her exposed pussy. But that's exactly what he did. She then realized that he had somehow managed to pull his penis out of his slacks without her noticing, probably because she had been too caught up in feeling. His penis felt warm and hot against her pussy. She didn't mind him stroking it against her flesh, but she noticed that he was dangerously close to the opening of her vagina. He hadn't asked her if they could go that far, and he hadn't shown her a condom.

"Tony, I don't like this," Desire said, struggling to remove her legs from around his back. Tony just ignored her, and pushed her legs open even wider. He used the muscles in his arms to keep Desire's legs open against her will. Before she knew it, he had ripped her panties so that he could start working his dick inside of her. He rubbed her pussy hard to spread out the wetness she had created, so that his job would be that much easier.

"Tony," Desire pleaded, fully aware of what was about to happen. "I ain't never done this before . . ." she cried loudly, hoping he would stop, and the bed began to make even more noise as they struggled. Tony was grunting and groaning as he rubbed against her like she hadn't said a word. She knew that she couldn't do shit with a nigga as big as Tony, and the fact that she was already high and underneath him had her doubting her ability to fight her way out of this one. She thought about all the people on the other side of the door, who would hear her screams and possibly interpret them as cries of passion. Even worse, what if all the strangers in the apartment turned on her and took Tony's side if she screamed rape? The pregnant girl had already given her bitchy stares. They could all jump on her rather than risk her going to the cops to rat out Tony. She heard laughter on the other side of the door, and saw shadows of feet breaking up the light that trickled underneath it.

Desire was stiff and tears streamed down her face as Tony smashed his way into her without a condom. He snatched down his pants and yanked up Desire's dress as he raised her to him once he had found the entrance to her pussy. It felt like her pelvis was splitting in two. Sharp pains shot up through her stomach. Tony's dick length matched his height, and he was hell-bent on getting all of it inside Desire. He pushed and pumped until they were both nearly hanging off the bed. He was lost in his own world and cared nothing about Desire's pleasure anymore. He held her down tight on the bed and covered her mouth so she couldn't scream as he pumped into her for as hard and long as he could hold out. Desire disappeared into a dream world, imagining she was at a party, letting herself focus on the music and laughter on the other side of the door.

Tony didn't even bother to walk Desire down the stairs so she could catch a gypsy cab when it was all over. He had immediately left the room and joined in the video game, leaving Desire to stare at the ceiling and contemplate the awful soreness between her legs. The insides of her thighs were badly bruised. She limped outside the back room, and Tony didn't even acknowledge her by looking up from the game. Once she arrived home, Hattie Mae was sleeping. Desire had wanted to wake her, as she had promised, but she could only go to the shower and let the water wash the horrible night away.

CHAPTER ELEVEN

As Desire grew into womanhood, her body went through transformations that would have made any brick house envious. Baggy jeans and sweatsuits were definitely things of the past. Prom night had shown her what the power of playing up her sex could do, and she had done it from that night on. Desire replaced her old stuff with sleek and sexy hoochie-wear. The memories of having to carry a few modest items of clothing around in a cardboard suitcase faded with each and every expensive purse, bag, shoe or dress that she threw money on a store counter for. The gear that she wore included nothing but top-of-the-line outfits, with designer labels the average person couldn't even pronounce and price tags that would make anyone stutter. She wouldn't be caught dead wearing anything the average chicken head from the neighborhood was wearing or could afford. Desire would joke, "I can't wear that cheap shit because I'm allergic to it, and I'd start breaking out in feathers."

Though Desire and Tiah were seventeen and sixteen respectively, their bodies and mannerisms attracted and demanded attention from grown men—and even women—everywhere they went. Sinister things had started to happen behind Hattie Mae's back. The girls made sure they were in church every Sunday, up front in the pews or singing in the choir. Carvelas and Desire avoided each other as much as possible. He was heartbroken, and had made it known. Desire was too proud to apologize or beg for his friendship, and so she lost it. Chanel had faded to the back, fearing that Desire was somebody she better not piss off if she wanted to keep her man. Desire changed, and Hattie Mae took notice but kept quiet. She had thought she was breaking the transfer of Nika's genes to Desire when with her teeth she had cut the umbilical cord that connected mother and child. She'd hoped and prayed that that one act meant Desire would never have the same hungers her mother had had. But Hattie Mae didn't know that exactly what she prayed didn't happen was actually happening. Life was stable and routine for a while, on the surface, but in reality things had dramatically changed.

It took money to look good. Desire and Tiah thought they needed money even to dream. Rather than looking at the blessings they had, they instead fantasized about being rich and famous in the future: the men they could pull, the clothes they could wear, the places they could travel, the cars they could buy. It was as if the four years with Hattie Mae had meant nothing. It had only provided them with the momentary stability they needed to catch a little breath before they started running the fast life again. This time, that meant experimenting in an area more dangerous than boosting, at least emotionally: stripping. They supported their lifestyle by working as strippers at a club in the Bronx. This is where they learned just how financially viable and lucrative the art of making love without penetration could be. They made as much as six hundred dollars a night for three hours work, while still in high school. They were amazed how much money there was to be made by simply gyrating and rubbing up on men.

Desire was an instant star from day one because she was double-jointed in both her legs and her arms. She could contort her body in any sexual position and had men busting nuts just from watching her perform. For those that were lucky enough to have enough dough to fuck with, she made it worth their while. Though Carvelas had probably been the one who deserved her virginity, Tony had taken it. But days later, he had acted as if he didn't know Desire when she bumped into him and Chanel in the lunchroom. He moved closer to Chanel as Desire approached, debating whether or not to confront him about raping her. But she was too ashamed that she had tried to steal Chanel's man, and it obviously hadn't worked. She decided then that the next time she had sex, the motherfucker would have to pay her. And that's exactly what happened with the first man she met in the strip club who wasn't satisfied by just watching her dance. And it was what happened with the next, and the one after him, until Desire could no longer remember the faces or the names. Desire was all about the paper and was a beast at what she did. She didn't discriminate. She didn't care if the dude worked for Microsoft or McDonald's.

As her reputation grew, so did her clientele. So much so, the club began to attract some of the biggest rappers and ballers from all over the city just to get at her. This was just about the time that she met the infamous rapper Lil Dollar, who was from Brooklyn. Though Lil Dollar was only nineteen, he'd been on lockdown since he was twelve, after he killed his stepfather on Christmas Day by putting rat poison in his collard greens for not buying Lil Dollar the bike that he wanted. He was an evil motherfucker. He was a seasoned "Razor Tag" vet on Rikers Island by the time he was sixteen, and had a record of 22–1: he slashed twenty-two men and boys in their face or neck, and got stuck only once. That one time left a scar down the side of his face, which he displayed proudly. He had such an unpredictable and moody personality that he would flip and set it off at a moment's notice on anyone at anytime. He and his band of young wolves were banned from two major hotel chains for trashing rooms and beating down the staff. He once kidnapped and hung a room-service waiter out the window for mistakenly bringing him a club sandwich with bacon. Lil Dollar was both famous and infamous. And he had heard of Desire.

On this evening, the club was full to capacity, but twenty minutes after Lil Dollar and his pack of young wolves rolled up, it emptied, because everyone mysteriously opted to call it an early night. Word among the dancers spread fast that the rapper was in the house. In addition to his thuggish reputation, he was equally known for being a notorious trick, spending tens of thousands in one sitting at a strip club. Thongs and G-strings flew everywhere as the dancers threw on the nastiest, sluttish wear they had, almost knocking down one another as they rushed to where Lil Dollar and his wolves sat.

Desire was unfazed by the competition. She showered and dressed slowly and waited for all the other dancers to play themselves out. When Desire finally emerged, she wore her Cat Woman outfit—a shiny black patent-leather G-string with a matching top, complete with mask and whip. When she reached the platform, she walked with the stealth and swath of a feline. She thought she had to grab Lil Dollar's attention. She didn't know she already had it. As soon as Desire saw Lil Dollar glance at her, with perfect timing Jay-Z's "I Just Wanna Love You" came bursting through the loudspeakers, and she worked hers and popped that coochie to the bass.

Lil Dollar and all his wolves caught notice of Desire, the Cat Woman, onstage, and pushed whatever girls were on their laps out of the way to get a better look. Desire knew she had the spotlight and really began to work it. She took one of her long legs and lifted it parallel to her head. The dancers looked at the expression on Dollar's face and knew it was a wrap. They wouldn't be fucking him that night after they saw his dick harden, as Desire was now on her back with both her legs behind her neck, giving him a clear view of the camel's toe. When she finished her dance, she slipped backstage. She wanted Lil Dollar to request to see her. She didn't want to give it to him easy. Desire knew she had a voice that was both powerful and radio-friendly; Lil Dollar could be her ticket into the singing career she had fantasized about since the day she took over the choir in church. It was Tiah who came and announced that Lil Dollar wanted a more personal visit at the bar.

Desire walked to the bar cool, calm and collected. She didn't want him to know just how impressed she was with his fame. The other dancers in the club glared at her as she made her way to where Dollar was waiting. A sparkling glass of champagne sat beside an ice bucket spilling over with cubes. A bottle of Cristal jutted out of the ice bucket, the steam still circling the lid, as Dollar had popped the cork only when Desire appeared.

"You wanted to see me?" she asked him. She let the champagne glass dangle between her fingers. She looked away as she sipped.

"You already know that," Lil Dollar said, running his hands along her creamy thigh without her permission. "That's why you guzzling the champagne I just bought for your sweet, sexy ass."

Desire immediately stopped sipping. If he thought she was about to be just another ho standing in line for one night, he was wrong. She smiled at Lil Dollar slyly, then slapped his hand away from her thigh. What happened next surprised even her. She quickly threw the glass of champagne in his face. Lil Dollar was too stunned to move. His entourage got up from their bar stools as Desire slowly walked away. But Lil Dollar waved them back.

"Keep your hands off that one," he told them, wiping the champagne from his face. "She's mine, and mine alone, to handle."

≥   ≥   ≥

Desire fucked Lil Dollar that night—mentally—as they spent the evening talking about all the men she knew who wanted her. She made sure to let him know she was a highly sought-after prize.

Her tales continued as they ate breakfast at M&G Diner on 125th Street the next morning, after she had spent the night in his huge loft facing the most famous black street in the world. Desire wanted to first separate herself from all the chicken heads and hoes that he was used to fucking. She decided she could work with Lil Dollar, use him to get closer to the fame and fortune she craved, so she pulled out all the weapons to hook him and make him believe that he needed her like humans need air. Desire intrigued him and he wanted to know everything about her: where she was from, who she be with, why she was stripping. Desire was masterful in manipulating Dollar as she flipped the game on him. She knew that if you can get a man to talk about their deep dark secrets, it put the chick in a class by herself. By the time they left the diner, Dollar had broken down and told her everything from killing his stepfather when he was a kid to how many other people he had fucked over in his life.

He was even more intrigued and impressed when their food came to their table and Desire said, "Excuse me," and spit a razor out of her mouth. He looked at Desire with amazement. Desire saw him staring and asked, "What?"

He smiled and spit his razor out of his mouth, and they both laughed. Desire found out that he also kept a razor in his mouth at all times, a habit from being in jail. Within days, they began having contests to see who could spit the razor in their hands and put it up to the other's throat the quickest. Lil Dollar was an expert spitter and always beat Desire to the draw. They had a sick, twisted attraction to each other. In the other, each saw themselves, as if they were looking into a mirror. They were two people who had survived the worst, and for whatever reason kept being drawn back to it. But what made Desire most like him, and so different from the other girls, was the focus with which she carried out her plans. She was the type who didn't just talk about what she wanted, she was dead-set on making some of them happen . . . and actually already had. He'd never met a girl like Desire, and he was hooked before he knew it.

*   *   *

Desire's patience with her seduction paid off big-time, in less than a year.

Within weeks, Lil Dollar began buying her expensive furs and jewelry. Then he started giving her unlimited spending money just so she didn't have to work at the strip club. It was clear that he was in love for the first time in his life. He no longer rolled with his wolf pack, no longer got himself into trouble, and rarely did he go out clubbing anymore. All he wanted to do now was concentrate on his career and spend time with Desire. Desire didn't want Tiah left out of the equation. Whenever they traveled, she made sure that he paid for Tiah to come along so she herself would feel comfortable. Dollar took them everywhere with him—from LA to Atlanta, to attend music award shows, or if he was on tour performing. He introduced them to everyone in the music industry, and they jet-setted and hung out with other millionaire rappers and executives. Desire and Tiah fit in like they were millionaire chicks themselves. This was the first time they saw how the other half lived, and the lavish living made their heads spin. She and Tiah were no longer the little girls who had traded secrets about expensive handbags in the middle of Macy's while they were broke. They now had the power to buy those handbags—and more—from not only the street, but also the real stores. In their minds, money meant power, and now they had it. They had to be a part of that world. It was mental insurance that they would never go back to being who they had been.

Hattie Mae was helpless to stop the change that became obvious in both of them. They came and went as they pleased, until finally taking up full-time residence with Lil Dollar. Hattie Mae's constant questions and preaching had started to get on their nerves. Not to mention they no longer saw church as a necessity or even a priority. Hattie Mae watched them pack for the last time, begging them to stay, knowing that if they walked onto the streets this time, they might never come back.

"Who is this Lil Dollar?" she asked Tiah and Desire after they had gathered a few of their belongings. They didn't take much from the apartment. Lil Dollar had replaced almost everything they owned with items that were much more luxurious and expensive. They ignored Hattie Mae as they continued to get their things and place them into Louis Vuitton luggage. Desire was convinced that Hattie Mae had previously sold them on a lie.

"Who is this man that y'all running to living with?" Hattie Mae repeated.

Desire sighed. "I told you, Grandma, he's my boyfriend."

"What kind of boyfriend can't even stop by here and introduce himself?" Hattie Mae's hands were on her hips as she followed the girls through the apartment, telling them everything they didn't want to hear. "He dragging you out of town but he can't drag himself to the front door to say, 'Hello, m'am'? That don't sound to me like somebody you need to running to live with. You almost eighteen. He can't wait till then to marry you? Valentine's Day. We could have something big at the church."

"Grandma, don't nobody want to get married in that broke-down church," Tiah snapped. The girls had gotten bored with all of it. They had tasted the fabulous life with just the tip of their tongues, they believed. They were ready to taste it all, and swallow it whole.

"Oh, so it's broke-down now?" Hattie Mae fought back tears. "It's broke-down now? This the same church saved yo life. This the same church saved mine."

Desire didn't want to hear it.

"Did it, Grandma?" she shouted. "Did it really save your life? Far as I'm concerned, sitting up in a tiny apartment in Harlem, with hypes and screaming babies everywhere, till it's time for my funeral ain't a life worth saving."

Hattie Mae ran up on her and snatched her arm. Desire buckled under the pain as Hattie Mae twisted it. Tiah knew not to get involved. She just stared. They had never seen Hattie Mae this angry. The feelings that had made Hattie Mae ready to fight Desire's mother if necessary, so that the demon would leave her house, were the same feelings that had her ready to fight Desire and Tiah so they would stay.

"This little apartment saved yo life!" Hattie Mae bellowed. She couldn't fight back the tears any longer. She had known the girls would grow up and leave, but she hadn't expected it to happen this way. "You wasn't even one foot long and half a foot wide when you had to come live here. You woulda died if I hadn't pulled you outta that snow, right out there in front of this window in this kitchen where you done fed your face for all these years!"

Desire wrenched her arm away.

"If I ain't careful, I'm gonna die in front of this window," she said. "Let's go, Tiah."

Tiah was torn. Her devotion to Desire was strong, but she knew they both had a debt to Hattie Mae.

"We just go'n be on 125th. We gonna come by here every day," she promised.

"Let's *go,* Tiah," Desire said, pulling open the front door. "Make up your damn mind. You can come with me and live the good life, or you can stay your ass here and be in church next Sunday. And the Sunday after that. Till you can't even walk to church no more. Then the van can come and pick you up, and take you to church in your wheelchair. That's what you waiting for, ain't that right, Grandma?"

Hattie Mae ran to the door. She raised her hand, and saw the devil himself in Desire's eyes when the girl didn't even cower.

"I want you out of my house," Hattie Mae said.

"I'm already gone," Desire told her. Tiah couldn't even look at Hattie Mae as she ran after Desire and onto the street, where a limousine was waiting to take them to Lil Dollar's. It was the last time either of them would see Hattie Mae for a very long time. Many, many months later, both of them would squint out from a bright stage into an excited crowd and see her face, but neither one of them would ever be sure if it was really her or if it was simply their imagination. And they would never find out. During the entire ride to Lil Dollar's, the words their grandmother had shouted after them haunted both girls, though neither one would ever admit it.

"Girls, I want y'all to promise me, promise me, that no matter what happens in life, no matter how hard it knocks you down, I want you to get on your knees and pray. Pray until you get an answer from God! Pray until you get an answer from God . . ."

CHAPTER TWELVE

Desire and Tiah had just hopped out of a cab on 117th and Manhattan after returning home from a whirlwind press trip to Las Vegas with Dollar. As soon they got their luggage from the cab and walked to their building, they ran into Lyfe, the dude they had given a beat down to several years ago. Lyfe hadn't changed much over the years and was now a crack dealer who regularly fucked over his customers by selling them speed. He still ran with flunkies, because he was a punk.

"Yo, Desire, what's up, baby?" said Lyfe as he and his boys stared at Desire and Tiah's asses and laughed as they passed. "When you gonna give me and my boys a private show?"

"Fuck you, nigga," said Desire. She and Tiah kept it moving.

He laughed and said, "Yeah, that's what I'm trying to do, bitch. So how much it gonna cost?" He pulled out a knot of money.

Desire turned around, furious. She spewed, "Nigga, your bummy ass don't have enough money to even have conversation with me, much less fuck me with your lil dick ass." His boys laughed as he tried to defend himself, but Desire continued. "Everybody know you be fucking crackheads, and they say you got a shriveled little dick that don't even get hard, so you better give that money to them bitches . . . Chump!"

Embarrassed, Lyfe managed to yell, "Fuck you, bitch. One day you gonna get knocked off that high horse, and I'll be standing there to piss on your black ass!"

Desire smiled and said, "You gonna be waiting a long time, faggot!" She disappeared into the building with Tiah, not thinking twice about Lyfe's prediction.

˜ ˜ ˜

Desire and Tiah were at Radio City Music Hall politicking with some industry execs at the Source Awards, which they were attending as guests of Lil Dollar. Desire heard her name being called from across the room. She turned and saw a guy smiling and waving wildly at her. She ignored him, because guys who recognized her from her stripping days often wanted to strike up a conversation when they recognized her. No sooner did she turn her back on him that she felt someone tapping on her shoulder. "Desire," the man behind her said.

Desire turned around, pissed, but her expression rapidly changed when she saw the man's face.

"It's me, Desire. Carvelas."

Desire took a step back, smiled, and asked, "Little Carvelas?"

His smile displayed a perfect set of white teeth as he nodded. "Yeah, little Carvelas." Desire hugged him and pulled back to look at him. He had the same cute baby face, but he was now much, much taller.

"Damn," Desire said, impressed. "You ain't little anymore. What happened?"

He chuckled shyly and said, "I guess I'm a late bloomer. Where your girl Tiah?"

"Oh, she running around here somewhere, probably getting her mack on. I'll find her, though. I'm sure she'd like to say 'sup."

They stared into each other's eyes.

"What you doing here?" she asked.

"Oh, I'm the assistant sound technician for the show tonight."

"So that's what you do now?"

"Yeah. It don't pay much right now, but I get to travel all over the world. It keeps me busy."

"I hear that," she said. They continued to admire each other.

"What's up with you? What you doing here?"

Before she could answer, Lil Dollar walked up. Desire introduced them. Carvelas smiled and extended his hand to shake.

Dollar sneered. "Who's this nigga to be shakin my hand?"

Carvelas had kept himself out of thuggish circles, but he certainly knew who Lil Dollar was and what his reputation meant. He decided not to dignify him with a response that would get something started. But Lil Dollar wouldn't let things die down easy.

"Fuck, who you be to be shaking my hand? Who is you to be talking to my girl?"

"Look, man," Carvelas said quietly, "I was just trying to say 'sup to my girl."

"You ain't asked me if you could do that, nigga."

Desire held Lil Dollar back as he moved toward Carvelas. Carvelas didn't budge.

"He's just one of my friends from off the block, from back in the day."

"Well, he callin you his girl and shit," Lil Dollar said. He threw Desire off. "I'm trying to figure out if he got a hidden agenda."

"No agenda, man." Carvelas was working and not trying to get involved with a fight that could make him lose his job. "Just wanted to speak to an old friend."

As Carvelas walked away, Lil Dollar grabbed him by the shoulder. He spit out a razor that was hidden in his mouth.

"What the fuck . . . ," Carvelas began, and Desire moved between them.

"Baby, no!" she cried.

Her cry caught the attention of one of the many security guards scattered throughout the crowd to keep watch on the big celebrities. He came over and asked if there was a problem. Lil Dollar quickly lifted the razor to his mouth, where it magically disappeared. He smiled at the security guard.

"E'r' thing's aiight. My girl was just telling this nigga to get the fuck outta her face."

Desire looked into Dollar's eyes and knew he was testing her loyalty. "Yeah, I was just telling him to get the fuck outta my face."

Carvelas knew that Lil Dollar wouldn't slash him with security right there. He stared at Desire long and hard, giving her a chance to prove that she could be loyal to an old friend by telling Lil Dollar the truth. She failed him as she drew nearer to Lil Dollar, who was getting ready to flare up again. Carvelas gave Lil Dollar a menacing glare and walked away, determined to forget about Desire Evans forever.

≈   ≈   ≈

When Tiah and Desire walked on the set of Dollar's next video shoot, they both were surprised at how much planning and how many people were involved in making a single video. All around them, there were makeup artists, lighting technicians, cameramen, production assistants and, of course, video hoes. Long weaves bounced atop the heads of girls who were all talking to one another cattily, not hiding the fact that they were competing for the spotlight. Some of the girls were so scantily clad, they may as well have been naked. They wore everything from Versace bikinis to Jimmy Choo shoes. The only thing excessive about what they had on was the dollar amount everything cost—not how much it covered.

Desire and Tiah stood on the sidelines and watched everyone at work as the video director described each scene to Dollar, to see what he thought. Inside, Desire was fuming. There had been many nights when, after lovemaking sessions where she gave Dollar every move she knew, she had tried to convince him to use her more in his music and let her sing. But he had always told her he liked to keep business and personal separate. Desire had decided that the benefits she received from just being on his arm weren't worth losing over this one issue. However, she was growing impatient with simply being in this world because she was some big rapper's bottom bitch. She put up with a lot including other bitches and his troubles with the law. She needed to set up some security for herself in case she and Dollar didn't last forever. And she knew from experience that almost nothing lasted forever.

Suddenly, the director yelled, "Bring the girls over." Moments later, his assistant went to him with three barely covered girls for Dollar to approve. Dollar smiled lustfully as the three girls struck their best poses. Desire and Tiah turned their faces up because they knew, by what they wore, that these were only low-grade Reebok bandits. The director said, "These the chicks who gonna be lip-syncing the hook throughout the video."

Desire and Tiah looked at each other as his words resounded in their heads.

Dumbfounded, Desire waited until the girls walked away before calling Dollar over.

"Dollar, why you didn't tell me you needed girls to sing backup in your video? I been asking you for the longest to hook up me and my sister, and then you go hire some knockoffs over your girl!"

Lil Dollar looked over his shoulder and cringed at the thought of anybody hearing Desire screaming at him. He whispered through his teeth, "Desire, chill the fuck out. I don't put this shit together . . . they do! I didn't even know."

Not satisfied, Desire pouted and smoothly said, "Then fire them and put us in their place."

"Desire, I already told you I ain't got no control over that shit. They pick the people who gonna be in the video!"

Desire wasn't having it. She exploded, yelling even louder, "How the fuck you ain't got no say in your own fucking video? What type of shit is that?"

Dollar remained silent as Desire pressed, "Who the hell I got to fuck to get a spot, Dollar? The director? 'Cause I see that he's the one that's really running shit. Toby!"

Dollar stared at her with contempt. Desire stared right back at him, then she signaled to Tiah. The girls headed toward the door.

Dollar grabbed Desire's arm. "Just gimme a chance, baby. Lemme go see if I can talk to the director, work something out."

Desire waited patiently as she saw Lil Dollar talking to the director and pointing in her direction. The director looked as if he was sizing up Desire and Tiah. Lil Dollar came back a few minutes later and told Desire exactly what she wanted to hear.

"I got you and Tiah on as their replacements."

Desire and Tiah jumped for joy. They had started out singing together in a small junior choir in a storefront Harlem church, and they had worked their way up to being front and center in a music video that was about to be aired all over the world.

"Hold up, hold up . . . it's only if they don't show up," Dollar stated.

"Oh, hell no," screamed Desire. "You got us on standby like we some fuckin groupies?"

"Desire, I tried, and that's the best I could do . . . it's either that or nothing."

Desire stared at him with malice for him being so weak. Here was a filthy-rich rapper that was paying for his own video, and he had to get permission from another motherfucker—who he's paying. A man that would kill another black man for looking at him too long, but who was out of his neighborhood and in front of crackers, cow-towing like he had to apologize for his existence.

"So you want me to put y'all names on the list or what?" asked Dollar. "I mean, if this don't work out, I promise you can finally get in the studio with me. Hell, we can fire them background singers. I can take my baby on the road and put her front and center with me."

Desire decided she was more interested in that promise than just being in the video. But she wanted the video too.

Desire smiled and said, "Yeah, baby, we could do that." She gave Dollar a seductive hug and kiss. "Now go get us on the list."

When Dollar was out of sight, Desire turned toward Tiah with a sense of urgency. "Tiah, listen, this is what I want you to do. I want you to find another girl who can sing and looks good—real good, no tramps, only classy. Meet me back here tomorrow at twelve sharp."

Tiah asked her, "Where am I gonna find another girl like that on short notice?"

"I don't know, but find one!" Desire said. "This could be our chance to shine just like we dreamed. We got to take ours."

As Desire signed the release form, she noticed the names, telephone numbers, and addresses of the three fleas that stood to steal her shine. She committed all their information to memory. And as she hugged Dollar, Desire stared over his shoulders at the three fleas rehearsing their dance routine.

⌀ ⌀ ⌀

The next day it was fifteen minutes before they were scheduled to start rehearsals and Tiah had yet to arrive at the video shoot. Desire paced back and forth, calling Tiah's cell phone for the hundredth time. Desire had corrected the flea problem that morning. She'd simply called each girl's house, posed as the director's assistant and told them the shoot was postponed until the next day. Everything was perfect, she thought, except Dollar had been performing shot takes since 6 A.M. that morning. The crew was now ready to shoot the background singers' scene, and Tiah wasn't there. Desire was just about ready to give up when she heard Tiah call her name.

"Yo, Dee . . ."

When Tiah turned the corner, Desire's jaw dropped nearly to her knees. She stared at the girl Tiah had at her side. It was Chanel, her worst enemy from back in the day, the girl who had taunted her in the lunchroom. The person who had been her arch nemesis during her high school years. She couldn't believe Tiah would actually bring her into the plan. She stared at Tiah, wanting to ask her what the fuck was going on, but she held back. She didn't want to ruin her chances of being in an actual music video by clowning. She decided to play the situation by ear. It could work out in her favor. They had less than an hour to learn the dance steps, the hook they would be lip-syncing and to get dressed. There was no time for arguing.

" 'Sup, Chanel?" Desire asked.

" 'Sup, Desire," Chanel responded. "Long time no see."

"Yeah, a lot of things have changed. You still with Tony?" She couldn't resist asking about the nigga who had stolen her virginity.

"Naw," Chanel said. "I cancelled that nigga a long time ago."

Desire knew that Chanel's words were just a front. The way Chanel had let him dog her out back in the day, she was sure it was Tony who had cancelled her. Desire had no idea where Chanel was now in life, but her guess was that she was still trying to become a star in a storefront Harlem church. Desire, however, had moved into the big leagues. And she was bringing Chanel into her world now. Desire did not feel the least bit intimidated anymore.

"I figured Chanel would be down for being in the video. She has the voice to go on the road with us on this," Tiah explained. Desire just put up her hand.

"You ain't gotta explain," she said. "We got work to do."

Desire, Tiah and Chanel were flawless as they executed every move, every harmony and every take without so much as a glitch. Toby commended them and added that they gave the video the class he'd wanted to achieve. Lil Dollar was even happier that his girl had satisfied the crew with her beauty and talent. After they finished, Desire pulled him to the side as the girls were getting ready to go celebrate with drinks at Midtown's swanky China Club.

"Remember what you promised me," she told him. She eased toward him and gave him the longest kiss she could muster without getting him so excited that he would want to take her into the bathroom and fuck her, as he had done before. She left him with her words and a hard dick on his mind.

At the China Club, the girls partied and drank. They talked

about how sexy they were and how men were going to drool over them when they saw them in the video.

"That's right," yelled Tiah. "When they see me, niggas gonna be creaming on themselves."

They all lifted their drinks and tapped their glasses: "Here's to creaming."

Chanel jumped in. "Well, when they see me, they're gonna be dreaming about me."

They lifted their drinks in unison: "Here's to dreaming."

Chanel asked, "So what they gonna say about you, Desire?"

Desire thought about it for a second. "Now, you know damn well what they gonna be saying . . . that bitch is my heart's desire!"

They raised their glasses.

"Here's to desiring." They laughed loudly.

As the evening dwindled, they reminisced about all the things that went on between them when they were younger. The girls were all grown now, and they saw that by putting past differences aside, they could all rise together. They talked about the good ole days when they all sang in the choir and how it had been such a good time in their lives. Right at the bar, they suddenly started singing "His Eye Is on the Sparrow." They sounded almost angelic in three-part harmony, as Desire and Chanel switched up on lead. By the time they finished the song, everyone in the restaurant was standing. The people gave the mysterious singers rousing applause. As they exited the restaurant, an older white couple asked, "What's the name of your group, so we can buy your CD?"

The young ladies looked at one another, speechless. Then Tiah spoke up: "Desire, Cream, and Dream."

≈ ≈ ≈

Dollar's boss was none other than Whip Daniels, record producer extraordinaire and CEO of Central Booking Records. He was the toast of New York City and had a lock on all the top hip-hop groups in the industry. Dollar's single was number one in the country, and it earned him a spot to perform during *Dick Clark's New Year's Rockin' Eve.* He would be seen all over the world.

On the strength of making Dollar's video so scorching hot, Whip invited Desire, Tiah and Chanel to lip-sync and perform with Dollar onstage to keep the same vibe as the video. The girls were beside themselves with joy to be part of something of that magnitude. They knew that the New Year's Eve celebration in Times Square was a wild party, which was broadcast all over the world. They couldn't even imagine the number of people that would be watching. Like always, Desire was going to milk this opportunity for everything it was worth.

Once again, as she stood facing a pivotal moment in her life, Carvelas came back into her head. He was on her mind for more than a favor. She had not seen him since the Source Awards. And they had not gotten the chance to exchange information then. Desire had not meant to hurt him that night, just as she had not meant to hurt him three years ago. She needed to be able to explain that to him. She knew Carvelas had to be a full member for Local 571, the Sound and Lighting Engineers Union. She wrote him a letter and hoped he would write back. She was sure he would, after she signed on an ending they had both avoided years before.

Carvelas,

I can certainly understand if you ain't trying to hear from me no more. I know I acted like a bitch that night. But you gotta understand. I was in a fucked-up awkward situation. Dollar ain't the easiest nigga to be with. He got a temper. But Carvelas, he do care for me. He's been taking care of me for a minute now, much longer than I had thought he would when we first met. And you know me, Carvelas. I'm just trying to take care of myself. I didn't mean nothing that night, just like I didn't mean nothing the night we went to prom. I ain't never apologized to you for that night. But the truth is, I'm really sorry. I was young, dumb. I wasn't thinking with my heart. I'd like for you to give me a call. The truth is, Dollar do a lot of work that I think you could benefit from. Don't worry, he ain't worried about us hooking up or nothing no more. But write me back, and put Tiah's name on the envelope. I'm sorry, but I got a jealous nigga. I do still want to keep in touch with you. We can be that team, like you said. Just in a different way.

Love, Desire

Desire hoped and prayed she still had the same effect on Carvelas as she'd had in the past. Even more, she hoped that they still had a friendship. Her hopes were reassured when Tiah brought her a letter from Carvelas one day, which she had already opened.

"This got my name on it, but piano boy is talking to you!" Tiah exclaimed, as they spread the letter on Desire and Dollar's plush king-sized bed—it had a canopy flowing down on it from the ceiling.

Desire,

Despite what happened that night, I am happy to hear from you. I know how it is. Time passes. Things change. You ain't gotta worry about it. I've moved on from that the same way I've had to move on from a lot of shit in my life. I see you still got your dreams of fame. All that shit you used to talk about back in the day seem to be coming true. That's good shit, kid. I'm proud of you. You always could get what you wanted. No worries about us being friends. You can call me anytime you want. I'm still living with my moms, trying to save up money to buy myself a place. I wouldn't mind meeting up with you to talk, long as Dollar don't get crazy again.

Love, Carvelas

They met up on a Sunday afternoon at Sylvia's, Desire's favorite restaurant from the old days. A small gospel quartet backed up by only a pianist and a drummer entertained the families and churchgoers who dined. Desire soaked up the warm, family atmosphere. She missed seeing this part of Harlem. After she and Carvelas caught up, she finally got to the point of why they had urgently needed to meet.

"Well, I got a chance to really make it big," she told him, and he stared at her, waiting for the punch line that he hadn't suspected was coming. "I think you can help me out . . ."

"So that's what this shit is all about? You need my help again?" Carvelas looked disgusted, and he pulled his napkin off his lap so he could throw it on the table. He signaled for the waiter to bring them the bill. This was not the same Carvelas that Desire had been able to sweet talk back in the day.

"Just do me this one favor, Carvelas, and I'll owe you bigtime!" she pleaded.

Carvelas curled his lip and said with sarcasm. "Gee, where have I heard that before?"

"Come on, Carvelas, I know I fucked up a long time ago, but we were kids then. Plus, I didn't do it on purpose."

"Desire, you fucking dissed me at Radio City for that punk-ass Dollar."

Desire quickly rebutted, "I just did that so you wouldn't get into the mix with him. You think I wanted something to happen to you?"

"Let me ask you something, Desire—why is it that the only time you seek me out is when you need something?" The waiter arrived, but Carvelas waved him away. He had a point that needed to be made. "You know I like you and always have. I ain't ashamed to admit it. But you never seem to give a fuck about my feelings—like I'm some piece of shit or something."

Desire turned from him, avoiding his eyes.

"The more I try to show you how much love I have for you, the more you seem to push me away. Just answer this one thing for me truthfully, and I'll do whatever you want me to do."

"What is it, Carvelas?"

"Why don't you love me back?"

Desire looked down at the ground for a moment and then lifted her head. Her face softened when she stared into his beautiful and caring eyes. She was bewildered that she couldn't find an answer to that question. Carvelas was everything a woman could ever want in a man, yet she had brushed him off since they were kids. She had no idea what she was still searching for, and could only conclude one thing, based upon the fact that she had kept searching for something else all her life, even during the times when she should have been content to be where she was:

"Because, Carvelas, I guess I just don't know how to love myself."

☙ ☙ ☙

Of course, Carvelas eventually caved in. He had a weak spot for Desire that amazingly had not toughened over time. After the meeting at Sylvia's, everything was set for the spectacle Desire knew she needed to create to put the spotlight on her—and keep it there. Desire was convinced that New Year's Eve was the ticket Desire, Cream, and Dream needed to hit the big time. They all knew they had to be flawless. This wasn't public access television. This was ABC, New York City and New Year's Eve. They rehearsed over and over for the New Year's Eve performance, until they harmonized and moved as one perfect machine. A huge stage for the performance was built right where Broadway split near 42nd Street. The stage's bright neon lights illuminated the night as if it were midday. Desire, Tiah and Chanel stood in awe as they looked out at the million or so faces that had withstood the winter cold to be a part of the biggest, wildest New Year's Eve celebration in the world. Despite the freezing temperature, they wore only all-black catsuits, and nothing else. No hats, scarves and certainly no jackets. Their hearts pumped rapidly, and inside they felt as if they were boiling in a sauna.

As planned, Carvelas had programmed a DAT tape to play the instrumental version of Lil Dollar's hit single. It was common practice for some rappers to lip-sync over a track at an outdoor event, because with the lack of acoustics, the rapper would run the risk of sounding horrible. Because the hook took up most of the song, background vocals were a must. Carvelas made sure to stay in the back where he belonged; he didn't want to ruin Desire's night by arousing suspicion in Dollar. Plus, he'd had about all he could take on the night of the Source Awards. He might have to show Lil Dollar that he was also from the hood if the arrogant rapper stepped to him again. But that didn't happen. Everybody was too focused on the performance. The energy made them all feel as if the air crackled. The crowd roared with anticipation as the stage lights began to flicker on and off to announce that the night's climactic performance was on its way. Tiah, Desire and Chanel huddled in the wings, pumping one another up as they sought shelter from the cold in one another's arms.

"This is it, y'all," Desire said. "We 'bout to get famous!"

"How many people y'all think watchin?" Chanel asked.

"Probably a billion!" Tiah exclaimed. Then, less excited, she asked, "Desire, you think Grandma one of them?"

Desire didn't have time to think about the question. Their time to hit the stage had come.

"THREE . . .

"TWO . . .

"ONE . . .

"Ladies and gentlemen, put your hands together for the artist with the number one song in America. Performing his hit song, 'Harlem Girl Lost,' we bring you Lil Dollar!!!!!!!!!!!!!!"

Lil Dollar strutted onto the stage with a vengeance as the crowd went bananas. Desire and the girls were dead center when the music came bursting through the speakers. Lil Dollar bobbed about onstage. Having given the crowd the glimpse of him that they craved, he moved back toward the fringes of the stage. He would wait until it was time for him to rhyme before he came back to center stage. The frenzied crowd before them appeared to percolate with uncontained excitement. Desire was frozen for a brief moment. Both Dollar and Carvelas were out of her sight. Tiah and Chanel had blurred out of focus, even though they were right beside her. The hundreds of thousands of faces before her seemed like an endless stream ready to devour her. She couldn't believe that she was being seen by so many people at once. She didn't know if her voice could soar through this crowd. This was definitely not the audience at church. It was a dream and a nightmare at the same time. But her fears disappeared once the girls actually began their routine. At that moment, only two people knew something had gone wrong—Lil Dollar and Whip, who listened in horror from the side of the stage. They listened for a few seconds more, until they were sure their worst fears were confirmed.

"Goddammit," Whip hollered. "They put on the instrumental version instead of the fuckin vocals!"

Lil Dollar turned from the audience and looked at his boss, unsure of what to do next. Whip was ready to race to the main engineer's booth. But a production assistant stopped him.

"No, Whip, listen," the young man said, and he pointed toward the girls.

Whip paused, and turned toward the stage. He watched and listened to the three unknown girls sing the hook to the song beautifully. Lil Dollar even seemed to have settled down as he rapped to his part, on time and to the beat. One by one, the girls stepped closer to the audience as Lil Dollar settled into the background. The millions upon millions of people who watched the performance that night saw history in the making, as the girls became larger-than-life performers, dancing, singing and vogueing without missing a beat. Suddenly, the spotlight and every network camera focused on the three girls. The frown on Whip's face disappeared, and Lil Dollar didn't seem to mind that he had lost the spotlight. The girls continued performing, and the crowd started to move forward just to get closer to them. They looked at one another and simply kept going. At the end of the song, Desire, Tiah, and Chanel stood in awe as a valley of people gave them a thunderous round of applause.

One person who was enthusiastically clapping was Carvelas, who had been watching with a pack of technicians from the sidelines. But Desire had already forgotten he was there. When the media stormed the girls after the performance, Carvelas found that he was not even permitted to move past security to tell Desire congratulations.

                                       *   *   *

Desire, Cream, and Dream were the stars that night, and they were flown by helicopter back to the New Year's Eve after-party at Whip's mansion in the Hamptons. The girls' heads were still spinning as they rubbed elbows and mingled among some of the industry's biggest celebrities. They stood around in amazement as singers, actresses and even athletes lounged on plush leather couches, sipping Krugs and Courvoisier. The number of expensive diamonds in the room outnumbered the people, and the bling sparkled like tiny spotlights, adding to the feel of fame oozing throughout the room. Every major entertainment magazine and television show was there to cover the event. For the first time in her life, Desire felt important.

Whip wrapped his arms around the girls while the reporters took pictures. He smiled widely and made sure he was in all of their pictures.

"Whip, tell us about the girls."

Without skipping a beat, he smoothly said, "I'm glad you asked. When I discovered these girls over a year ago, when I heard their voices, you could have knocked me down with a feather." The girls hid their shock well. They were all experienced hustlers and knew exactly what Whip was doing.

Whip paused as if he were too overwhelmed to continue. "I had to rub my eyes and pinch myself to see if they were real, 'cause my ears don't lie. So I said to myself, 'Whip, God musta sent you these three girls, 'cause they sound like angels.' So I waited to bring them out in a big way. And what better way to introduce to the world the greatest girl group since the Supremes than in the epicenter of the world, the city that's so nice they named it twice—New York, New York!"

"So what's the name of the group?" one reporter asked.

Whip smiled, "I'm gonna let them tell you." He took one step back, and the girls announced who they were. They said their names individually, then in unison they proclaimed: "We're DE-SIRE, CREAM, AND DREAM."

Whip smiled as he applauded loudly, then said, "Yes, Desire, Cream, and Dream, the next big thing!"

Lil Dollar, who arrived late by limo, stood by and watched his boss steal the credit. He grew even angrier as he watched Whip offer the girls a record deal on the spot.

CHAPTER THIRTEEN

The music business is a multibillion-dollar industry, and hip-hop is a major reason why. The five major record companies consisted of aging white men who wouldn't know real rap from Reynolds Wrap. As hip-hop morphed into a great leviathan, they would pay, handsomely, A&R reps who could find them artists, then sign them to the companies for pennies. But game recognizes game, and many blacks, mainly hustlers, had the vision and hindsight to capitalize and take advantage of the industry that was riding off their talent. Geniuses such as Russell Simmons, Sean "Puffy" Combs, Jay-Z, Damon Dash, Jermaine Dupree, Master P, and others were smart enough to learn that ownership and control were the keys. They created monopolies by signing the most talented rappers and singers the 'hood had to offer, forcing the majors to come to them on their terms and make them young millionaires in the process.

Whip Daniels was one of those geniuses. He became 'hood rich before the age of fifteen by running short cons on old people and fools. He got into the rap game in 1981 by default, when a friend who managed a rap group borrowed a thousand dollars from him to buy studio time and press some records. Whip's silver tongue and penchant to manipulate and swindle paid off handsomely, when two months later the song became a hit. When the guy arrived to repay him, Whip reneged on the deal. He claimed that he lent him the money with the understanding that they would be partners. The friend rebutted, and Whip challenged him in court.

Whip won the case because he made his friend sign a blank piece of paper before he lent him the money. By the time they got to court, that same blank piece of paper was neatly filled in, stating Whip owned all recording rights and fifty percent of the publishing rights to the single—thus making him his first million. The friend walked away with virtually nothing because of the expenses he incurred promoting the group. To add insult to injury, the judge also ordered that he repay Whip the thousand dollars, with interest. Not only was Whip a shark when it came to business, he was no better in his personal life. His only friends were celebrities and the people who he was producing music with at the time; usually, once he got finished with his pet projects, he had made enemies of former friends, who would never talk to him again. Even worse, he was married to a woman whom he kept hidden in a huge brownstone in the Mott Haven section of the Bronx. She had two children with Whip, but he never brought his family around. Furthermore, his escapades with the women who flocked around him because he was in the industry were legendary. He had fashioned a grandiose image of himself as a terrible Wizard of Oz–like ruler that nobody could get close enough to to really know, let alone take down. However, in the public eye he had the image of being a musical genius, the Quincy Jones of hip-hop.

There is no loyalty in hip-hop, because rap fans are fickle. And like rap fans, Whip had no use for washed-up performers. As soon as their records failed to produce, he'd drop them from their contract like a hot potato. Whip disposed of artists if their last album was weak and failed to make money. He didn't believe in hustling backwards. Almost immediately after his background singers upstaged him on New Year's Eve, Lil Dollar's career took a serious nosedive. Although he had made a lot of money, he was a lavish spender who had accumulated hundreds of thousands of dollars of debt. Whip had filled Desire's head with the promise of stardom. Lil Dollar became a has-been within a couple of months. He was a liability to both her and CBR now, not an asset. She decided to be at Lil Dollar's loft when Whip told him that he wasn't hitting the numbers CBR had hoped he would. Desire knew it was time to leave Dollar alone and fly solo. She had planned to tell him after Whip left them alone. Her plan went horribly wrong.

"What you want to talk with me about, Whip?" Dollar asked as he reached for a bottle of Heineken. He had two blunts rolled and ready on the opulent crystal-and-glass coffee table that centered the room. Whip stopped him. This was not a party, in his mind. Desire was tense as she waited for Whip to drop the news. She lay back on the couch in pink silk pajamas, sipping a cup of chamomile tea since she'd had a long day rehearsing at the studio.

"Man, this isn't an occasion to celebrate," Whip said. Dollar looked concerned and took a seat next to Desire on the couch. Whip remained standing.

"There's really no easy way to say this," Whip began, "so I'm just going to have to spit it out. CBR has decided not to renew your contract."

Dollar took a long sip of the Heineken he had placed on the table, next to the blunts and all the jewelry he had just removed. He nodded his head quietly as if he had been expecting this announcement.

"I can write another hit," he told Whip. He grabbed Desire's hand for support. She held it limply. She would have an announcement of her own as soon as Whip left.

"That's the problem, Dollar," Whip continued. "Unfortunately, it takes money to produce. CBR just doesn't think you've given them the numbers to make that investment again. One hit single doesn't make you a success."

Whip held up his hands as if he was ready to box. Dollar stiffened and then calmed down. He looked toward Desire as he tried to regain composure. Desire said nothing. Her silence was strange. She usually had his back.

"I'm sorry, Dollar," Whip said. "There may be some opportunities for you to produce—"

"Fuck producing, motherfucker!" Dollar swept the champagne glasses he'd set out on the table for them onto the floor.

Glass shattered everywhere. "I'm a star, man. I ain't no background nigga."

"Baby, calm down," Desire said, standing to grab Dollar's shoulders. Dollar turned toward Desire so that Whip couldn't see him. She wiped his tears and hugged him as Whip stood uncomfortably in the middle of the living room with his hands in his pockets.

"I'm sorry, Dollar," Whip said. "Man, I really am. I mean, you now how these things are."

"Yeah," Dollar sneered. "You promised me you was gonna have my back. You promised me you was gonna take care of me. But now I'm just a washed-up rapper to you, and you ain't got no use for a nigga!"

"This happens to everybody, Dollar," Whip said. "You can't be on top forever."

"Not unless yo name is Whip and you controllin all the shit. Then you stay on top forever. You stay rollin in dough forever."

"Dollar," Whip pleaded, "my time is coming too . . . one day, I might not be able to produce hit records anymore. You don't think the public's gonna spit me out too?"

"Yeah, but you'll make sure your pockets are fat and go'n stay fat before that shit happen. Get out of my house, motherfucker!" Dollar pointed to the door.

Whip gathered his briefcase and shook Desire's hand. He then made his way to the loft's elevator alcove. Dollar threw Desire off of him as soon as the elevator arrived to take Whip down.

"There has to be somebody else you can talk to," Desire said, following Dollar as he tore into every pillow, picture frame and statue in his massive living room. Desire could not stop him. She decided now was not the time to let him know that she was thinking of ending the relationship. Then, he turned on her.

"Did you know about this, bitch?" He grabbed her by the shoulders and shook her violently. "Whip done fucked up yo head now too. Got you thinkin you 'bout to be a star too. Well, yo ass would still be turning tricks in a strip joint if it wasn't for me. He told you about this, didn't he!"

Dollar had been angry with Desire before, but he had never put his hands on her. She was suddenly terrified of him. She had the thought that he might pull a razor out of his mouth and slash her with it. And she did not have a razor in her mouth this time to compete with. Desire cried out, but Dollar did not stop questioning and shaking her, no matter how much she told him no. He had lost control. The beautiful Harlem loft he still had to pay for wasn't so beautiful anymore. He went to the parking lot at Seventh Avenue where he kept his vehicles and busted the windows of his Benz and Escalade. But before he trashed the cars, he beat Desire until she was unconscious. Tiah and Chanel found her the next day on the living room floor when they arrived to take her to the studio. They had to cancel the session because Desire's mouth and eyes were so bruised, she did not want to be seen. The next day, after the rescheduled studio session, they found some small belongings Desire had brought to Dollar's house sitting on the curb of 125th Street.

Once Desire was able to make it to the Greenwich Village apartment where Whip was putting them all up until recording was over, she noticed a pile of papers stuffed in between the wrinkled clothes Dollar had smashed into huge garbage bags. The papers were a bunch of letters that had been ripped in half. With her hands shaking, Desire put the pieces together and realized that Dollar had been opening letters addressed to Tiah. Carvelas had been writing to her for months, and she hadn't even known.

❧ ❧ ❧

With Dollar out of the picture, Whip could concentrate on turning Desire, Cream and Dream into his next sensation. Desire was the lead singer on every record that the group recorded for the new album, which would launch their careers. "Harlem Girl Lost" had burned up the charts, mostly because of them, and the public couldn't wait to hear more. To everyone at CBR, Desire was the real cash cow. The girls played several small concert venues around the country to keep their names and faces in the public eye after the New Year's Eve moment and before their first album came out. Whip knew he had to continuously promote the group, because in the relatively short amount of time it was going to take to produce a hit album, the public would forget the three girls who had torn up the stage on New Year's Eve. The concert crowds always went wild over Desire. As far as CBR was concerned, whatever Desire wanted, Desire got. And she knew it. Whip would grant her every request to keep her happy. But when it came to giving the group a better contract, he stuck to his guns and would not give an extra penny. He told her that a deal was a deal. They would make much more if they didn't worry about money and worried about producing a hit record.

The more Desire learned about the music industry, the more she realized how bad a deal the group had signed. From what she heard, other, less talented artists were receiving a much larger portion of profits than Desire, Cream, and Dream, seemed to be getting. Still, Whip spoiled them with shopping and spa trips as he tried to ease their minds so they could save all their energy for the studio sessions. After a tiring day of recording, Whip would often treat them to dinner at one of Manhattan's most exclusive restaurants. But that didn't keep Desire from obsessing over the fine print she had noticed in the contract. Fine print that only guaranteed them pennies for every record they sold, while Whip and CBR would receive the bulk. Desire wanted to get out of the contract, by any means; she was just waiting for the perfect time. And the eve of releasing their first record was certainly not the perfect time.

* * *

Whip was in a meeting when Desire stormed into his office. The three white accountants, already nervous simply by being in Whip's presence, nearly hit the floor when the singer they had all heard about came in with a hellish look on her face.

"Whip, what the hell is this shit?" Desire fumed. She held up a piece of paper. Dazed, Whip turned a light smile toward the accountants, as they quickly stood, embarrassed, pretending to wipe lint off of their suits.

"I'm sorry, gentlemen," Whip said. "Let me introduce you to Desire Evans. Desire, this is—"

"Fuck them," Desire interrupted, not even looking their way. "I want to know what's this bullshit with my advance check?"

Whip cleared his throat. "Desire, give me a minute, and then we can discuss this in private."

Desire was not having any of it. "I ain't waiting a minute. I'm about to put this place on blast if you don't tell me what happened to my money!"

One of the accountants anxiously interjected, "We . . . we can come back a little later, if you like." Whip waved his hand toward them to indicate they should leave.

He remained silent as he watched the three men exit. Whip turned to Desire and said, "Now, what do you want to talk about?"

"This small-ass check, that's what the fuck I want to talk about!"

Whip sighed and rolled his eyes. "Desire, how many times do I have to tell you, that is handled by the accounting department."

"Bullshit, this shit happened on my first check, and you said the first checks are always small and that I'm gonna see a bigger check the next time. I trusted you."

"What do you want me to do, Desire?" Whip said. "Everything is in black and white. Every dime, every nickel, every penny!"

"Whip, we been doing shows all over the country and promoting this record well before it's coming out. We was already famous after New Year's Eve. Where all the money from our shows? What happened to the money you said we was getting for workin our asses off every day? How the fuck I receive only four thousand dollars?" screamed Desire.

Whip shrugged. "Desire, I told you before, that is based on monies after everything is recouped—traveling expenses, hotels, food, and you got your video budget, production costs, publicity, then don't forget, you girls' personal account . . . shit, that's damn near a million right there."

He watched her closely as he spoke in a winding tone. Desire was definitely the real deal, because she was one of those rare commodities that was respected by both the R&B fan and the ever-fickle hip-hop heads.

"Now, I would understand if you were a solo artist and were upset, but you got to remember—" He paused to ensure he had her attention. "The money is split three ways, and everything you do is always gonna cost you three times as much."

Whip smiled and told her to sit down so he could further explain the business to her.

"See, Desire, there is no such thing as loyalty in this business. Either you are a shark, or you are a victim. It's all about survival of the fittest in this game, sink or swim, you decide. If you show any weaknesses, you'll be eaten alive. This is the only business where a person can start as a lowly intern who gets someone's coffee, and two years later, that same intern is your boss and making you get his coffee. If you remember one thing from this meeting, remember this, a golden opportunity comes around only once. When it does, you got to be able to do two things: one, recognize it; and two, don't give a fuck on how anyone feels about it. If it's in your best interest, fuck loyalty, because they would do it to you if the shoe was on the other foot."

Desire remained silent as she absorbed everything he said.

CHAPTER FOURTEEN

Desire's plan was to make a solo record behind Chanel and Tiah's back while they continued to work on their group album. Whip knew that she was the real star in the group; the other girls paled in comparison and were more suited to be backup singers than larger-than-life divas. Desire had that potential, Whip recognized it, and he had no problem helping her cultivate her stardom. In a matter of time, Desire turned into a person that nobody recognized. She began to isolate herself from Tiah and Chanel. She replaced them with an entourage of hangers-on and flunkies. While Tiah and Chanel rode the tour bus to the venues where they opened for more established singing acts, Desire flew with Whip and other executives. After shows, the requests for Desire's autograph were overwhelming, and Desire loved every minute of attention from the mobs who rushed her after performances. She was also flooded with requests from men who wanted to date her, but she had found a way to get rich on her own and decided that she didn't need men for anything—not even their dicks. The fact that Desire was so elusive simply made men want her more, and pretty soon, street hustlers caught on and began printing posters from her promotional photos. Desire, Cream, and Dream had just one song playing on the radio, yet it seemed everyone in the world knew Desire's name. The girls complained about the favoritism that Desire received, but it fell on deaf ears. The strife and bickering began to take its toll on all of them, especially Tiah.

The bond between Desire and Tiah was now nonexistent. Tiah occasionally phoned Hattie Mae, but Desire never bothered. Hattie Mae did not even know where they were living. Desire barely talked to Tiah. She was more interested in penning her solo songs, or planning and carrying out secret recording sessions with Whip. The only time she and Tiah's paths crossed was when they were onstage, at a photo shoot or doing a group interview. The beating from Dollar had hardened Desire even more. She had watched him carry out his wrath on others, but had never thought he would do it to her. He became just one more person she added to the list of those who had let her down. Ironically, she avoided the two people who never had—Carvelas and Hattie Mae. She didn't want anyone in her life who would try to talk her out of her decisions, try to make her see things their way. Desire enjoyed the flash of jewelry, expensive cars and furs that were being thrown Desire, Cream, and Dream's way to keep them happy so they would produce. However, she also remembered that when Dollar threw her out, he had kept everything he ever bought her. She knew the group didn't own anything that was being given to them. It was all contingent upon satisfying CBR; if they didn't produce, they would be kicked out and left with nothing, just as Dollar had been. As such, Desire did not care about anyone but herself anymore.

During concerts dates, unusual things began to happen. Once, everyone's wardrobe except Desire's came up missing. When this happened, Tiah and Chanel had to literally wear the clothing on their backs, while Desire wore a glamorous sequined gown, making both girls look like baggage handlers onstage. Another time, the bus driver was given the incorrect itinerary, dropping Tiah and Chanel off at the wrong concert hall, two hours away. By the time they made it to the designated venue, Desire was already bowing and thanking the audience. Ultimately, both girls' roles within the group began to diminish, and they were reduced to backup singers within weeks of their album's release.

Tiah and Chanel were so disgusted with the situation that one day they showed up at the recording studio and refused to sing. Inside the booth, Desire pressed her earphones to her ears and sang her heart out. When it came time for Tiah and Chanel to join the song, they remained silent, and crossed their arms.

"What the . . . ?" Whip stopped the music, and the sound technicians and engineers were given their cues to exit. Desire had been oblivious to her group members' lack of participation. She had no clue that they had finally caught on to the fact that they were slowly but surely being phased out of the group, before it was even truly a group.

"Can either of you tell me what the fuck your problem is today?" Whip asked. Desire started to speak, but he put up his hand to stop her.

"We ain't singin today," Chanel answered.

"And may I ask why not?" Whip demanded. Desire ripped off her headphones and put her hands on her hips, glaring at the other girls.

" 'Cause we ain't really a part of this group," Chanel said. "It's all about Desire. So let her ass sing the whole song."

"This is a group effort, ladies," Whip said. "Let me decide what's best for the music."

"What's best for the music, or for Desire?" Chanel asked.

"You wouldn't even be here if it wasn't for me," Desire spat. "Your ass would be singing in a raggedy-ass church uptown if it wasn't for me, crying to your uncle, married to one of the choirboys and spittin out babies. You just mad you ain't got the spotlight!"

"Despite what you think, Desire, you ain't the only one in this studio who can sing!" Chanel shot back. Tiah remained quiet, feeling too hurt that it had come to this between her and Desire. She took her anger out on Whip. Desire was shocked that Tiah was actually vocalizing the feelings responsible for the ice that now coated their relationship.

"Fuck you, Whip," Tiah spewed. "You let Desire do whatever she wants, and when we complain, you don't do shit. Since she do whatever the fuck she want, I'm gonna do what I want! So fuck you, thank you."

Whip for the most part took the insults on the chin, but as time went on, Tiah became more hostile toward him. She started to cuss him out like he had stole something. And then Whip got angry.

"You need to calm your little black ass down and remember who got you to this point," Whip said. "Don't fuck around and fuck up the biggest chance you're ever gonna get in your life. In one second, I'll send you back to Harlem to live with your grandmother. All I gotta do is say the word."

"If you fuck around and try putting me out the group, I'll sue your big black ass. I spoke to a lawyer."

The mention of lawsuits or lawyers made Whip's hair stand up. Almost every artist that ever recorded for him was already suing.

"She said that if you try, motherfucker, you got to pay me to use our group name, since I invented it," Tiah continued. "And if you even think of doing some grimey shit, I'm gonna do some grimier shit. I know about all the illegal shit you done to artists and I know how you been doing it. I bet a lot of your former rappers would love to see the shit too. And it don't stop there, I know all about your little secrets, and I bet your so-called wife and *her* lawyer would love to know them."

Tiah had had enough, and she stormed out of the studio, with Chanel on her heels. Desire saw the girls' outburst as just another chance for her to get closer to her own goals.

"Whip," she said, putting her earphones back on, "let's rehearse that song we wrote the other night."

Whip called the producing team back in, and they did just that.

ι. ι. ι.

The stress and strife in Tiah's life began to take its toll on her emotionally. She became disenchanted not only with Desire and CBR, but with herself as well. Soon, she began to seek solace and relief in pills and alcohol. The first person who had ever given Tiah uppers and downers had been one of the other dancers at the strip club. After Whip took her and Chanel's threats as a challenge, and began to exclude them even more, Tiah spiraled into an anxious depression. She called up the former dancer and put in a request to pick up everything from cocaine to ecstasy from a reliable supplier. As soon as Tiah got her hands on the drugs, she started using them regularly. She also started arriving late or missing concerts and promotional appearances. In a couple of showcases, where industry and media executives were given a private party and performance, she was out of sync with her steps and forgot the songs' lyrics. She was always either drunk or high. It began to get so bad, they had to cancel shows because she could barely remain on her feet. Tiah's erratic and inconsistent behavior forced the promoters to pull the group from venues, just as their first self-titled album was hitting the record stores. Desire was furious.

ι. ι. ι.

Two months had passed since the album's release. Although an extraordinary amount of momentum had been put forth to make a name for the girls so the public would be dying to buy their album, sales were slow. The group had quickly gotten a reputation for being unreliable performers, so Desire, Cream, and

Dream missed many crucial concerts. Furthermore, a drug supplier had leaked the news that Tiah of Desire, Cream, and Dream was one of his biggest customers; it created a press scandal that caused many consumers who were concerned about their kids to not buy the album. A big meeting was scheduled between the group and Central Booking Records, at Whip's central office in Midtown Manhattan. Whip decided to cease and desist all their future dates and appearances until further notice.

Desire and Chanel were already sitting with Whip and his henchmen when Tiah, an hour and a half late, staggered in. Before, Tiah's long hair had always been styled meticulously, but that day her hair—now a mini Afro—was a mess. The unusual clothing she wore also raised a few eyebrows, as it sagged off her body. Tiah leaned against the wall and lit a cigarette, glaring at Desire the whole time.

Whip spoke first, while pointing to a chair far away from Desire. "You can sit over there if you want."

"I don't want to sit down, motherfucker. Just give me my money so I can get the fuck out of here," snapped Tiah. Whip had had her assets frozen to recoup monies lost as a direct result of her behavior. According to CBR's lawyers, Tiah's unpredictability and unreliability meant she had reneged on her contractual obligation to the company, and the money was no longer hers.

A small white man stood up. "Ms. Tiah, I'm an attorney for Central Booking Records. On behalf of the company, I must inform you that your contract, as of this day, is null and void, and CBR is relinquishing your services for any and all future recordings and performances. As it states in section seven of your contract, if the majority of the group find a member detrimental to the group as a whole, each member can elect to vote said member from the established entity. You were voted out of Desire, Cream, and Dream on the fifteenth day of June of this year. It's out of the generosity of CBR's heart that we present this check to you. This will be the last money that you'll receive from the company."

Tiah stood speechless as his words registered in her mind. Chanel ran out the office with tears running down her cheeks. She had not been in favor of this decision. Desire and Whip had threatened to find action against her as well if she didn't vote against Tiah.

Desire had her head lowered. Tiah's eyes fell on her sister.

"Desire . . ." Tiah said as tears welled in her eyes. "You gonna let them do this to me?"

Desire kept her eyes on the floor.

Tiah yelled, "Look at me, Desire!"

Desire slowly lifted her head and looked Tiah straight in the eye. "Yeah, I voted you out, and it's your own fault! You was the one who started fucking up, not me. I wasn't the one getting fucked up and missing dates."

Tears flowed freely from Tiah's eyes as she listened to her sister cut into her. "You was the one who made me start doing that shit in the first place, Desire."

"Started you doing what, Tiah?" Desire snapped. "I wasn't the one forcing you to shoot up and snort up. I know by now you got a glass dick in your mouth!"

Ashamed, Tiah shook her head. "If you knew I had a problem, Desire, why didn't you offer to help me?"

Desire rolled her eyes. "I've been helping you your entire life,

Tiah. I'm tired of covering your ass. That shit was turning into a fucking job and I resigned from it."

"But we're sisters, Desire. Sisters. And that's what family do for each other," cried Tiah.

Desire threw her hands in the air as she stood up and said, "Family? I ain't got no fucking family. We're only make-believe sisters, and . . ."

The words cut through Tiah like a knife. And Desire was fighting back tears.

"Only make-believe sisters?" Tiah asked. "After all the shit you told me and everything we been through, we're only make-believe sisters? Well, fuck you, Desire!"

Tiah surveyed everyone in the room. Her stare settled on Whip. "As for you, motherfucker, I ain't finished with your ass, cause I know you the snake behind all this shit. And since you fucked me, I'm gonna fuck you. I know this guy who takes pictures, and he got some of you that he will sell to the highest bidder." Tiah held up the check in her hand. "I'm about to cash this bitch and go picture shopping. Or maybe I'll just drop off the ones I already have to your wife."

Tiah started to storm out the room, and Whip summoned his henchmen to go after her. They grabbed Tiah and brought her over to Whip who snatched the check out of her hand.

"Bitch, I was being nice giving you some money. Now you ain't getting shit!" He ripped the check up before her eyes and threw it in her face. "Show my wife that, bitch!"

Tiah gritted her teeth and kicked him in the groin. Whip bent over in pain. Then, fighting for control, he stood up straight, and punched her repeatedly in the face, showing no mercy. Overcome, Tiah pleaded for Desire to help her, but Desire sat frozen. Memories of the beating from Dollar flooded her, and she was afraid of having Whip's vengeance turned on her. She stayed in her seat and watched the revolting beating. Desire had forgotten how the two girls had met in the first place, with Tiah rescuing her from receiving a like beating in Brooklyn.

The henchmen took hold of Tiah, and each took turns kicking her. Tiah tried in vain to escape their clutches. Desire put her hands over her ears. She could not stand to hear Tiah's cries. She finally couldn't take it any longer.

"All right, y'all, that's enough!" Desire finally attempted to help, grabbing the henchmen, who refused to stop their assault on her feeble sister. Tiah was still trying to fight them off, calling them every bitch and motherfucker in the book. But she simply could not keep them from overpowering her. Finally, Whip grabbed Desire and led her out of the boardroom. Desire knew there was no use trying to talk him out of whatever he had planned for Tiah. So she left. Whip watched Desire walk down the hall. She was silent, and took small, slow steps, as if she were in a trance. Finally, when she had turned the corner leading to the building's exit, he started back toward the boardroom. Tiah's cries for mercy had stopped, and the henchmen simply held her down until they got further orders from Whip.

Whip walked back into the room, took off his belt, and looked down on a beaten and broken, Tiah. "Now beg, bitch."

CHAPTER FIFTEEN

Junior's Restaurant in Brooklyn was already crowded when Desire arrived that evening. She walked briskly past a hostess with a huge smile.

Desire went toward the back. She lowered her glasses when she came to the table of a disgustingly fat white man digging heartily into a whole roasted chicken.

She had little doubt that it was the man she was meeting, even though he hadn't described how he looked. Over the phone, he'd told her she would know it was him, and to bring fifteen thousand dollars in cash.

As she stood before him, she asked cautiously, "Are you the Camera Man?"

The grotesque man didn't even bother looking up. He

only kicked out the chair front of him. It was his way of gesturing to her to sit down.

Desire was there to purchase some explicit photos of her performing unspeakable sexual acts on three men during her stripping days. Desire had been contacted about a year and a half ago by the infamous Hip-Hop Camera Man, but had paid it no mind at the time. The Camera Man was well known in the industry, and recognized as a square dealer, willing to give the person in question first dibs on purchasing his photos of them.

Desire sat a full five minutes and watched him tear into the bird as if he hadn't eaten in weeks. Finally, he grabbed his napkin and wiped the residue of chicken grease and sauce from his mouth.

"You got the money?" he grunted.

Desire tapped the boot box in the shopping bag she'd brought, which contained the money, and said, "Yeah. You got the pictures?"

He eventually looked up, but instead of looking in Desire's face, he ogled her breasts. Once again there was silence. While he stared hungrily at her breasts, Desire noticed his hand slip under the table. His eyes began to flutter, and his mouth began to quiver. Desire was unmoved as she watched slobs of spit formulate and drip down his turkeylike chin. When he was done, he took the table napkin and wiped his hands.

"Give it to me," he growled.

"Like I said"—Desire looked into his beady red eyes—"show me the pictures."

He reached inside his overcoat and pulled out a long yellow envelope. "Don't even think about running off without payment, sweet tits. I have backups." He eased open his overcoat and showed her another yellow envelope, and smiled.

Desire looked over her shoulder and then proceeded to rip open the package. She instantly recognized the three men involved, a once well-known rapper and two of his boys. She recalled the night, almost four years ago, when she was taken to the Marriott Marquis Hotel, in Midtown Manhattan. They must have arranged to have someone in the closet, because the dude who was hitting it from behind was looking into the camera with a wicked smile on his face and waving.

Desire looked up at the Camera Man, who was enjoying every moment of her discomfort.

"How do I know these pictures won't turn up again?"

"They won't . . . at least not from me," he growled. "Listen, this is what I do, how I make my living. People come to me with explicit pictures and I buy, sort of like an investment. Do you know how many strippers wind up marrying entertainers and celebrities, or how many actresses, singers, rappers, started off as slutty strippers? Then one day, the person gets famous, and my investment just grew into a great return. Sound familiar? Hell, if you got enough money, I can dig up dirt on anybody, anywhere. But for you, my dear, I'm willing to do it for an even exchange any day.

"I hope you charged them boys plenty, because by the look on their faces they were enjoying every hole on your body." He broke out in roaring laughter, and his belly and neck shook like Jell-O.

When Desire retrieved the money from the boot box, she pushed it toward him. He then gave her the second yellow envelope. As he began stuffing the money inside his coat pocket, Desire snatched a stack out of his hand. "What the fuck are you doing?"

Desire leaned back in her chair as she put the money in her purse. "I hope you enjoyed the nut you just busted, cause my services don't come free either."

"Damn, girl, I like your style." He lifted the napkin he'd wiped off with and said, "Judging from how sticky this rag is, it was worth it."

Disgusted, Desire got up and walked out the restaurant and to her car. There was something else that had brought her to Brooklyn today. Desire had been thinking about Tiah a lot. No one had heard from her since that day in CBR's boardroom. It was as if she had vanished into thin air. The only connection anyone had to her was a voice that came on the radio occasionally. Desire wanted to search some of their old haunts in an effort to find her sister. She wasn't planning on inviting her back to the group. She just wanted to know she was okay. As Desire walked toward her car, she noticed what looked like a parking ticket on her windshield. As she got closer, she realized it was a note attached to her windshield wipers. She pulled it from underneath one of the wipers. "Turn around!" yelled a voice from behind her. It was her old boyfriend, Lil Dollar.

Desire hadn't seen him since he beat her up. She had heard he'd been searching for a record deal ever since. Lil Dollar eventually fought Whip in court, and lost. Desire noticed that he no longer wore the expensive jewelry that he had become famous for. Even though he had on a fresh pair of white Uptowns, a nice sweatsuit and a small platinum chain and cross, he looked pretty average compared to how he used to look. She was even happier that she had decided to wear a tight-fitting Donna Karan dress and sexy Jimmy Choo slingbacks that day. Dollar could see first-hand that he hadn't brought her down. She was doing better without him.

Desire flinched as Dollar gave her a hug and told her that he missed her. She couldn't say the same. "I recognized the Lexus while I was walking by and decided to wait for you."

"Yeah, Whip gave it to me," Desire said, wondering how many others he had promised fame and a Lexus to before snatching both away, passing the Lexus—and sometimes the fame—on to someone else. She was shocked to see Dollar, and was not at all happy about it. She still could feel where he had hit her that day.

"So how you been?" Lil Dollar continued, as if nothing had ever happened.

"Busy," Desire replied blankly. "You know how it is."

"I hear that. But what you doing in Brooklyn, Desire?"

She wasn't about to confess that she was searching for Tiah. She wanted Dollar to think everything was all good.

"Oh, I was checking out these shoes at the mall, but they ain't got my size."

He nodded, his eyes traveling up and down her body. "You still looking good, ma. You want to—?"

Desire cut him off. "Dollar, listen, I got to be somewhere in a lil while, so 'mma go."

He shook his head. "Aiight, give me your number and I'll call you later."

She couldn't believe his nerve. He had beat her mercilessly, then dumped her things onto the street. And now that she was on top and he had slipped, he thought he could weasel his way back into her life. Well, he wasn't about to hop on her moving train.

"Dollar, I don't think so," Desire said. "Me and you really ain't got shit to talk about, not after that day."

She clicked the alarm on the Lexus. Dollar grabbed her arm.

"Yo, I just remembered," Dollar said, interrupting her. "I saw your sister, Tiah, out in Bed-Stuy."

Desire tried to hide her interest in what Dollar had to say, and get information at the same time. "So? All her brothers live out here. She be out here all the time."

He put his head down. "Not for nothing, yo, but your sister is out here smokin crazacks like a motherfucker. She's selling her ass and everything."

Seeing she was affected by what he had said, Dollar continued. "Yo, if you want me to take you up to where I saw her, I will."

Desire shook her head. With the new pictures Dollar had painted in her head, the idea of reunting with Tiah lost its flavor. She couldn't think about saving Tiah when she had to set up her own future. "Naw, that's okay. And listen, I really have to go now. I'll talk to you later."

Dollar was furious. His old colors started to show.

"So it's like that now, Desire, huh?"

"Yeah, nigga, it's like that." Desire had decided that she had no more time to waste. She eased into her Lexus and prepared to take off. When Dollar started to talk mess, she jumped out of the car anyway.

"I should have known you wasn't gonna be nothing but a fake-ass bitch," he told her. "You got you a little shine and now you don't know a nigga. In fact, I bet I see your grandmother more than you do."

"Oh, please," Desire shouted. She got up in his face. He couldn't beat her down in the middle of Nostrand Avenue in Bed-Stuy. "I stood by your ass all those times I caught you fuckin all them bootleg bitches. I stayed with you every time your black ass was in and out of jail. So don't even try it, I did enough for your ass."

"What the fuck? If it wasn't for me, your stank ass would probably still be selling pussy and stripping in the Bronx. I made you who the fuck you are today, so you should get down on your motherfucking knees every fucking day, thanking me, you fuckin unappreciative bitch!"

Desire hopped into her car. She decided that she was above arguing with him. Lil Dollar ran to the driver's side and pleaded, "Desire . . . I didn't mean what I said. It's just that I still love you, and—"

"Motherfucka, you can wipe my ass with that bullshit," Desire told him, putting the keys in the ignition. "Did you love my ass when you was wiping your floor with my face? Just do me a favor and act like you never knew me, nigga! Next time you see my ass, you betta be asking for an autograph!"

Desire put the car in gear and sped out, leaving him standing in the street.

*   *   *

In the months since Tiah had been ejected from the group, Desire had fallen fast and hard for someone Whip introduced her to:

his best friend, Sterling Rivers, the NBA's poster boy for success. In the league for only five years, he had already won four championship titles, three MVPs, and was scoring champ for two years in a row.

Desire had never met a man like Sterling. He didn't smoke, drink, or swear. And to her surprise, he didn't believe in sex before marriage. He and his family were strict Christians and he'd been raised to live according to God's law. He and Desire spoke daily, and they spent many nights in each other's arms, talking about the Bible.

When Desire met his parents, who'd been married for thirty-three years, they embraced her as if she were their own daughter. She'd never seen a family that was so close. They did everything together—eat, pray—and they even had the house with the picket fence, and a dog named Spot. Desire felt she had truly hit the jackpot. She was the hottest chick in the game, with the hottest guy on her arm. She was going to have everything she ever dreamed of.

ɞ ɞ ɞ

Desire and Chanel had never gotten along. Recently, they had begun to fight even more. Worse, the only thing keeping Desire, Cream, and Dream in the public eye was their image, not their music. Even though the girls had sensational voices, Tiah's absence had meant that they couldn't shoot the videos that were crucial to a music artist's success. Without a video, their songs were not favored by the DJs. The songs that everyone responded to the most were ones that had videos to go with them. "Harlem Girl Lost" had long ago fallen off the charts and been replaced by new hits. Desire's sexy image—plastered inside schoolboys' lockers, on teenagers' walls and on posters sold on the street by vendors—had become the primary reason for their continued success, rather than their music.

But on this night, Desire had Sterling by her side as she, along with Chanel and Whip, were celebrating the fact that their album had made the *JET* magazine Top 20. They were at a VIP party in Atlanta, with plans to leave for New York the next day. The music was booming loudly. A call from Hattie Mae came on Chanel's cell and Desire excused herself from the group. Someone had gotten word to Desire, through Chanel's people, that Hattie Mae was desperately looking for her. She placed her hand to her ear to drown out the noise. It had been so long since Hattie Mae and Desire had spoken, Desire barely recognized her own grandmother's voice.

"What did you say, Grandma, I didn't hear you."

Desire had just assumed that her grandmother wanted to congratulate her on their accomplishment of being featured in *JET.* When a person made it in between the covers of *JET,* they had arrived. Hattie Mae was elated to finally speak with Desire. After checking to make sure Desire was okay, Hattie Mae began to talk about herself.

Speaking louder, Hattie Mae said, "I said I don't feel well."

Desire took a breath and asked: "What's wrong, Grandma?" Hearing Hattie Mae's voice on the phone was comforting. Desire was always surrounded by people, yet she always felt hopelessly alone. For the first time in a long time, she wanted to run back to her small twin-sized bed in the Harlem apartment she, Tiah and Hattie Mae had shared. But she was a long way from home.

"I don't know," Hattie Mae sighed. "I just don't feel good 'bout a lot of things."

"Grandma, why don't you go to the doctor if you feel sick?"

"I don't know. I'm just so worried 'bout Tiah these days, you know. She come by the house here sometimes. I know she got kicked out of y'all group."

"She got herself kicked out, Grandma," Desire corrected. "Tiah had a lot of chances. She just didn't want 'em."

"I tried to get her to go to a program, but she never showed up for me to take her."

Desire frowned. "Grandma, you gotta stop worrying so much about Tiah. She's grown now. And stop letting her in the house. All she'll do is steal and beg you for money."

"Desire, I don't want to hear you talk like that 'bout yo sister no mo. You hear me, no mo!" Hattie Mae screamed. "Now, she's ya sister, and she just made a damn mistake!"

That was what Desire had always loved about Hattie Mae. Grandma always wanted to see the good in everyone, never the bad. Desire winced as she thought about the fact that all of her nice things seemed to come from Whip, at his discretion. Here she was, pushing a status whip and rocking designer gear, and she couldn't even buy Hattie Mae anything, because she and Chanel rarely saw liquid cash. Every time she questioned Whip about it, he told her not to worry, that money was coming soon.

"Grandma," Desire asked softly, "is everything all right, is there something else you not telling me?"

There was a long pause.

"Grandma, you still there?"

"Yes, baby. I'm sorry for yellin. I just miss you and want to see you."

"I'll be home tomorrow, and I'll make you my first stop when I get off the plane. I miss you too."

Desire could sense Hattie Mae's smile beaming through the phone.

"Praise Jesus, I knew you wouldn't let me down. I just wanna see both my babies together again. It's . . . it's just that I don't wanna see you and ya sister not talking to each other. Y'all gonna need each other. So promise me when you come home you also go see about her."

Desire rolled her eyes. She had decided to let her worries about Tiah go. She knew that Tiah knew the streets as well as she herself did. Her sister would survive.

"Grandma, I'll do what I can. But I'll see you tomorrow. Love you!"

Those were the best words Hattie Mae had heard in a long time.

"I love you too, baby," she responded.

When Desire returned to her table, she could not help but notice the unusual stares cast upon her by everyone in the room. She turned and faced Sterling, and suddenly the music stopped playing. Sterling rose to his feet.

"Desire, I want to ask you a question, and please don't lie to me." Desire's palms began to sweat. She stared into Sterling's eyes.

"Do you love me?" he asked.

"Yes, Sterling, of course."

"Well, if you truly love me, you would . . . marry me!" Sterling reached in his pocket, pulled out a ring box and handed it to Desire, who was speechless. She gasped when she saw the size of the diamond.

After getting over the initial shock, Desire emphatically said yes, over and over again. Everyone in the room started clapping, and suddenly Whip allowed all the photographers into the room to take pictures. Desire was overwhelmed by the number of them.

. . .

On the way to Atlanta's sprawling Hartsfield-Jackson Airport, Desire used her cell phone to call her grandmother. There was still no answer. She had been calling the house since early that morning, to let Hattie Mae know exactly when she'd be home. Desire had not seen Hattie Mae in so long, she had almost forgotten her face. She couldn't stop fidgeting on the plane because she was so nervous with excitement. She couldn't wait to tell Hattie Mae about Sterling, and wondered what Grandma was going to cook that night, since she always had warm soul food waiting. As soon as her plane touched down at LaGuardia Airport in New York, Desire and Chanel went to the waiting limousine. The driver dropped Chanel off at the Greenwich Village apartment, and then hit the West Side Highway to take Desire straight uptown. Desire called Hattie Mae's apartment again as New Jersey and the Hudson River flew by. When they reached the 125th Street exit, which would lead them into Harlem, Desire suddenly felt more at home than she had in months. The cars, shoppers, stores and restaurants of 125th Street seemed much more welcoming than they had when she'd actually lived on the street. It was as if her whole perspective had shifted.

Oddly, Hattie Mae still hadn't answered her telephone, even though Desire knew that she *must* be expecting her. When they arrived at Hattie's building on 131st and Lenox, Desire asked the limousine driver to wait. She had long ago misplaced her keys to the apartment. The lock to the entry door was broken as usual so Desire entered the building. Fearing something was wrong with Hattie Mae, she dropped her luggage and ran into the apartment. In a panic, she ran into every room and yelled for Hattie Mae. No one answered.

Desire went across the hall to Ms. Benny's apartment. Desire banged on the door, kept banging until Ms. Benny answered.

"The ambulance come get Hattie Mae late last night, say something wrong with her heart or something," Ms. Benny told Desire. Desire's own heart was pounding as she thought back to the conversation she had shared with Hattie Mae the night before. She wondered if Hattie Mae had some sort of premonition and had been afraid to tell her.

"Where they take her?" asked Desire.

"They took her to St. Luke's, over on—"

Desire ran down the stairs, yelling to the limousine driver that they had a new destination.

※　※　※

For Desire, hospitals were nothing but miserable reminders of all the pain and suffering she had endured in her life. She was unable to think straight as she walked through the entrance of St. Luke's. The sanitary white cleanliness of the hospital blinded her as she walked through all of the maze-like corridors and hallways in order to reach the intensive care unit. She had called both Sterling and Whip, but neither of them had answered, or called her back, despite the fact that she had left messages for each, stating that something was wrong with Hattie Mae. Desire recognized several of the women from Hattie Mae's church. They were huddled together, in prayer, with doctors and nurses surrounding them. Desire was caught off guard when she saw Lil Dollar leaning against a wall. Even from the back, she could see he was crying. Desire burst through the crowd and placed her arm on Lil Dollar's shoulder, turning him around to face her. He pulled her into his arms.

"Desire," he cried, "Hattie Mae is gone . . ."

The words hit Desire straight in the chest, and if she hadn't been in Lil Dollar's arms she probably would have fainted. She was totally and completely numb, unable to shed even one tear for the woman who had saved her life when she was just a newborn baby. Her mind swirled as she thought about all the time that had been lost while she was out doing her own things, trying to forget where she had come from, climbing to the top, all while neglecting and disrespecting the woman responsible for her life. No amount of fame or fortune would ever fill the hole that burned through Desire's heart that day.

CHAPTER SIXTEEN

Hundreds of people had come to Bethel A.M.E. Church to show respect to Hattie Mae Evans on her final journey home. She had been a pillar of the Harlem churchgoing community for decades. That entire week, Desire was devastated and took her anger out on those closest to her. As she sat in the front row with Sterling and Chanel, she wept silently. Whip had had too many meetings to make the effort to attend. Carvelas sat quietly in the back pews with other church members who had known and loved Hattie Mae. Desire's celebrity didn't mean a thing to all the people who had come to celebrate Hattie Mae's homecoming. It had quickly spread throughout Harlem that Desire and Tiah—of the Desire, Cream, and Dream singing group—

had lost their grandmother. Sure enough, a crowd of people collected outside the church just to see if they could get a glimpse of the stars. Once Chanel caught wind of this selfish plot on the part of fans to exploit Hattie Mae's passing, just for a photo or an autograph, she called in bodyguards to keep the crowds at bay. The people outside were only interested in seeing the famous Desire, but those inside the church saw the real Desire, Hattie Mae's beloved granddaughter.

Just as the junior choir started to sing the song that would introduce the pastor's eulogy, a tear-ridden woman nobody recognized came into the church and walked down the aisle toward the altar where Hattie Mae's casket lay. Her clothing was tattered and dirty. She had a grotesque, twisted-looking jaw, which had clearly been broken at one time and hadn't mended well.

One by one, as the woman got closer to the casket, people began to recognize her—it was Tiah. The gossip spread fast, as those filling the pews began to point and whisper. Some even laughed. A member from Desire's entourage knelt beside her to give her the heads-up, but Desire refused to even look at her sister. She was ashamed and embarrassed by what Tiah had become. Plus, she couldn't imagine what Tiah smelled like now that she was most likely using on a regular basis. There was no way Desire was going to let Tiah dishonor Hattie Mae's legacy by sitting in the first pew, an awful reminder that not all Hattie Mae's good deeds had turned out good.

"Get y'all hands off me, that's my grandmother lying there!" Tiah said to one of the pallbearers attempting to restrain her.

"Just calm down, Tiah," the man said in a hush. "Desire said there's no more room up front. Why don't you sit in the back."

Tiah looked over at Desire, and all the people she didn't even know sitting in the pew reserved for family members.

"I ain't sitting in the back," she said. "That's my grandmother, and somebody is gonna hafta get up."

She glared at Chanel, ready to fight her if she had to, just to claim her place with the family. Tiah tried to brush past a pallbearer, but he and two other men stopped her. She struggled to get past once more, but they wouldn't budge. She began punching the men as they restrained her.

"Desire . . . Desire, tell them I'm family. Tell them I got a right to be here."

Her pleas fell on deaf ears as Desire ignored her. Tiah's sadness gave her ferocious strength that she had been unable to harness the day Whip and his henchmen had given her a beat down. She struggled free from the men as if they were weak schoolboys. To the choir and the funeral attendees' dismay, she paraded to the front of the church, as if caught up in her own private service. Tiah looked at the casket and walked toward it. The only woman who had ever loved her unconditionally was gone. Tiah got on her knees and prayed the way Hattie Mae had always told her she should. She regretted the fact that she hadn't done so in years, until now. She broke down and cried for a brief moment. Then she realized the best way she could honor Hattie Mae. She stood and began singing her grandmother's favorite hymn, a spiritual that Hattie Mae would often hum while cooking, sewing, or just when she wanted to show she was in a good mood. Though Tiah's voice was hoarse, cracking, a fraction of what it once was, she still moved people in the crowd to tears. Chanel was overwhelmed with emotion and buried her face in her hands. Desire could not stand to see a visual representation of all that could have been, and how all that was hadn't been enough to save Tiah. Desire walked to the back of the church with her head held high and was blinded by fans' flashing cameras the minute she walked out of the church doors.

        ⁑ ⁑ ⁑

Over the next few months, Desire totally submersed herself in her work and finishing her solo album, to ease her mind over Hattie Mae. The whole experience of her grandmother's death, the strain between her and Tiah, the constant battle with Whip over her contract. All of the drama and instability eventually took its toll on Desire. Sterling was on the road with his team, and she found herself exiting the studio and going straight home, to spend her nights smoking weed and flipping channels. It was like she was able to create her own little dream world, where she had no problems, no obligations, no one to satisfy but herself. And in this dream, she had everything she wanted without having to work as hard as she was now working to get it.

She had years of plotting, scheming, fighting, partying and fucking behind her. What had it gotten her besides material things that were subject to seizure at Whip's discretion, and at less than a moment's notice? She didn't understand what the point of it all was anymore. None of it had brought her happiness. She eased off the couch—where she had made a mess of melted Häagen-Daz and Doritos crumbs—so that she could roll herself another blunt. Weed had been an aphrodisiac for her and Dollar back in the day, and was just a party thing for her now. But lately, she had been feeling more lonely than ever, especially on the nights Chanel was soaking in the streets with Whip and the rest of their crew. That lifestyle had lost a little of its lure for her. At home, alone, and blazed, she could let her mind wander through some of the good old days: confiding in Hattie Mae, the silly little rivals in school and church, battles she and Tiah fought in the streets, even passing notes with Carvelas. She blew out a cloud of smoke so thick from her second blunt of the night that she could barely see the television, when a news flash came on that instantly sobered her:

"MTV reports that Tiah Denton, former member of Desire's Dream, was found overdosed in a Harlem crack house. It was reported that she had no pulse when paramedics arrived. They rushed her to Harlem Hospital, where doctors worked feverishly to revive her. It is speculated that she was depressed after she was ousted from the group by its lead singer, and her sister, Desire Evans, after Ms. Denton became addicted to prescription drugs. More news as it comes in."

Desire was so high that she was only mildly concerned with the report on Tiah. She was actually more concerned that the secret was out that Whip had been working feverishly behind Chanel's back to change the name of the group so that the name of its biggest ticket stood out even more than it already did.

CHAPTER SEVENTEEN

With the finishing touches finally put on her solo album, Desire had everything just as she imagined it would be. She and Sterling were the "it" couple. She had used Whip and CBR to make a hot product that didn't have a single corporation's name attached to it. At least not yet. Her contract with Central Booking Records was for just one album from the group Desire, Cream, and Dream— not Desire's Dream, the name she had already picked out for her first album. Best of all, she had used Whip to work behind the scenes to change the name of the group so that it was already being branded into the listening public's head. She had fulfilled her obligation to CBR, Tiah had disappeared and Chanel was just tired and ready to get out of the game. That left Desire right where she wanted to be—alone. She was now a free agent, sought after by all the major labels, particularly Sony. Whip was confident that he could re-sign Desire, this time as a solo artist. And when he offered her some bonus money, Desire gave him her word that she would stick with him as her manager and producer.

But things changed when Whip found out about Desire's secret meetings at Sony. Though it made billions of dollars each year, the music industry was a rather small network of business associates and executives. Although she'd done everything possible to keep the Sony meetings under wraps, there were plenty of ladder climbers waiting to sell out whoever crossed their paths, and there were plenty of others who recognized the value of favors, favors that would be recognized later. Whip received a favor from an old business associate, who had noticed Desire's name on the roster of Larry Cohen's meetings for the day. Whip drove to Sony's office building when Desire refused to answer his phone calls. And when he spotted Desire walking toward the building with Larry Cohen, one of the most powerful megabrokers in the business, he hopped out of his car and confronted her.

"Desire, can I have word with you?" He looked at Larry Cohen. "Alone!"

Mr. Cohen wasn't afraid of Whip, unlike most white men in the industry. He stood his ground. "Talk to him another time, Desire. We're busy."

Whip scowled at the man, but Mr. Cohen didn't back down.

Avoiding a potential confrontation, Desire elected to speak to Whip. "Listen, Larry, just gimme a second. Okay?"

Larry looked at his watch and said, "Okay, but we're pressed for time." He moved toward the fleet of shiny black limos that were always parked outside of Sony, waiting specifically for the never-ending rotation of important people who regularly emerged from the building.

Desire knew that Whip was no fool. There was one reason and one reason only why she would be going into Sony's offices with Larry Cohen. She put her hands on her hips and waited for Whip to light into her. She'd just let him tire himself out.

"How could you do this to me Desire, after all I did for you? I gave you your start, I made you famous, I made you rich, I saved you from Dollar—and you turn around and stab me in the back!" He was so angry he could hardly contain himself.

Desire simply stood there and listened. She had known it was vital to do her homework before plotting her break from Whip.

"Now, we had a verbal agreement. I done spent damn near a million goddamn dollars on you. No. You ain't gonna fuck me. I'll have your ass in court before I let you get away with that."

Desire snapped, "Save the drama, Whip, 'cause you can't do shit to me. All the while you was cheating me and the group, you were making money hand over fist."

She turned her back to the fleet of limos so Larry Cohen wouldn't have any idea just how serious the conversation had gotten. She balled her fist and shoved it in Whip's face, right under his nose.

"I'll let you in on a little secret, I'm not as dumb as you think. Once you fucked me on my first advance check, I hired a damn lawyer, and he schooled me on everything. He told me you skimmed over a million and a half from our show profits alone. I knew damn well that if you knew *I* knew you'd cheated me, I would never have a chance at getting that money. You woulda had me in court for years, just like you've had every one of your other artists. It would have cost me the same amount in legal costs as the money I was owed. I knew from the giddyup I wasn't going to re-sign with you."

"How long you been playing me, Desire?" Whip wanted to know.

"The question is, how long did it take before somebody got the chance to play you before you played them? Me and Dollar mighta fell out in the end, but don't think I didn't watch what you did to his ass. Don't think I wasn't taking notes."

"Dollar had to go because he was too much of a risk."

Desire wasn't about to let Whip continue. She jumped in quickly. "I remember your tiny-ass advance checks, all the lies you told me about shit that was going to come in the future." She pulled a Louis Vuitton wallet out of her leather coat pocket. She snatched a couple crisp Benjamins out of the wallet's slivers and threw them in Whip's face. "Right now, I just came out of a meeting where I know I'm about to get advanced about . . . you guessed it, a million dollars, give or take a few hundred thou. I have Larry, who happens to be a lawyer, ready to file a countersuit if you even think about coming after me on some stupid-ass verbal-agreement shit."

"You know they ain't giving you all that money at once," Whip said.

"Oh, I know. But they gonna give me enough. Enough so that I don't have to be one of your fuckin stupid-ass puppies no more. I ain't no puppy dog, motherfucka. I'm a shark."

Whip's jaw twitched out of control. Desire had him over a barrel, and there was nothing he could do about it. He was powerless, only able to race his mind back and forth on ways to sabotage Desire's new album. "Fuck you, Desire. I'm not gonna let you get away with this shit, not for a minute."

Desire started to head toward the limousine Larry had just stepped out of, waving to her that it was time for them to get going to an important meeting.

"Nigga, I already got away with it. You shouldn't be mad at me, 'cause you was the one who taught me that there was no loyalty in this business."

Whip watched Desire stare over her shoulder at him before Larry helped her into the back of the limousine. Suddenly, a sly smile expanded on his face. He would let her think she had chumped him . . . for now at least.

CHAPTER EIGHTEEN

Hundreds of people were on hand for the ceremony that was dubbed the "Wedding of the Year" by insiders in entertainment circles. The media from the sporting and music worlds were there to cover the event. Hundreds of people crammed into Riverside Church to catch a glimpse of the famous couple.

Desire was in the dressing room, nervously waiting for the groom. The wedding was supposed to start over an hour ago. It was so unlike Sterling to be late. Suddenly, one of the bridesmaids told Desire that the groom's limo had just pulled in front of the church. Relieved, Desire looked out the window, and saw Sterling exit the limo, looking sharp in his perfectly fitted tuxedo. She frowned when Whip, who was the best man, hopped out the limo behind him.

Sensing something was wrong, Desire lifted her gown and ran out of the room and down the main entrance to the church. Sterling stood scanning the foyer with his eyes. Whip pointed to where Desire stood, holding the hem of her dress. As they approached her, Desire felt her knees wobble when she saw Sterling holding a manila envelope. Sterling was sweating profusely. His jaw was tight.

"Do you know what this is?" he yelled.

Desire stared at the envelope.

"Come on, baby, let's not do this here." Desire took Sterling by the hand and guided him to the back room for privacy.

Sterling broke the silence. "Once again, Desire, tell me what the fuck this is."

"Sterling, baby, that happened a long time ago. I was young."

His faced turned flush. "So you knew about this all along?"

Desire put her head down and nodded.

"You was just gonna keep this to yourself. Is that what you saying?"

"I would have eventually told you, but I didn't know how . . . I felt ashamed." Desire shook her head.

"You would have waited until you infected me to tell me, is that what you saying?"

"Infected? What are you talking about?"

"Our blood tests came back," announced Sterling, "and yours came back positive—for HIV!"

CHAPTER NINETEEN

Desire had completely avoided the phone, television and newspapers after her aborted wedding. She could not believe what was happening to her. Sterling refused all contact, had even changed his telephone numbers. Desire had stayed in her apartment—high, drunk and delirious after Sterling dumped her at the church. She was oblivious to the media storm brewing while she was in seclusion. She only agreed to meet Larry Cohen, at his request, in his lavish Fifth Avenue penthouse one evening, after he called her out of the blue to say that he needed to speak with her. He sent a limo to pick her up. Larry was the first person she'd seen in nearly a week; and when riding the elevator up to his apartment, she mistakenly thought that he was exactly the person she needed to see.

The elevator finally reached his three-story penthouse, and she stepped out into the most majestic home she had ever seen. The floors were shiny Italian marble. Greek-like sculptures were scattered throughout the apartment. The ceilings were nearly twice as high as the ones she was used to. Every piece of furniture before her looked custom-made, from bookcases to a huge desk to a couch covered with Thai silk. The largest paintings took up entire walls. Larry had several black maids and butlers running around. One of them met her at the door and escorted her to Larry's home conference room.

Despite all she was going through, Desire was determined to keep up a good front. He wasn't about to see any cracks in her exterior. She had purposely pulled out the most expensive suit she owned—a hand-tailored Christian Dior black number—just so she could give the impression that nothing was wrong. She had also painstakingly curled her hair to perfection. She looked like a Wall Street power broker, and her three-inch heels comfortingly echoed her footsteps throughout the penthouse. Desire was surprised when she entered the room and found several white men seated around the nearly fifteen-foot conference table. Larry hadn't warned her this would be a group meeting. He sat at the head of the table, with a copy of the latest *New York Post* in front of him. Everyone bristled with tension as soon as Desire walked into the room.

"Have a seat, Desire," Larry said. He wasn't talking to her in his normal tone. She suddenly preferred to stand, and shook her head. He offered her water, scotch, wine or coffee—all of which were sitting in the middle of the table. Desire signaled no with her hand.

"What is the occasion for this meeting, gentlemen?" she cautiously asked.

It was clear Larry was the only one who had authority to speak, at least for now. He rose from his seat and walked over to Desire. He spread the newspaper on the table in front of her. A celebrity gossip item was highlighted in yellow:

It has been reported that Desire Evans, formerly of the group Desire's Dream and now a solo artist, is suffering from the HIV virus. Having risen to the top of the charts as part of the group Desire, Cream, and Dream with the hit "Harlem Girl Lost," the group is now disbanded because of contractual disputes and member Tiah Denton's drug problems. Though medical authorities at a private clinic in Manhattan refuse to confirm the diagnosis, Evans is reportedly seeking treatment at that facility. Evans could not be reached for comment. Representatives from Sony, her current record company, did not return this newspaper's calls.

She knew that her doctor was ethically responsible for protecting such sensitive information. She had obviously been found out and sold out, but by whom? When thinking back to who could have possibly wanted to tarnish her reputation and leak her misfortune to the world, Whip became her primary suspect. She couldn't imagine Sterling, Chanel or even Dollar turning on her in this way.

"Desire, is this true?" Larry asked.

Desire was too stunned to speak. The dozen or so white men in the room shuffled the papers in front of them. She recognized some of them—various sales, marketing and PR representatives Larry had introduced her to as the team who would be orchestrating her solo career. She knew that the faces she did not recognize were mostly lawyers, who were probably present to explain to her how her contract had to change. Desire did not know how to answer Larry's question. She could only look at him and shake her head. She put her hand over her mouth to keep from crying, but she couldn't stop the tears.

"Please help me, Larry," she begged, as she fell into his arms, and he had to keep her from tumbling to the floor.

                                           ะ ะ ะ

Whip had been right about one thing: there was no loyalty or friends in the music business. Sony was under no obligation to forward Desire any more of her promised advance, because they had officially dropped her from their artists roster. She was given legal documents that explained how she was now a great risk to the company, and that she could be sued for breach of contract for not divulging information about her HIV status, since it was directly related to the image they were investing in. Desire did not have the energy or time to explain that she herself had just learned of the diagnosis. She had to figure out how she was going to support her lifestyle and pay her bills now that she was not going to be receiving money from Sony. She still had the music from the solo album she had created—the album Sony had contracted to promote, to solidify her star status—but no record company would invest in her now that she had the stigma of

HIV. She had not been smart enough to pay cash for things, and with her mind so scrambled with all that was happening to her, she began to spend money like water without even thinking. Her bank accounts quickly dwindled to almost nothing, and she maxed out her credit cards buying liquor, eating at restaurants all the time, and shopping to take her mind off her pain. The nearly six thousand dollars' rent was due on her Village apartment, and Desire discovered she didn't have it.

The ramifications of the public news hit Desire immediately. Now, whenever she was recognized, she could hear the snickers and sense the apprehension in others. Instead of admirers, she now had hecklers who called her shit like "a rotten pussied bitch" as she passed. She had gone from a beautiful, glamorous, famous star to an infamous HIV victim in a matter of weeks. Desire did not think she could get any lower. The worst part was she had no one to take her anger out on, and she was still worried that there could be a hit out on her life. Her instincts told her that this was a more devilish way for Whip to get back at her, though; if he had her killed, he wouldn't be able to witness how much he was making her suffer over the long term. Desire had no way to reach him as she found her face plastered throughout the tabloids. The papers always referred to the informant as "a source." Desire knew in her gut that Whip was behind all of this. He never liked anyone having the upper hand on him, and he always found a way to bring his "enemy" down when things didn't go his way. And if he was behind all of this, he had certainly found a way to bring Desire down. The funny thing was, she was so down that she could not even think about plotting revenge.

One day, she bundled herself up in a dark hat, scarf and glasses so she could ride the D train uptown. No one recognized her as she sat alone in the last car. She slipped quietly into Bethel A.M.E. Church just as a deacon was straightening the church after the day's prayer service. He recognized Desire as she unbundled herself and sat alone in the first pew. Of course, the whole church was talking about the news that was blasted from the radios and in the newspapers. Radio talk shows and BET news programs had even run call-in discussions on HIV, unfortunately using Desire's situation as the launching pad for their talks. There was no way most people who had known her wouldn't have found out the news by now. The deacon decided not to bother her.

As Desire sat alone, her whole life flashed before her eyes. Every sin, every iniquity, every injustice and every evil that she'd imposed upon others seemed to have been returned to her with a vengeance. She had learned in the worst way that the best way to determine who your real friends are is to wait until trouble comes. When the smoke clears, most will have disappeared, and those who remain by your side are the true friends. In Desire's case, not a single person came to her side and offered their support, a kind word or a simple hug. Not one. Even Carvelas had not sought her out. She felt even more that everything she had ever thought about being alone was true. She knew she could not afford the medical insurance Sony had originally given her, so she needed to reserve any money she made from selling her material things, for the medicine and care she would need to stay alive. Desire knew that she had no one to call for a place to stay, and there was no way she would be able to afford her apartment without Sony's money. Luckily, her name was still on a lease in the projects. She'd had a grandmother who thought ahead, and always paid her rent on time, often even a couple of months in advance. As such, the management respected Hattie Mae so much that they were taking their time to find a new tenant to inhabit the apartment she had lived in for years. Desire was relieved when she called and found out the place was still empty. She moved back into Hattie Mae's apartment in Harlem the next week.

＊　＊　＊

Desire turned into a recluse, opting to stay a prisoner in the confines of the apartment. She had nobody, and she wished that Hattie Mae were there to hug her tightly and tell her everything was going to be all right. She watched television only to see if they were reporting anything on her, and was happy to see nothing was being said. The world had moved on to other celebrities' problems in order to feed people's insatiable appetite for controversy. Desire would only go out at night, right before the stores closed, to pick up food and liquor.

Fear became a constant, as morbid thoughts of death began to consume her mind. She had not spoken to anyone at the clinic since a nurse had called her the day after she got the diagnosis, begging her to come in. Desire did not feel sick, so she did not see a reason to go to the hospital and face the truth. She figured with HIV the best thing she could do was stay away from people who would make her sick. And staying away from people was exactly what she wanted to do. She drank more and more alcohol to get her through the day, to dull her thoughts. She bought dirt weed from the small-time pushers who hovered around her building then bragged to their friends that they were selling nicks and dimes to *the* Desire. When the weed and liquor stopped working, she would cry until her eyes were bloodshot. Soon, with each depressing day, she began to hear voices telling her to put herself out of her misery. Finally, there came a night when she decided to do just that.

In one hand, Desire nursed a fifth of vodka. She sat on the couch, listening to one of her grandmother's favorite gospel albums. All cried out, Desire staggered uneasily toward the bathroom. She looked at herself in the mirror with disgust. She opened the medicine cabinet and randomly selected a bottle of pills. She didn't know if they had been for Hattie Mae's high blood pressure, diabetes or some other problem. She didn't care. She opened the cap, turned on the faucet and downed the entire bottle. Putting her mouth to the faucet, she guzzled some water. She slowly wiped her mouth, and kept her head down for a moment before looking in the mirror once again. She saw her grandmother standing behind her. In a panic, Desire tore the shower curtain down to cover her as she scooted as far back into the tub as she possibly could.

"Don't be afraid, baby," Hattie Mae said, smiling softly down upon her.

Desire blinked rapidly, trying to adjust her eyes.

"Grandma . . . is that really you?"

Hattie Mae nodded. "Yes, baby, it's really me."

Desire smiled for the first time since she'd found out about her disease. She tried to stand up, but her legs had no strength.

"Save your energy. You know this ain't the way I raised ya, Desire."

Desire began to cry. "I know, Grandma, but I can't take it anymore. I don't think I can go on like this any longer. I'm so alone."

Hattie Mae's presence grew stronger. "Find something to live for."

"Grandma, I'm sorry," Desire cried. "I'm sorry for everything . . . the lies, the scheming, leaving you, not being here when you died. I'm sorry for all of it . . ."

"Now, baby," Hattie said, and Desire could feel her grandmother's hug, "don't you worry about all that now. You 'pologizin' for stuff I done already forgave. All that in the past. You just worry 'bout how you gonna make yourself better. You got a lot of living to do. You ain't no old woman, like I was, yet."

Desire closed her eyes wearily and when she opened them again, she was sitting on the couch. She looked around for her grandmother, but Hattie Mae wasn't there. All Desire heard was the CD player playing her grandmother's song: *"Pray until you get an answer from God . . . you got to pray until you get an answer . . . pray until you get an answer . . ."*

Desire tossed the bottle of vodka to the floor. She went into the bathroom and wiped a cold rag on her face and neck.

CHAPTER TWENTY

It was a warm, beautiful summer evening when Desire strolled into an upscale bar in her old stomping ground of Greenwich Village. She was on the prowl, dressed in a conservative Donna Karan blue suit with a matching pair of blue Manolos. She looked every bit of the part of a working woman. A long blond wig hung over her expensive Prada glasses, which gave her a seductively glamorous appearance. No sooner had she ordered a drink than a potential victim slid up behind her, offering to pay for it. It didn't take long for the suited-up white man to proposition Desire for a rendezvous at one of the many 21st Street hotels that charged by the hour.

* * *

Desire figured there was a better way to use all the clothes, shoes and bags she had collected from her years in the spotlight than selling them for cash. The liquor and weed had taken a toll on her looks: her eyes had yellowed and she had bags around them; there were dry patches all over her body, her lips had become darker and her face was often bloated. She'd gained weight from all the alcohol, despite the fact that she was HIV positive, and she had cut her hair short so people wouldn't recognize her. Desire soon found that she could walk around in public. Not to mention, most of the images people had seen of her had been airbrushed anyway. Desire began hitting the streets at night, disguising herself each and every time. She didn't discriminate, as she picked up black men, whites, Latinos, Arabs, and Asians. She even allowed herself to be picked up by other women.

She loved rich immigrants the most; they were the least likely to know she had once been a big star. And they were the most likely to have cocaine to add to the party. The money that rolled in helped Desire pay her meager rent, buy food and other necessities and support her alcohol and drug habits. She never thought about saving. In dark bars and corners, and even darker hotel rooms, no one ever suspected that they were sleeping with a woman who had been among the most famous in the country.

As she retreated deeper and deeper into her private misery and self-pity, Desire became more and more brazen about taking as many people as she could with her. Rather than causing her to change her life, she had misinterpreted her hallucination of Hattie Mae as a sign to fight evil with evil. Desire began convincing her lovers to have unprotected sex, then she started leaving messages on the bathroom mirror written in red lipstick:

YOU ARE NOW A MEMBER OF THE ELITE!
WELCOME TO CLUB HIV!

Or

Roses are red, violets are blue,
I have AIDS and so do you!

Word quickly spread that there was a woman sleeping with people with the intention of infecting them with HIV. However, that did not deter the steady stream of johns Desire found to support her scheme. She even began calling late-night radio stations to warn them that she had the AIDS virus and had already slept with over a hundred men and women in the metropolitan area, and that she planned on infecting hundreds or thousands of others before she died.

So many people were calling the radio stations, trying to get through, it was nearly impossible for the authorities to trace her calls.

"And what exactly is your reason for doing this, Miss . . . Miss . . . ?" the evening DJ of Hot 97 asked when Desire called in.

"Whisper Daniels," Desire said into the phone, just hoping that Whip was listening and would recognize her voice. She had just heard a remix of "Harlem Girl Lost," and gone into a rage that made her want to call the station. Not one person had returned her calls demanding to speak to Whip, to find out where her desperately needed royalty checks were. She walked past posters of her former self, past cars blasting her music from their stereos. There was no way she'd be allowed into the many VIP music parties that took place throughout New York City. Security would hold her at the door, and tell her that her name was "not on the list." She had been a star! She deserved to be paid like one. Whip and CBR had used her up and thrown her away, not thinking of her anymore. And unfortunately, they had the bogus contracts that allowed them to do it.

She wanted him to know that by hurting her, he had caused the potential hurt of many people. She had given up on finding and killing him. She had gone mad, taking her rage out on others.

"How are you convincing people to have unprotected sex with you?"

The show's producers had to bleep out most of Desire's response.

"When you can suck and fuck like I can, it's easy to get people to do whateva the fuck you want. This pussy is golden. Always has been, always will be. The first motherfucka I ever fucked wanted this pussy so bad, he fuckin raped me to get it."

"It sounds like you've had a lot of pain in your life," the DJ said. "Have you ever considered getting help or going to therapy, rather than causing pain for others?"

"I don't need no motherfuckin therapy!" Desire threw the vodka bottle she had just emptied, with one gulp, onto the floor. "The motherfuckas who out there cheating on they wives and girlfriends gonna need therapy. If they wasn't out fuckin somebody over in the first place, they wouldn't have to worry about me—now, would they?"

"So do you see yourself as acting out some sort of punishment on people?"

"Hell yeah," Desire said. " 'Cause motherfuckas ain't never gave a fuck about punishing me!"

She hung up the phone and began to roll another blunt.

՞ ՞ ՞

Desire eventually found that this stronger weed was better than alcohol at soothing her pain. At first, it worked magnificently, making her instantly forget her troubles. But as her money ran low, she found herself on the prowl for crack cocaine. In a matter of just three short months after Desire first hit the pipe, her mission to conquer and destroy mankind took a backseat to destroying herself. In the beginning, since Lyfe's crew had the best product in the neighbohood, she would send another hype to cop for her. Even though she got robbed half the time when the addict ran off with her money, or chipped pieces off the top, she took the risk just to keep Lyfe from knowing she had a habit.

Ultimately, saving face was no longer an option. She became so strung out and thirsty that nothing else but getting a blast mattered. The first time she had to stand in the long line of addicts who were Lyfe's customers, Desire wore a black hoodie and a cheap pair of dark sunglasses. She stood with her head down, waiting to be served.

"Aiight, y'all motherfuckas make a straight line and have your money out," screamed Lyfe, as his man served the crackheads. "No singles, no change, and no fuckin shorts."

The crackheads responded by checking their pockets to make sure they could meet Lyfe's requirements. He looked down at them with disgust, from his perch on the staircase. If they said something slick to violate the rules, they risked not being served. A crackhead's tolerance for being humiliated was without parallel. If someone beat a crackhead down and put them in the hospital, the very next day the drug addict would be back on the same line, missing front teeth and all, smiling and thanking the abuser for allowing them to purchase crack from him.

As Desire moved closer to the front of the line, she prayed that Lyfe wouldn't recognize her. But Lyfe was so suspicious of being hunted by the NYPD that he always made sure an unfamiliar face was identified.

"Yo, who the fuck are you?" Lyfe barked as Desire extended a twenty and asked for two. "Yo, you ever served this bitch before?"

His man nodded. "Yeah, I served the bitch before."

Still not satisfied, Lyfe asked, "Yo, why you wearing them dark motherfuckin shades at night, you police or something? Take them shits off."

Desire raised her head slowly and took off her glasses. His eyes lit up like a Christmas tree. He had waited years, ever since the day she had punked him on a Harlem curb, for the opportunity to make good on the promise that Desire would one day need him.

"Oh, shit, if it ain't the world-famous singer Desire Evans. Yo, give that bitch back her money . . . as a matter fact, give her three more on me. Yo, bitch, next time I want you to sing into my microphone, aiight?"

꽃 꽃 꽃

Lyfe knew exactly what he was doing. Courtesy of him, Desire became an all-out crackhead. There was no shame in her game.

She no longer used disguises. All that mattered was the hit, and she had been reduced to using various means to get it: selling her body for ten dollars, running off with other people's money after they sent her to cop a hit or straight up pickpocketing tricks for their wallets. Her favorite spot to trick was underneath the Metro-North train station on 125th Street. She had gotten so deep into her habit that she'd even forgotten to pay rent. She was unfazed the day she woke up and found an eviction notice under her door. The management had decided they could do no more to help Hattie Mae Evans's granddaughter. Hattie Mae's paid-up rent had run out, and Desire was putting no more money toward the apartment. They needed to get a paying tenant, not to mention providing a needy family some housing. Desire had less than thirty days to find somewhere else to go. She knew how long eviction proceedings took in the city. She chose not to even try to look for a new place to stay, deciding that the city marshals were actually going to have to come and put her out if they wanted the apartment back.

Lyfe still had the best drugs on the West Side, and Desire was forced to deal with him, even though his humiliating antics had begun to bother her. One time, he wanted her to sing for him and his boys, promising that if she did he'd give her anything that she wanted for free.

One night, Desire was broke and fiending badly for a hit. She couldn't find any vics or tricks to earn some cash. At that moment, she was the spitting image of the woman her mother, Nika, had been over twenty years before. She walked the streets for hours and ended up standing right in front of Lyfe's crack spot. Her mind told her to walk away, but her body's cravings told her otherwise. She stayed in front of the crack spot, knocking on the door.

One of his workers peered through the peephole and opened the door. He placed his arm over the door and gave her a cunning smile.

"Yo, El, it's ya girl . . . the singer," the man yelled over his shoulder. Lyfe told him to let her in. Desire took a deep breath before she entered, and then walked to the back room. She noticed fifteen or so crackheads already busy smoking themselves into oblivion. In the back, Lyfe sat at the table, smoking a blunt, with both his rottweilers beside him. Desire knew he was lit up because his eyes hung droopy and red. He smiled smugly at Desire and extended his arm, holding out his half-smoked blunt.

"You smoke?" he asked, as he choked loudly. Desire shook her head. Weed had lost its lure for her.

"You sure?" Lyfe said while holding the smoke. "This that purple, B." Desire declined again. She stood with her arms folded, looking around impatiently.

Finally, Lyfe spoke again. "So how many you buying tonight?"

Desire eyed the ground like a child. "I came to sing for you," she whispered.

Lyfe sat up and put his hand to his ear. "What? I didn't hear you, you got to speak up."

Desire cleared her throat and started singing the group's first hit song, "Harlem Girl Lost."

"Louder, bitch!" Lyfe screamed as he jumped up and did the two-step. The crackheads in the room paid her no attention and continued getting lifted.

Lyfe clapped his hands and began to mock her by doing the

Wop and the Cabbage Patch. "Owww, it's ya birthday . . . it's ya birthday!" He was ecstatic that he had brought Desire to this point.

Desire finished singing for him and stood with her head hanging down. She wanted nothing else but to get out of there and take a blast. She extended her hand out for her drugs.

"Now you got to entertain my dogs," said Lyfe, and his smile disappeared. "I tell you what . . . jerk off my dogs and I'll give you ten of those thang thangs."

Desire stared at him for a moment. When she thought about the ten dimes, she felt her stomach flip with excitement. Then she looked at the huge, bullish dogs who sat loyally at their master's feet. Their tongues were wagging as they ran their eyes all around the room, guarding Lyfe against anyone who got out of line. Desire was so delusional in her painful cravings, the dogs appeared smaller and more innocent than they actually were.

"All I got to do is jerk them off?" she asked, strongly considering it just so she would have a day or two's supply of crack.

"That's all," Lyfe said as he grabbed his dogs by their collars. He moved both dogs into the middle of the floor. Desire bent down on her knees next to the dogs and slowly reached for their penises. Lyfe had reduced several others—men and women—to this madness before. The dogs were used to it, and became excited that they were about to be pleasured. Desire squinted and twisted her mouth in disgust once the dogs' red, moist penises came out. Several men gathered around to watch. They laughed when the aroused dogs began to try to mount Desire from behind so they could hump her. The dogs were worked into a frenzy that needed to be satisfied, and pretty soon they were barking with frustration, and Desire began to cry out in fear.

Lyfe couldn't take it anymore and waved his hands, "Aiight, aiight, that's enough." Lyfe's boys grabbed the dogs' collars and led them away from Desire. The dogs protested by refusing to budge, but a few hard jerks on their collars finally subdued them.

"Hold up, Desire," Lyfe said. "One more thing."

Desire looked at him as he began to unzip his pants. She stayed down on her knees, waiting to give him some head so she could infect his ass. But he told her to lie on her back and open her mouth. Dread filled her eyes as she watched Lyfe's boys surround her. They waved long, thick pieces of two-by-fours in their hands. When Lyfe walked up with his dick in his hand, she closed her eyes. She closed her eyes tighter when she felt the warm urine hit her face.

"Open your mouth, bitch!" yelled Lyfe.

As he finished, she nearly choked, coughing up spit-up and urine. Lyfe stared down at her. He nodded to his partner, who handed him the crack.

"I knew you wasn't shit."

He tossed the crack on the floor and watched Desire scurry to retrieve the rocks. When she picked them all up, she went into a corner of the room and put the stem to her mouth as fast as she could.

* * *

The difference between an addict and a junkie is that an addict goes though hell as they fight for their soul. But a junkie has gone to hell without coming back. He or she no longer has a soul. Desire was now a junkie. She became a mere shell of her former self, a walking zombie, and her health declined. There is no way anyone would recognize her now as the once famous Desire Evans. She epitomized the image of an AIDS patient, weighing a shrunken and shriveled ninety-three pounds. Her neck was so skinny that people who stared at her wondered how it supported her head. The deep, dark circles under her eyes told tales of horror and suffering. Her ability to function as a human being was annihilated. She had no regard for herself, or for life as a whole. The situation became even more ghastly once the city marshals showed up to remove whatever belongings Desire had not sold from the apartment. She turned into an animal who lived in alleys, abandoned buildings, crack houses or rooftops, anywhere she could lay her head for a few hours. Nothing was beneath her, and she generally dined in fast-food Dumpsters. Usually, her daily snacks consisted of twenty-five-cent cakes, potato chips and cookies from the local bodegas.

The drama Desire caused on the ho stroll on East Harlem's Park Avenue made her an outcast. She drew heat from police and other hoes because she would rob and beat every trick she encountered, making it bad for everyone else. As soon as they saw Desire, the whores chased and beat her down. There seemed few options for this fallen angel. She had to either go crazy, go to jail or die.

≈ ≈ ≈

Desire was walking down 127th between Lenox and Fifth when she heard the car honk at her. She knew better than to waste time. She ran to the car.

"What's up, honey, you looking for a date?" asked Desire. She tried to hide her rotted yellow teeth as she smiled only slightly.

The Hispanic man was ugly, with sunken-in eyes and skeleton cheeks.

"How much?" he asked her, turning down the salsa music that blasted from the stereo of his red Nissan.

"Ten dollars," said Desire.

"You got it, honey," he replied, and Desire jumped into the passenger side of the vehicle.

He drove them to a secluded area on 128th Street between Madison and Park Avenues. As soon as he parked, Desire began to unbuckle the dirty jeans she wore, with no panties underneath. When she looked up, he just stared at her without saying a word.

"What's wrong, baby?" she asked. "I ain't got a lot of time."

Again, he remained silent and just stared.

Desire grew frustrated. "Listen, if we ain't gonna do nothing, I'm leaving."

He smiled and said, "You don't remember me, do you?"

"I ain't got time for your games." She attempted to leave. He wrapped his huge hand over her arm and pulled her closer to him. He took off his hat. Desire did not recognize his face. She was too strung out to realize that about a year before, he had picked Desire up on Park Avenue. She had pickpocketed his money as she gave him a blowjob.

Desire knew she was in trouble just as the trick punched her in the head and jabbed her in the eye. Dazed, Desire's body began to shake as she pleaded for him not to hit her anymore. Her fear made his penis hard. He grabbed her by the leg and began to rip her jeans off her body. He unzipped his pants and pulled out his penis and began rubbing it rapidly.

"Open your fucking legs . . . *wide*!"

Desire lost the air in her chest as she stared at the scarred, sore-ridden skin around his genitals.

"Mister, please, I . . . I got the virus, I got HIV!" Unmoved, the man continued to assault Desire and hold her down. Desire felt the head of his penis begin to enter her. He punched her once again as she struggled. She felt herself drifting back to the day Tony Evers had raped her virginity out of her. She was not going to remain frozen, as she had that day.

"Bitch, I do you one better than HIV." His eyes lit up. "I got full-blown AIDS."

In him she saw herself—an angry person who no longer cared about anyone else's life because there was no more hope for his. Desire struggled to no avail to free herself, but he was much too strong. The pain was excruciating as she felt the ripping and tearing of her insides. She cried and begged for mercy, but it was a fruitless plea. The wild man began choking the air out of her. She lifted her arm to her mouth and spit her ever-ready Oxford razor into her hand. It was a habit she had never broken. She then felt for his penis, and with one swift move she cut into it with all the remaining strength she had. She watched his eyes light up and then she heard a loud, howling scream. Air came into her lungs once again as he released his grip. He reached madly below his stomach, trying to wildly hypnotize himself to numb the agonizing pain. The stump of his severed penis spewed blood everywhere. When Desire looked down, the other half was still inside of her bruised vagina. It expelled itself when she stood up and got out of the car.

Desire ran, almost nude, up 128th Street, screaming at the top of her lungs. It was as if her life had come full circle, a catalog of experiences that her soul could no longer bear. She had been born near here, was living virtually the same life her mother had, was dying the same way. She was being raped, robbing, stealing, thieving, lying, and dying. She was alone, beaten and in a state of health that had her on a tightrope separating life and death. Desire was literally running for her life. She didn't stop running until she ran right into a man's arm, the force of which nearly knocked her senseless. She was hysterical as she begged the man to save her.

"Please, please help me . . . a man just tried to kill me."

"Desire?"

Desire looked up, miraculously, into her old friend Carvelas's face.

PART THREE

This is the part of the story where it ends at the beginning. The day when the story told from the beginning has come around again. This time, the girl might be older. The street may have changed. There might be more people in the story. But it's the same story still. Less than a quarter of a century later, there's again a terrible February night in Harlem. Only now it's no longer news. Now almost nobody will hear or talk about it. It's been the same story heard for so long, by so many people, that it can't even get anybody's attention anymore. There's nothing sensational about the details. Nobody cares anymore how the story got to this point. Another fucked-up drug addict is now off the street. That's all most people care about. For most people, that was the end of the story. But not for its victim. She wanted to start her story all over again.

CHAPTER TWENTY-ONE

When Desire awoke, she was on a hospital gurney at Harlem Hospital's mental health unit. The attending medical staff from that night had admitted her for detoxification and a mental evaluation.

Once she regained her sense of reality, she screamed as loud as she could, as if she had suddenly awakened from a nightmare. She saw a familiar face nearby—Carvelas—talking to a doctor. When Carvelas saw her try to rise, he rushed to her side.

"Desire, it's okay, it's okay," he repeated as he wrapped his arms around her frail body. "Everything is fine now . . . you're in the hospital." Desire was mortified as she stared into his eyes, still unsure that she was safe. Carvelas didn't even seem to notice that Desire now looked closer to a monster than the girl he would have fallen in love with.

"Don't let me go, Carvelas," Desire begged. "Don't ever let me go . . . please hold me. I don't want you to let me go."

"I won't, Desire, I won't," said Carvelas as he continued to hug her nearly lifeless body and softly kiss her battered skin. Her running into his arms had been a moment when he'd hoped he was dreaming. He had hoped that the nightmare running down the street wasn't the person he had thought she was. He was heartbroken he had been wrong.

"You don't have to worry no more, I got you and I'm never going to let nothing happen to you again."

"You promise?" Desire asked.

Carvelas pulled back to look in her eyes. He was someone she had seen before, yet he seemed totally new. She was correct, because he had been born again. He said softly, "Desire, on the beneficent and merciful God Allah, I promise that I will sacrifice my own life to protect you from another moment of pain."

෴ ෴ ෴

Desire was scheduled to stay in the detox unit of Harlem Hospital for the next ten days. Carvelas promised her that he would be there when she completed the program and that she need not worry about not having a place to stay. Desire thanked him repeatedly and promised him that she would work hard to beat her addiction.

Over the next ten days, Desire rested, listened to the staff and learned many things about her addiction. However, she wasn't so open with her assigned therapist when it came to talking about her past. She was willing to confess to some of the people who had left her, the experiences that had changed her. She was willing to talk about the highs, but avoided the lows. The therapist told Desire that her drug addiction was merely an extension of bigger problems that she had yet to address. The first step to liberation is to trust someone and have the courage to talk about it. The therapist recommended that Desire be placed into a long-term drug program after she left detox. Desire opted instead to beat the addiction with her own willpower. The doctor informed Desire that it would not be that easy.

"It seems that you've had quite a life," the therapist warned her. "Many of the things that you have talked about have been very traumatic, and psychologically debilitating. Those things need to be dealt with, or you may turn to drugs again."

"Well," began Desire, "I've been taking care of myself most of my life, and been through shit you could never imagine. Things that I'll never tell anybody about. And each time, no matter what the circumstances were, I survived. I just did what I had to do. I didn't cry about it like y'all white people, lay my problems on others, like those suckers in groups. If I say I ain't gonna do something no more, that's it! I'm disciplined. I got willpower."

"Desire," the doctor said, "willpower alone is no match for drug addiction. That is why they say it is such a cunning, baffling and insidious disease. Try taking a box of Ex-Lax and see how much willpower you have not to go to the bathroom."

"That's all about your body," Desire told the therapist. "This is about my mind. I know I can stop using."

The therapist had no choice but to accept and respect the patient's wishes. Help was always a choice.

ʕ   ʕ   ʕ

At the end of her ten days on the unit, Desire had gained sixteen pounds and felt reasonably better. As promised, Carvelas was there to meet her. He took her to the apartment that he rented in a rehabbed tenement building on 116th Street in Harlem, near many of the mosques that he frequently attended. Over the years, Carvelas climbed the ladder and became a top-wage union employee. During Carvelas's travels, he began to explore different faiths and religions, one of which was Islam. After partaking in several services at local mosques, and studying the Quran, he'd gravitated toward Islam ever since. It was apparent that Carvelas eagerly anticipated Desire's arrival to the small, modest apartment. He had gone all out and stocked the refrigerator and cabinets with food. He'd also bought new CDs and DVDs, so Desire wouldn't get bored. He even went out and bought her a lot of female toiletries, some pajamas and ladies underwear.

Desire was secure and at ease for the first time in over a year as hope once again came into her life. She and Carvelas spent hours upon hours reminiscing about the good times, and crying over the bad. For the first time in a long time, Desire felt as if she would never be alone again.

ʕ   ʕ   ʕ

The air was crisp and cool as Carvelas and Desire strolled happily hand in hand from the movie theater on 125th. Laughing, Carvelas suddenly felt Desire's hand grow tense. Lyfe walked in their direction, with his dogs on a leash. Three of his boys were also with him. Desire put her head down. Carvelas's face turned stone cold instantly, as he saw Desire cower. It was as if their lives moving on was blocked by constant interruptions from the past.

"Yo, El, ain't that you girl . . . the singer?" Lyfe looked up and stared at Desire.

"Oh, shit, yeah, it is," Lyfe walked closer and looked her up and down. "Damn, you almost don't look like a crackhead no more."

Carvelas stepped in front of Desire.

"What you say, nigga?"

Lyfe's dogs began barking aggressively. Lyfe recognized Carvelas and chuckled. "Oh, shit, dis that nigga Carvelas. I use to whip his ass back in the day. What, cause you got some size, you got heart now, nigga?"

Carvelas was a little nervous, but he was more sad to be confronted with someone who had gone absolutely nowhere in life. Lyfe was up to the same old thing, only in a worse way. Carvelas was on a different level now. He was no longer afraid of a thug who had terrorized him for far too long. He felt as if Lyfe was a warring spirit who could not possibly win anymore.

"Lyfe, I would like it if you left me and my girl alone," Carvelas began calmly. "However, if you don't, then you can get ready for the fight of your life."

Lyfe seemed amused, but one of his boys reached for his pistol. They were all stunned when Carvelas did not move one inch. They had never had someone respond to the threat of a gun like this. Carvelas refused to budge as Lyfe's boy moved closer and closer, until the gun was pointed almost directly at Carvelas's heart. Carvelas had no fear as he decided it was time for him to defend himself. He was fast. The dude didn't even see it coming as Carvelas suddenly and swiftly struck him in the throat. While Lyfe stood scared of Carvelas's self-assured power, his boy gasped for breath. Carvelas pulled the pistol from the boy's hand and placed him in a headlock. Lyfe was motionless. Carvelas threw the boy to the ground and grabbed Lyfe so fast, Lyfe couldn't stop him. Desire had no idea what was going to happen next, but she stayed quiet and still as Carvelas put the gun in Lyfe's mouth.

Carvelas stared at Lyfe as he spoke: "I could kill you right now, if I really wanted to. A part of me tells me I should. But even though I can, I won't. Son, this is my word, if you ever talk sideways or even think about giving your drugs to my girl again, I'm taking *your* life!" Carvelas pushed the pistol deeper into Lyfe's mouth. Lyfe began to gag as Carvelas held him up and made him take nearly the entire barrel of the gun down his throat. Desire had no idea if Carvelas was going to kill the man who had terrorized them both. She didn't care. It was broad daylight, but Carvelas didn't have an ounce of worry as people from the neighborhood stood by and watched the drama unfold. Many of the mothers and older regulars on the block starting clapping.

"If I ever find out you so much as call out her name again, so much as point a finger at her, I pledge my soul on Allah that y'all niggas will die a million deaths. Now, if y'all niggas want rage, I'm gonna make the front page!"

They were in a standoff. Lyfe knew Carvelas was not going to shoot him—at least not today. But Carvelas had shown Lyfe that he should never even risk taking the chance again. Carvelas eased the pistol out of the Lyfe's mouth, staring at him all the while.

Lyfe only stared and mumbled, "Fuck you, nigga." The young dude fixed his collar and asked Carvelas for his pistol back. Carvelas slapped him viciously across the face with the weapon.

"I'm taking this shit off the street, punk."

He grabbed Desire's hand and they walked through the crowd, which was roaring with excitement that somebody, *anybody*, had finally put Lyfe in his place.

~ ~ ~

Over the next few weeks, Carvelas stayed by Desire's side as she planned all the goals that would help her get her life back together. Desire fell head over heels in love with him. To have a man who was willing to give up his life for her was a gift Desire could not comprehend, especially since she hadn't been there for him nearly as much as she could have been. His devotion was beyond her understanding. Although she was comforted by it, she still could not help feeling suspicious of it. Carvelas slept on the couch and gave Desire the bedroom. He wanted her to know that he didn't need to have sex with her, even after she had gotten healthier and looked almost like the girl he had met years ago in church. Desire actually wanted it that way, because she had not yet confessed to him that she was HIV positive. Carvelas made it clear anyway that it was more than sex that he was interested in.

"Desire, I wasn't about that then and I am not about that now. I've totally changed my life. I look at you and see somebody who used to love life and living. I know your past. I know what you been through. It's going to be hard for you to go back to that. I just want to try and help you do it."

Desire had never heard a man speak like that. She was overwhelmed, and could not believe that she had had to sink so low in life to truly listen to Carvelas. She thought about all the letters he had written her that had gone unanswered. She thought about how he had probably avoided her at the funeral of a woman he had loved because he couldn't stand to see what her granddaughter had become. Or maybe he couldn't stand to look at what could have been between them. Desire could not believe or understand how someone was still with her, despite everything.

"Baby . . . what's wrong?" Carvelas asked.

"I'm thinking about how wrong I did people. I know I did you wrong . . ."

"You don't have to worry about any of that. It's a past life. People make mistakes. I knew you would eventually come around."

"But it wasn't just you. I've hurt so many people . . . and Tiah, I did her so wrong. She might be dead because of me, and I don't know what to do."

"I know you're hurt, Desire, but all you can do is pray for her."

"But I feel so guilty. I judged her and put her out the group for using drugs and then I became a fucking crackhead myself."

"Don't think like that, Desire, you just got caught up. That's not who you are. You are a strong and beautiful black woman who made some mistakes. You don't have nothing to ever be ashamed of. I'm sure that God is looking over her right now, protecting her no matter what."

Desire was calmed by his words and looked into his eyes with passion. They approached each other and kissed passionately. Desire lay back slowly as Carvelas caressed and stroked her body affectionately. Their breathing became heavier as she began to unbuckle his pants. Carvelas worked his tongue down her neck and to her breast. Desire moaned loudly then stiffened.

"What's wrong?" Carvelas asked, still in a zone.

Desire shook her head. "No, I can't do this."

"I'm sorry, Desire, I didn't mean to . . . This is not what I want to do either."

"Carvelas, I got something bad to tell you." She wasn't going to beat around the bush. "I caught the virus."

Carvelas was silent as her words swirled in his head. Desire waited for him to say something—anything. All at once, Desire wished she had never told him, as she could not stand the thought of him leaving her again.

"Desire, I already know," announced Carvelas. "I read the newspapers. I hear what's going on in the street. I wanted to reach out to you . . . but I didn't know where you were."

"And you still want to be with me?"

Carvelas grabbed Desire's hand and kissed it gently.

"Desire, when a man really loves a woman, there is nothing in the world that he won't accept about her. And I've loved you too long to just stop now. I asked my pops a long time ago how can you tell if you really, really love a girl. He said, 'There are two ways. One, when she takes you through all kinds of shit and you still want to be with her. Two, when you can only think of her two times a day—that's day and night.' Desire, there wasn't a single day that went by that I didn't think about you . . . not one single day. I used to see you on television and wish I could kiss you through the screen, just so I could feel you."

Desire was overwhelmed by his words. She wiped his tears

away and pulled him to her chest and caressed him in her arms as she rocked him like a baby. Carvelas fell asleep in her arms. Desire lie awake, smiling, too happy to risk dreaming.

≈   ≈   ≈

Carvelas had been on leave from his job for over a month when he received a call from his union boss. There was a convention in Chicago and his boss asked if he was ready to come back from the extended leave he had been granted for personal reasons. Since Carvelas was now the top technician and the job paid maximum-scale rate, Carvelas would make upwards of three thousand dollars a day for the eight-day event.

Desire sat in the bedroom, listening to Carlvelas's conversation. She knew that Carvelas was missing out on a lot of money to stay at home with her. The same man had called at least twice a week, to see if Carvelas wanted to work local events, but he had always refused.

"Listen to me," Desire said seriously. "You can't keep babysitting me. I'm going to have to stand on my own eventually, so why not now? I know how much you like your job, and how much they need you, so do me this favor, baby . . . go. I'm gonna be all right."

The next day, Carvelas relunctantly left for Chicago. He would be gone one week. Desire sighed when they parted. She knew she would have to sit alone, without her man by her side, for the first time in a couple of months. Before Carvelas left, he assured her that if she needed him, all she had to do was call him and he would be right there. He gave her all the information that she would need to reach him at all times. Before he left, he also placed money in the top drawer in the bedroom in case of any emergency.

On the third night Carvelas was gone, Desire scanned the Chinese take-out menu, then picked up the phone to have some food delivered. After she placed her order, she turned on the TV and waited for her food to arrive. She watched a high-speed car chase on *Cops,* saw the police pull two white males out of the car. As they were handcuffed, the cops searched their vehicle for drugs or weapons. They pulled out a small cellophane plastic bag and shined their flashlights on it as they poured the contents out of the bag. Large chunks of crack the size of Now and Laters lay on the hood of the car.

Suddenly, without warning, Desire's stomach began to flip. The way it began to growl and shake, it felt as if she had to go to the bathroom. Her body was reacting to the euphoric recall of the cocaine, releasing adrenaline throughout her body.

Desire cut off the television as her heart pounded and palms got sweaty. She recognized what was happening and immediately picked up the telephone to call Carvelas. She breathed rapidly as she waited for him to pick up. She was about to try the other number he'd given her, but the doorbell rang, startling her. She went to the door, and saw that it was the Chinese delivery man. She opened the door, then went to her drawer to get the money. When she opened the envelope, she nearly lost control of her bowels. Desire fingered through the thick wad of cash; it was all fifties and one hundreds. The delivery man's voice broke her out of her trance.

"Must deliver other order, ma'am."

Desire pulled out a fifty and told him to keep the change. She snatched the bag of food. After she had locked the door behind the delivery man, she threw the food in the trash can and ran to the bedroom. She grabbed the envelope from the drawer again and with shaky hands began counting. Twenty-seven hundred dollars. She grabbed her coat and left the apartment, heading back into the mean, dark streets of Harlem. It was as if she weren't even herself anymore. She just wanted to get one hit, one rush of ecstasy from the crack she could already taste in her mouth. She planned to go right back home, to not get caught up in the streets, to only buy a little taste and then start rebuilding things immediately. But when Carvelas returned home four days later, his apartment was bare, and Desire was gone.

CHAPTER TWENTY-TWO

It is believed that if a drug addict or alcoholic in recovery relapses, they return with a higher tolerance for their drug of choice. A heroin addict who needed a bundle a day to get high before rehab now required double that amount.

Several weeks after she returned to the streets, Desire's addiction was worse than ever before. That first night, Desire copped an eighth of a brick, rented a motel room and smoked herself into oblivion. She had not wanted to smoke it in the apartment, because it was only going to be for one night, and then she'd go back to real life. But the minute she took that first hit, her real life became the one she had escaped mere months ago. It became the only one that mattered. By the time she had smoked an unusually high amount of crack cocaine, and all the money was gone, her entire being had warped. She had finally lost her mind.

*. *. *.

On Valentine's Day night in 2007, Desire Evans stood on the corner curb, freezing as she watched the fluffy white snow rapidly rain down. She looked like a woman over twice her age. There was nobody on the street that she could beg any change from, no cars on the road to flag down to offer her sexual services to, nothing. Broke and destitute, she cried, because her body craved the drug and she didn't have the means to feed it. Her mind raced to think of her options, and there was only one.

Desire knocked faintly on the door, and heard heavy footsteps approach. The door opened, and the same young teen that Carvelas had taken the pistol from stood looking at her as if she were a ghost.

"Yo, Lyfe," the boy chuckled. "You ain't gonna believe this shit."

When Desire entered the apartment, she saw Lyfe lying back lazily as he smoked a blunt. He was rubbing one of his rottweilers. A devilish grin crept across his face when he saw Desire.

"So we meet yet again," he snarled. The taste of the barrel of his own boy's gun in his mouth rushed to his tongue. He was about to take all the hatred and fear he had felt for Carvelas in that instant out on the woman Carvelas had been trying to protect. They both had punked him for far too long, and way too many times. He was about to show Desire just who she was fuckin with.

He whistled for his dogs to group together in the middle of the floor. As if he were a Roman emperor, he raised his arm and commanded them to sit, indicating that Desire should get on her knees. She complied without a word. She had been through this before. She had no soul left. She was just a body, living and existing only for the drug. If it wanted her to commit this senseless act, she would, because it truly had become her. The two dogs knew it was mating time, as their moist, red penises were already protruding. She attempted to massage their penises, but Lyfe snapped, "Don't put your funky ass hands on my dog's dicks, bitch! I want you to suck them, like the dirty bitch you are."

Desire obeyed quickly, without words, as if she were a robot. She had lost all feeling, all shame. She bent awkwardly and put the first dog's penis into her mouth. She closed her eyes and squinted tightly as she worked one dog, then switched to the other.

This went on for nearly twenty minutes. Desire had lost all track of time, was only concerned with the minute when Lyfe would hand her the drugs. Finally, Lyfe clapped his hands and said, "Cease!"

When Desire stopped, she could see that Lyfe was in a psychotic haze. Eyes bloodshot and aflame, he glared down upon her with hatred and reached for his zipper. "Lay the fuck down and open your mouth—wide." Both of Lyfe's flunkies glanced at each other and snickered. Desire cringed but assumed her position slowly. On her back, she closed her eyes to fight back the tears of total shame and humiliation—but lost. Desire's pathetic life at that moment flashed before her eyes; she began to cry even harder, when suddenly, the words of Hattie Mae entered her mind as clear as day.

"Desire, I want you to promise me that no matter what happens

in life, no matter how hard it knocks you down, I want you to get on your knees and pray. Pray until you get an answer from God!"

A surge of strength entered her body as she said, "Yes, Grandma, I'm gonna pray, I'm gonna pray."

Desire rose, got on her knees, and began to pray silently. Lyfe glared at her as if she had lost her mind, and sneered, "Bitch, what the fuck you doing?"

Tears fell heavily from her eyes. "My grandmama told me to pray," Desire said, choking back the tears.

"Bitch," yelled Lyfe, "are you crazy? Did I tell you to get up? Lay the fuck back down!"

"My grandma told me to get on my knees and pray." She cried again.

Lyfe grew angrier and kicked Desire viciously in the face. Desire lost her balance, but got back on her knees and repeated, as if she was in her own space and time, "She told me to pray if I'm in trouble. She was the only one who loved me."

Lyfe's eyes grew wider and then he said, "Oh, this bitch thinks I'm playing." He motioned to his flunky. "Yo, bring me the two by four."

All the while, Desire continued to babble incoherently as if she was losing her mind. "I never knew my momma. She left me."

The boy handed the thick piece of wood to Lyfe, who gripped it firmly. "Bitch, I'm gonna teach you to listen now."

Desire never saw the blow coming, as Lyfe swung the wood behind his shoulder and delivered a sickening blow to her face. Both his flunkies cringed at the sound of her facial bones cracking. Desire slumped over, bleeding from her mouth and nose.

Lyfe began to circle his victim. "Bitch," Lyfe yelled, "you bring that nigga of yours to step to Lyfe and think you can live after that? You lost your mind, bitch? My name is Lyfe, son, and I handle mine."

With will from the heavens, Desire suddenly began to rise to her knees again. "My mama had me on the street, my grandmama saved me and her," she mumbled through her swollen mouth.

This infuriated Lyfe even more. "Oh, this bitch really want it," he said as he backed up. Lyfe then ran toward Desire full speed and knocked her senseless across her skull, splitting it instantly. Desire's body lay limp as blood spewed rapidly out of her head. Lyfe continued to pound Desire all over her body. The two boys turned their heads in shame as they listened to the sickly cracking of Desire's bones. They could no longer watch the brutal beating. "Take it, bitch, yeah, take it!" Lyfe screamed, as spit flew from his mouth. "Where ya punk-ass man now!" Desire's body was lifeless.

One of the boys began to cry; he could no longer take it and rushed his boss and grabbed him before he delivered another violent blow. "No more, man! You killing her! No more!" Lyfe struggled to be freed, but the other boy helped contain him. Lyfe's chest heaved in and out rapidly, as his eyes fluttered hysterically. "You won, man, you got her back," cried the boy.

Lyfe began to return to sanity and looked at both boys, who slowly released him. He looked at the wood that was still in his hand, and that was now saturated with blood, and tossed it aside. Wiping blood off his face he blinked and gazed down upon Desire's broken and twisted body. He looked at both boys, who had their heads down, and said, "Take this bitch outside and shoot her!"

Desire once again made headlines in the newspapers:

"HARLEM WOMAN FOUND SHOT, LEFT FOR DEAD IN SNOW."

Forty-eight hours after Desire was rushed to the hospital and the bullets were removed from her body, she finally opened her eyes. The trauma surgeons had done the best they could, but they didn't give her much chance for survival. She opened her eyes for only the second it took for her life-monitoring machines to record a crucial spike in brain activity. Then she slipped back into a coma. One of her lungs had collapsed, and she'd been placed on life support.

On the sixth day, Desire opened her eyes again, and came out of her coma. Being the seasoned hospital veteran that she was, Desire knew immediately where she was; however, she wasn't sure what she was there for. When she tried to sit up, crippling pain hit her like a ton of bricks. She tried to scream, but something was holding her jaw shut, so she could only moan like a wounded cat. The pain was so awesome, she wanted to die. She saw a nurse appear, and her eyes began to feel heavy shortly after she sensed the nurse injecting a shot in her arm. She passed out.

≈ ≈ ≈

It would be another full day before Desire would find the strength to awaken again. The first thing she saw was Carvelas's smiling face. Again, he appeared to her like a miracle. A warm, soothing calm came over her as she felt the loving stroke of his hand against her.

Desire tried to speak, but she cringed in pain. She sensed a stiffness in her face that she had never felt before.

"Your jaw is wired shut," Carvelas carefully explained. "And both your arms have been broken. Lyfe beat you and had you shot. He was found by police, running from the scene after somebody called 911. The bullets in his gun matched the ones pulled out of your body. He's been arrested on attempted murder charges. I'm here. He can't hurt you anymore."

Carvelas broke down in tears, and he lowered his head and begged her to forgive him.

"I'm sorry, Desire . . . it was my fault they did this to you . . . If I hadn't let my anger get to me, hadn't challenged him, this wouldn't have happened . . . I'm sorry. I'm so, so sorry . . . If you had died I . . . I wouldn't know what to do . . ."

Desire squeezed his hand tightly. "Thank you for saving my life . . . again," she whispered.

Carvelas shook his head. "Did I? Desire, there's somebody here to see you."

Desire looked at him, silently questioning.

"It's your sister, Tiah," he announced.

At that moment, Tiah walked into the room. It was as if she and Desire had reversed their appearances. Desire stared at Tiah, and saw a nearly spitting image of the woman she used to be. Even better, Tiah looked nothing like the woman she had been when Desire had last seen her at the funeral. Carvelas stood up, gave Desire a light kiss on the forehead and left the room.

Tiah approached Desire cautiously. She smiled and bent down to give her sister a gentle hug.

There was a deafening silence as they looked at each other uneasily. But Tiah could no longer hide her true feelings, and she began to cry.

"I miss you, Desire . . . I miss you so, so much!" Tiah looked at Desire and wrapped her hands around Desire's. "I want you to consider going to a placed called Visions after you're released from the hospital. The rehab program saved my life."

Desire was unable to speak, but it was a moment when words were not needed.

ε   ε   ε

Several weeks later, Desire got stronger. She and Tiah bonded as they filled each other in on what had happened after they lost contact with each other.

Tiah was now attending John Jay University in Manhattan and was working on her bachelor's degree is social work. During her free time she counseled runaway teen girls for a nonprofit in Brooklyn. And just like Desire, she had yet to receive any royalties from her time with Desire, Cream, and Dream.

Desire spent a total of six weeks in the hospital. Upon her release, she entered the Visions Drug Rehabilitation Program, under a false name.

CHAPTER TWENTY-THREE

Visions housed over two hundred men and women. Many of the residents were plagued with issues such as mental disorders, homelessness and criminal pasts resulting from their addictions. Visions was considered the last stop on the rehab train, with the next stop being jail or death. The government-funded program accepted anyone that sought recovery. From the outside looking in, one would think that with so many dysfunctional beings under one roof, it would be anarchy, but real relates to real; most of the fine staff of men and women who worked there had been patients at one point themselves. They were the best type to help others because they knew everything there was to know about the mind of a fellow addict.

Since the Visions program had stringent rules, Desire was not allowed to have contact with anyone from the outside for sixty days. This was done to keep the clients' focus on their recovery and to avoid additional stress from family members or significant others.

Desire spent the vast majority of the first morning staring at the mounds of paperwork that needed to be filled out. Even though her jaw and bones had mended and the casts had been removed, her arms and hands were numb. Desire flexed her fingers and grimaced at the papers in front of her. The intake administrator empathized, "It's a lot of paperwork, I know, but it's necessary that it all be filled out to process you into the program. If you're not up to doing it all right now, you can stop and go have lunch, then come back. Would you like to do that?"

Desire kept her head down and remained silent. The lady waited for a response. Most addicts that walked into the program were timid and scared. Many had been on the streets for years and had dealt on a daily basis with human animals, the grimiest of grimy cutthroats, who were constantly plotting and scheming. Now that they were off of the streets and the drugs and in a new environment, around new people, their social skills were absent.

The administrator smiled and tried again to connect with Desire. "By the way, my name is Cheryl. Welcome to Visions."

With her jaw still wired shut, Desire turned and gave the other woman a light smile. Cheryl smiled back even as she stared at Desire's twisted and deformed mouth and face. Desire admired Cheryl's strength. The administrator barely blinked at the sight of Desire's grotesque face. Cheryl extended her arm to shake Desire's hand. Desire tried to lift her hand slowly, but it was too painful. The kind-hearted administrator leaned over and gave Desire a gentle, sincere hug.

"My name is Desiree . . . Desiree Vera," Desire strained to impart. She smiled inwardly at having taken Carvelas's last name.

≥   ≥   ≥

Desire's transition into the new program was touch and go, as she basically was quiet and kept to herself.

The first week took a lot out of her. Because Visions was a structured and controlled environment, Desire had a hard time with the strict rules, such as 5 A.M. wake-ups, house duties and mandatory group discussions and meetings that lasted into the night. She often wondered if she had bitten off more than she could chew. In her second week, she was assigned a managing counselor.

Desire had been assigned to the head counselor because her case was so severe. Mrs. Avery was despised and hated by staff and residents alike. She was a no-nonsense, micromanaging tyrant who would fire any counselor or staff member for even the most minor infraction. Residents fared no better, as she would show the door to anybody who wasn't inclined to follow the rules of the program. Mrs. Avery was a former addict. It was rumored that the she had once been married, but her husband left her when he found out she couldn't have any kids because she had polluted and abused her body so badly.

Desire had a one o'clock meeting with Mrs. Avery.

"Excuse me," said Desire as she peeked into the office. "Um, I'm supposed to see Mrs. Avery. My name is Desiree Vera."

Mrs. Avery didn't look up from the paperwork on her desk. "Ms. Vera, you were supposed to be here at one P.M."

Desire looked at the clock on the wall; it read seven minutes after one.

"I know," said Desire, "but I'm new, and I didn't know my way around and—"

Mrs. Avery rudely cut her off, saying, " 'But' is a word used by procrastinators who are doomed to failure. Failure is what brought you into this program. Have a seat outside and think about your failures."

Desire stared at her, not saying a word. She backed out the door and sat in the hall.

Desire sat there for nearly three hours, until she heard Mrs. Avery call her name. She walked into the counselor's office and stood before her desk as Mrs. Avery continued writing on a piece of paper. Desire stood for another full minute, until Mrs. Avery gestured that she could take a seat.

After she finally stopped writing, Mrs. Avery slowly and methodically filed each piece of paper in different folders and closed her desk drawer. She took off her glasses.

"Ms. Vera, why are you in this program?"

The question caught Desire off guard and she stammered, "Um, because I want to stop using drugs."

"Ms. Vera, did you get high today?"

"No!"

"Did you get high yesterday?" she asked.

"No!" Desire said, a little annoyed.

"Well, it seems to me that your problem isn't stopping, your problem is staying clean. You can stop when you want to. But then you go back. You are here because you do not know how to live on society's terms and your life has become unmanageable. Is that right, Ms. Vera?"

Desire nodded.

"Since that's the case, Ms. Vera, you are to follow all rules, participate and show up *on time* to all scheduled meetings. These are copies of all the house rules and regulations you received and signed on your first day. Read and sign each page *again,* and come back tomorrow at six thirty—*that's A.M.*—to have a one-on-one for an assessment plan."

She handed Desire a spiral notebook and stared at her with cold, dark eyes.

"You are expected to keep a daily log of your feelings and the events that go on in your life. That is your personal journal. It is for therapeutic purposes only. It is not to be read by anyone else unless you want them to. I'll expect you to write at least one page a day. You are dismissed."

Desire's pride had been wounded by Mrs. Avery. She knew that she had gotten to the lowest point a human being could possibly get, but she still didn't think she deserved the type of treatment Mrs. Avery had dished out. It was as if everybody was afraid to cross her. Most of all, Desire resented the way Mrs. Avery had talked to her. Who did the woman think she was? Desire laughed as she thought about the fact that there was a time when Mrs. Avery would have been begging her for an autograph. She decided she was only going to speak when spoken to as far as Mrs. Avery was concerned. So there was an icy chill each and every time the two women were near each other. Mrs. Avery acted like she didn't even care.

* * *

Not everyone was in the Visions program by choice. Some of the residents were mandated by the courts or as a condition of their parole. One man, J.D., was a Midtown pimp and crack addict. He was only biding his time, fulfilling a requirement imposed on him by his parole officer when his urine came up dirty. He noticed Desire during group on several occasions, but never paid her any mind. Over the weeks, however, Desire's wounds began to heal and her bandages were removed. J.D. then saw a potential sex partner to help him pass his time.

As Desire sat eating lunch one day, J.D. walked up with his food tray.

"Anyone sitting here?"

Desire rolled her eyes, as except for her, the entire table was empty.

"I know that was a stupid question, but I didn't want to be rude and just sit down, nah mean?"

He placed his tray on the table. Moments later, he said, "Damn, I forgot to get some juice." He rose and asked Desire if she wanted him to bring her some since he was going. She declined. Before he left to get the juice, he asked her, "Excuse me, ma, do you mind watching my tray?"

Desire nodded. He thanked her and smiled as he walked away. It was a small gesture of trust. J.D. went on to extend many little gestures such as that, and in no time at all he and Desire were on friendly speaking terms. They sat together at breakfast, lunch and dinner. Desire told him everything about her family and being strung out on drugs. The long conversations and constant contact filled the hole left by Carvelas's absence. She found herself thinking more and more about being alone, and about how J.D. made her forget all about it.

One day, as they both sat together eating and laughing during lunch, Mrs. Avery approached them.

"Ms. Vera, I'd like you to come with me."

Desire and J.D. continued to laugh, only quieter, as they watched her walk away, in her extremely masculine style. J.D. mocked her in a deep voice. He began posing like a bodybuilder. Desire smothered her laughter and asked J.D. to watch her bag while she went to see what Mrs. Avery wanted.

Inside her office, Mrs. Avery told Desire to sit down. Taking off her glasses, she wasted no time getting down to business. "If you spent as much of your time with the rest of your peers as you do with Mr. Davison, you would be doing much better than you are now. Remember our policy on fraternization—we can put you both on focus," said Mrs. Avery. Desire nodded.

"Oh, by the way Ms. Vera, all resident members are required to join an activity group after sixty days." She handed Desire a list of activities: choir, writing, painting, computers, pottery, gardening, cooking and dance.

Desire read the list, and saw Mrs. Avery's name listed as the music instructor. She knew for sure that she would not be joining the choir. She settled on pottery, simply because she wanted to try something she had never done before.

≈　≈　≈

A few days passed and Desire had a strange feeling that J.D. had been avoiding her. Every time she'd see him, he would say he was busy and had to leave. She missed having someone to talk to. There were many other women and men in the facility, but most people were so caught up in becoming rehabilitated, they just attended required activities and otherwise stayed in their rooms. She grew concerned that she was losing a friend, and confronted J.D. in the cafeteria. When she sat down in front of him, he avoided eye contact with her.

"J.D., what's up with you? Why you been avoiding me?"

J.D. continued to play with his uneaten food. "I'm aiight, it's just . . ." He shook his head, and said, "Oh, never mind."

"What's up?" Desire asked again. She sounded like a schoolgirl who was about to get dumped.

"I should be asking you that," J.D. said.

Desire was confused. She had been busy with her required group meetings, therapy sessions, medical checkups, exercise time and journal writing. Not to mention the fact that she was starting to like pottery. It was slow, dirty and sometimes long work, but she had made some nice pieces that she could actually see giving as gifts. She had decided she wanted to practice it even more. She had even started fantasizing about selling her pottery at a table on 125th Street. She had thought J.D. knew she would make time for him when she could. She had begun to notice that whenever they were together anyway, he did nothing but talk about the life of crime he'd had on the street, and how he planned to get back on top once he left Visions. No matter how much Desire tried to tell him he could do other things, he still insisted on focusing on the past.

"Are you mad that whenever we talk, I'm trying to tell you that you gotta change?" she asked him.

"Somethin like that," J.D. responded. "It's like you done got too high and mighty for a nigga . . . trying to forget where you came from."

Desire was stunned. She had thought they were friends. Desire still hated the thought of being alone. But she thought about Mrs. Avery, and all the other addicts floating around Visions trying to get clean. She realized she was alone in here, but not lonely.

"Damn right I'm trying to forget," Desire said, rising up from the table. "I'm in here cause I gotta forget. If I don't forget, I might as well leave here right now and shoot myself."

"Oh, so you one of those?"

"One of what?"

"Junkie motherfuckers who think this shit in here matter," J.D. said. "Think you gonna sit up in here and get betta and ain't gonna use shit again."

"That's why I'm here, J.D.," Desire said. She couldn't believe he was talking like this to her. "That's why you should be here too."

"I'm here 'cause I gotta be," J.D. growled. "Hell, if I didn't have to be here, I wouldn't be. This shit don't matter. It ain't nothing but some big-ass fantasy world. What's gonna happen to your ass when you gotta get back out there on that street, huh? What's gonna happen when you ain't got a million motherfuckas you don't know who ain't go'n be there when you need 'em holding you off from suckin' that glass dick? What's gonna happen then?"

Desire looked at J.D., and felt guilt that she had ever even entertained the thought of him coming in between her and Carvelas. She knew she would never talk to J.D. again after she spoke these final words:

"J.D., I can't answer that. I really don't know what's gonna happen. All I know is, I gotta try. I gotta believe."

⁊ ⁊ ⁊

The next Saturday afternoon people started filling the lobby of the Visions Rehabilitation Center. It was Visitors Day. Carvelas and Tiah were the first in line. Carvelas was especially anxious to see Desire. He could hardly get any sleep the night before in anticipation of seeing his boo, his baby, his soon-to-be lady. He carried a bouquet of expensive roses for her.

By the time they all found a corner in the cafeteria, the room was already filled to the max. It was tense for a long period as J.D. stood lurking by them, visiting with some of his partners from the street. Desire looked over at him and could tell that he was up to no good. She didn't even smile in his direction.

"Desire, what's up? You don't know me all of a sudden?" yelled J.D.

"No, J.D.," Desire said. People like J.D. no longer had an effect on her. "It ain't nothing like that . . . I'm just happy to see my visitors."

"Is that the reason you can't look me in the eye?" he said, nodding toward Carvelas.

Carvelas met J.D.'s glare with a steady look of his own. Carvelas had been through a lot with Desire. It seemed as if she was either always leaving him or throwing him off. He knew every time he left her alone, there was a chance that she would leave him. He had come to peace with that, and decided to let the cards fall as they would.

"Who is he, Desire?" Carvelas calmly asked, knowing that he would be able to sense the honesty of Desire's answer.

Desire looked over at J.D. and saw him and his boys throwing up signs. She saw them showing off their brand-new tattoos and counting out imaginary dollar bills on the table. Desire shook her head.

"Nobody," she told Carvelas. "Just somebody I used to talk to up in here."

CHAPTER TWENTY-FOUR

"Hello family, my name is Pam and I'm an addict. I'd like to thank my Higher Power for another day clean and sober, for without Him, I would not be here today."

That's how the speaker began. It was the Wednesday night women's group session and every female in the center was required to attend. The guest speaker that night was an alumni who had come back to share the experiences that she went through as an addict, and how she was able to arrest her addiction. Desire sat in the rear of the meeting room, fully prepared to sleep through the lecture as she usually did, but this speaker caught her attention.

"With that out the way, ladies, I'm going to let you know from the very beginning that I'm not the kind of sister to sugarcoat shit when it comes to sharing my past. I keep my shit real and I keep it raw, because that's the only way a bitch like me knows how to bring it. Don't get it twisted. I ain't here to preach to you, lecture you or give you a sob story on how bad drugs are, because there ain't nothing I can tell you that you already don't know. I'm here for one purpose and one purpose only, and that is to save my life. Yeah, I know that sounds selfish, but this is a self-ish program, and I'm about saving my life today. The way I save my life is by ridding myself of all the pain that's been tearing my insides apart for so long. So I free myself by telling others my pain, my hurt and my secrets. The shit that's been keeping me down for years. My story is no different from most of yours. I smoked crack and I lost."

Desire sat upright, hanging on to Pam's every word. The woman couldn't be more than thirty, Desire thought, but her dead eyes made her look much older.

"How many girls in here were ever raped? Raise your hand. How many of you ever sold your body for crack? Raise your hand. How many of you ever sold your baby's diapers or infant milk to get a hit? How many of you ever lived in the train station tunnels? How many of you ever went to the bathroom thinking you had to piss real bad, but instead of urine coming out, a fetus plops out of your pussy? How many of you got HIV, hepatitis C or Herpes because you let men go up in you raw dog?"

Everyone stared at the speaker as she held her hand high. Her eyes scanned the silent room.

"Well, every one of those things I've mentioned applies to me, and as I look in many of you women's eyes, a lot of those same things apply to you too. I'm here to tell you today that it's okay if they do. It's okay if you aren't ready to talk about it yet, because it took me years to get past the shame. But that same shame kept me out there on the streets, sick and suffering, because I kept being ashamed of myself. Then one day, as I sat in this very room, I heard a powerful woman share her experience, strength and hope, and as she told her story, it was like she was telling mines and that's when I realized I wasn't the only one ever raped. I wasn't the only one who lived like an animal, nor was I the only person that had caught the virus. Then she said the most powerful words I've ever heard. That I would always be as sick as my secrets. She said that I would always remain an addict, always remain miserable and always suffer from them if I didn't give them up. And ladies, this is why I'm here tonight, to give up my secrets and save my motherfuckin life!"

After the meeting Desire headed to the front lobby for her final smoke break before lights out. She couldn't stop thinking about the speaker's words, and how much she had been drawn to the woman. It was almost as if she had known her before, like at some point they had been one and the same. Desire had decided not to wait in the long line of women who mobbed the speaker after she finished giving them all the tongue-lashing they needed. She felt as if the woman was so real, she would be able to look right through Desire and predict her failure or success. Desire wasn't ready to know that truth about herself. She wasn't ready to confront someone who had come across as strong as Pam.

When she got to the bottom of the steps, she saw J.D. involved in a huge argument with some staff members. They had found his urine positive for cocaine for the second time, and security was ordering him to leave the program and return to police custody. The police had not arrived yet, and obviously J.D. was plotting how he could escape before they got there to return him to prison.

"Fuck y'all, fuck y'all!" J.D. yelled. He was completely out of his mind, out of control.

When Desire got closer, J.D. spotted her. "Desiree, c'mon, baby, we gettin' the fuck outta here. Let's take all these motherfuckas."

Desire stood torn. She remembered how once in between all the bullshit talk, J.D. had hinted that he really wanted to change his life. She was given chance after chance and knew that maybe if he had just a little more time, he might be able to do it.

"Y'all 'bout to kick him out of here for one little-ass mistake?" she said to the staff. At that moment, Mrs. Avery arrived. She was responding to the call for staff that had gone out over the loudspeaker. In an effort to get to the front of the small crowd, she pushed Desire out of the way, but Desire continued to speak. "You sending him back to prison? Y'all supposed to be trying to help us!"

"This man don't wanna be helped," a staff member said as he and a security guard moved J.D. toward the door, where another security guard was waiting to cuff him.

"Who are you to tell somebody whether or not they wanna be helped?" Desire said.

"Ms. Vera," Mrs. Avery said, "I think it's best that you smoke your cigarette elsewhere."

"I ain't going nowhere. I'm staying right here, and so is he."

"Fuck you, bitch," J.D. screamed at Desire. "Yo stupid ass is stayin here. I'm getting back to life."

Desire was speechless. J.D. threw the first security guard off of him, snatched up the garbage bag of belongings he had come to Visions with. Punching the security guard who waited with handcuffs, he slammed the glass door and stormed out. Everyone heard the police cars that would soon swarm J.D. As soon as they saw the police overtake J.D., everyone breathed a sigh of relief . . . everyone, that is, but Mrs. Avery.

"In my office, Ms. Vera," she shouted to Desire.

ɛ   ɛ   ɛ

Desire was a nervous wreck as she waited outside Mrs. Avery's office.

When Mrs. Avery finally arrived, after making a brief statement to the police and filling out an incident report, she gestured for Desire to enter her office. Desire didn't know whether to sit or to stand at attention. She decided to sit. But when Mrs. Avery slammed the door closed, Desire jumped to her feet.

"I'm not going to waste any of your time, Ms. Vera, so I'll just get down to business," Mrs. Avery began. "I'm going to make a recommendation that you be asked to leave the program. Like I told you from day one, this program doesn't necessarily have revolving doors. For every one person that comes here, there are twenty more people waiting in line to get in, people who really want to be clean. You are simply unable to be honest with yourself. You fraternized with somebody who was obviously not a good influence. Then you interfered with our efforts to keep the peace here. Far as I'm concerned, you obstructed justice. The whole time you've been here, you've skated through this program without saying so much as a word about who you are or about your past. I truly wish you well in your future endeavors, Ms. Vera, and I really hope you find what it is you're looking for, but we cannot help you. Now leave."

Mrs. Avery turned in her swivel chair toward the computer, to close out Desire's case file. Desire stood paralyzed, her mind racing, wondering what her future would look like. With one last glance at Mrs. Avery, she forced herself to move. As she approached the office door, she again froze.

"I ain't got nowhere to go, Mrs. Avery," she cried. "I can't leave. I really, really need help!"

Mrs. Avery seemed unmoved by Desire's plea, simply turning her head. Broken, tears fell heavily from Desire's eyes.

Desire stared at Mrs. Avery with malice. "Well, fuck you and this fucked-up program, too, you heartless bitch!" Desire turned on her heels and stormed out of the office slamming the door violently behind her. Desire's mind raced a thousand miles an hour as she headed toward the steps, but suddenly she stopped in her tracks. She began to break down and cry as she used the wall for support. She turned and looked toward Mrs. Avery's door through her tears and grew angrier. *"No,"* Desire thought, *"I'm not letting her get off that easy."* She gritted her teeth and pushed herself off the wall and scurried back to Mrs. Avery's office. When she opened the door, it was as if Mrs. Avery was expecting her as she sat at her desk eyeing her smugly. Her arrogance infuriated Desire even more as she readied herself to tear into her, but at once she lost her bluster. Desire stood speechless; her mouth moved, but not a word came out. She trembled as she finally found the words. "Why did God do this to me, Mrs. Avery?" Desire cried, searching the woman's face for answers. "All my life I was walked on and beat up on, Mrs. Avery. Why they always doing that to me?" Desire struggled for the words. "Why me, Mrs. Avery? Why me? Why me? Why me?" Desire asked the question over and over as she continued crying.

Mrs. Avery stood up, walked toward Desire and embraced her. "I don't know, but everything will be okay if you keep opening up like that."

Desire pulled back and pleaded, "Mrs. Avery, I don't want to go back out there. I'm scared and I need help. I'm sorry for everything I said to you." Mrs. Avery assured her that it was okay, and they embraced again. Desire pulled back in desperation. "That means I can stay?"

Mrs. Avery smiled and nodded. "Yes, you can stay. But . . . ," she added quickly, locking eyes with Desire, "under strict stipulations."

The counselor told Desire to sit down, and walked back to her desk and began writing in a notepad. When she finished, she handed the pad to Desire.

"This is your contract. Read it aloud, then sign it," Mrs. Avery ordered.

Desire spoke slowly and softly, concentrating on each and every word: "I, Desiree Vera, promise from this day forth that I will participate in all groups, by sharing and partaking in all discussions and meetings. I will sit up in front at all times, and answer all questions if called upon. I will also meet with Mrs. Avery one hour each day, during two o'clock free time Monday through Friday, to have intense therapy. An infraction to any of the above will be considered a violation to this contract, resulting in immediate expulsion from this program."

CHAPTER TWENTY-FIVE

During Desire's first week of probation, she participated in all group meetings, all discussions. The one-on-one therapy with Mrs. Avery started off slow. One day Desire reached Mrs. Avery's office early, before the counselor had arrived. Desire was humming and singing her mother's song, when she noticed Mrs. Avery standing in the doorway. Desire had not sung that song for years, but as she was opening up about her past, many memories—good and bad—were coming back to her. When Mrs. Avery entered the room, Desire ceased singing the song. Mrs. Avery walked toward her desk and gave Desire a rare smile.

"Ms. Vera, I didn't know you had such a beautiful voice."

Desire eyed the ground, a little embarrassed.

"Oh, it's nothing, I just sing sometimes when I'm bored."

"What is the name of the song you were singing?"

"I don't know, it was just a song my mother sang to me when I was little," replied Desire.

"I thought you said you never met your mother?"

"Can we talk about this some other time, Mrs. Avery? I don't feel like talking about it right now."

Mrs. Avery changed the subject and went on with their therapy for that day. At the end of the hour, just as Desire was heading out the door, Mrs. Avery explained that she was taking the liberty of placing Desire in a mandatory social group. She opened her desk drawer and pulled out a piece of paper, wrote down Desire's name and signed her own. Desire had to join the choir, which met twice a week.

๙ ๙ ๙

The Visions Rehabilitation Choir was known throughout the community for their uplifting praise in song. The fifty or so members performed weekly at a community church. People from all over the world came to Harlem to hear them sing. All of the members were former addicts. They delivered an inspiring message through their own personal testimony on how God pulled them up out of their circumstances and saved them. Each week, Mrs. Avery selected two members, usually senior members, to give their testimony before the audience, followed by a song of their choice.

When Desire first entered the choir room, the members were already split into three sections. Mrs. Avery was standing in the middle, directing them.

"This way, Ms. Vera," Mrs. Avery said, pointing to a place near where she stood.

"Do you know 'The Lamb of God'?"

Desire nodded.

Mrs. Avery walked over to the pianist and whispered in his ear. He began playing. Desire hadn't sung in over two years. Her hands began to perspire as she looked around at all the choir members, who were staring at her. She decided to close her eyes, block everything out and concentrate on the music. She let the music take over and began singing. As if Desire had never left Bethel A.M.E. Church, or as if second nature had kicked in, she became engulfed with the Holy Ghost. She belted out the song, sending chills down the spines of every member in the room. The audience applauded, praised and stomped their feet at her rendition. At the end of the song, as if she were in a trance, Desire slowly opened her eyes and with surprise watched the room go wild for her. She glanced over at Mrs. Avery, who was clapping too.

During weekly rehearsals, Desire couldn't be happier as she reconnected with God through the gospel. The more she rehearsed, the more it reminded her of the days she spent in church with Hattie Mae and her sister, Tiah. Tiah and Carvelas continued to visit, filling Desire with hope as they described the three-story building they had purchased in the Bronx; Tiah had the top floor, Desire and Carvelas would have the second and they were searching for tenants for the first. Over the next few weeks, Desire and Mrs. Avery grew closer as Desire finally began telling her bits and pieces of her past. The more comfortable she became, the more she opened up. She even told Mrs. Avery her real name and what she used to do for a living.

In one session, as Desire looked at Mrs. Avery, she could have sworn that she saw a tear in the counselor's eye. Desire took a deep breath. She couldn't imagine what she had told Mrs. Avery that would make her so emotional.

Mrs. Avery approached Desire, caressed her hand and said, "I'm proud of you. I'm so proud of you. But you can't stop freeing yourself. I want you to give your testimony in church tomorrow."

"Do you think I can invite some people, Mrs. Avery? Please?"

Mrs. Avery paused a moment and then submitted. "Sure."

❧ ❧ ❧

When Desire and the rest of the choir came out of the dressing room, the auditorium was already filled to capacity. Dressed in matching burgundy and gold uniform gowns, the choir approached the pulpit. As they settled onstage, Desire scanned the audience. She smiled when she saw Tiah in the front row. Her smile widened when she saw, seated right next to her sister, Chanel. And just as she had begged Mrs. Avery to make it happen, Carvelas was seated at the piano. The only person missing was Hattie Mae.

The reverend stood behind the podium and welcomed all those in attendance. After a brief, fiery sermon, he introduced the Visions Rehabilitation Choir. Mrs. Avery stood up, centered herself in the middle of the choir and lifted her hands to cue the song. The performance was jubilant, and the entire room began to sing along. At the end of the song, the audience gave a rousing applause.

Mrs. Avery took the microphone and set it in the middle of

the aisle. "Hello, ladies and gentlemen, my name is Mrs. Avery, and I am the choir director of Visions Rehabilitation Choir." They responded with loud applause. She nodded and smiled, waiting until they finished. "Thank you, thank you. This portion of the program will focus on two of our members. I selected them to share a testimony of their life and how they overcame their circumstances. We do this for two reasons: to show you that no matter what happens in one's life, no matter what you go through, no matter how hard life gets, you can call on God. Amen. To see you through it no matter what. The second reason is, to purge oneself of all the pain, shame and secrets that can weigh you down. It's called 'freeing ourselves.' "

Mrs. Avery put the microphone back in the stand and returned to her place with the choir. She lifted both arms and the choir rose to their feet in unison. Carvelas started playing softly. Desire stepped forward, out in front of the choir. She walked nervously toward the center aisle, where the microphone stood. Desire scanned the hundreds of eyes upon her. She closed her eyes and asked God to give her strength, or a sign that she could do this. When she opened them, Carvelas had stopped playing and came to stand beside her. Suddenly all her fears and uncertainties faded away. She turned toward Mrs. Avery and smiled. Desire surveyed the crowd once again, and the words just suddenly came out.

"Hello, everybody. Please forgive me if I appear to be a little nervous, but I haven't been to church in a while. I'm not the kind of person to go around quoting scriptures from the Bible, but I find this one almost fitting. 'As a man thinketh in his heart, so is he.' Well, ladies and gentleman, I'm here to testify to you today that my entire life I had lies in my heart, so I became a liar. My name is not Desiree Vera. It is Desire Evans, and I'm the former lead singer of a group called Desire, Cream, and Dream. As a man thinketh in his heart, so is he. I had greed and envy in my heart. I've sold records and become famous, but today I am a homeless recovering drug addict who is HIV positive. I've been trapped all my life because I was a street girl and didn't want to accept who and what I was and covered it up with material things to be the person others wanted me to be. See, I was born in the street—and when I say 'born in the street,' I mean just that. My mother, who I never knew, was also a junkie, and she gave birth to me prematurely, right on 127th Street, on the sidewalk. She dragged me by her umbilical cord through the snow. I don't want to bad-mouth the woman who was my mother, because before I came to Visions I was exactly where she was, and now I understand. And I don't want to turn this into a pity party, so please, if you don't mind, lift your heads and help me free myself. The only thing I really remember about my mother was her voice as she sang a gospel song on an old cassette tape. I played that tape every night before I went to sleep, until it was embedded in my mind. Would y'all like to hear it?"

The audience applauded loudly.

"Trouble in my way, I have to cry sometime, so much trouble, I have to cry sometime, but I know that Jesus, Jesus He will fix it, my sweet Jesus, He will fix it after while, after while!"

Everyone in the church was shouting and jumping up by the time Desire sang the last verse, but to Desire it was as if they had all disappeared. She again spoke, letting God give her the words:

"I can't count the number of times I sang that song when trouble came my way. It was almost like my mother knew there was going to be trouble for me, and she was teaching me how to deal with it. Over the years I suffered in unimaginable ways, but I had no one to blame but myself after a certain point. I believed it was my destiny to suffer like my mother did—a family curse. The only way out of it was a lifetime of misery and a horrible death. I accepted my fate until a speaker named Pam came to Visions. She said something that, finally, made sense to me. Something that really stuck in my head. She said that I should only worry about the here and now, and that I would always be as sick as my secrets if I didn't release them. She told me that the only way to rid myself of this toxic shame that's been keeping me in bondage for so long was to get honest with myself and my God. Just for today, I choose life, and if it requires me to tell on myself to free myself from addiction, then so be it. As I thinketh, so I am, and my whole life I became the sum total of everything I thought I was, a no-good street girl. Over the years I learned to accept my curse, and I relished it. Then, at thirteen, my luck changed—the same person who saved me and my mother from freezing to death the night I was born, a lady named Hattie Mae, somehow found me and adopted me. Hattie Mae, or Grandma, loved me, y'all, more than she loved herself, and she was the first person to tell me something, something I never heard my entire life—that I was beautiful. I thought if I became rich and famous everyone would love me and I would be happy for the rest of my life. In my journey to get to the top, I hurt and used so many people. I hurt my family. I hurt friends. I hurt the ones who loved me the most. But out of all the things that happened to me in life, all the hurt I did to other people, nothing equals the hurt that I've done to myself.

I now know that before someone can find love in you, you have to have love for yourself. Today, ladies and gentleman, the person who stands before you is a lost little girl who's finally learning how to love herself. A girl who finally knows that being rich doesn't necessarily mean monetary wealth. One can be rich with family, rich with friends and rich with happiness."

Tears began to fall from Desire's eyes, and she stood proud and tall as she said, "I'm no longer ashamed of who I am. I can finally say that in my past I was a street girl, a street girl named Desire."

Everyone stood and applauded wildly, and Carvelas returned to the piano and began to play "Trouble in My Way." The booming voices of the choir filtered through the speakers, as if they had all clung to the song at one point in their lives too:

"Trouble in my way, I have to cry sometime, so much trouble, I have to cry sometime, but I know that Jesus, He will fix it, my sweet Jesus, He will fix it after while, after while!"

By the end of the song, Desire had the entire church on their feet, giving her a thunderous applause. When the church finally settled down, Desire walked back toward the choir. Mrs. Avery gave Desire a long hug and whispered, "Congratulations" into her ear. Desire received hugs from all the choir members.

Mrs. Avery then began to speak. "Ladies and gentleman, that's the good thing about praise and testimony, it can affect anyone at any time, even me. I too would like to free myself of secrets that have been haunting me for years. As long as I could remember, I was on one sort of drug or another. Finally, after God gave me the strength to beat my addiction, I vowed to help others who suffer from the agony of addiction, and that's the reason I became a drug counselor in the very place where I got clean over twenty years ago."

Emotion crept into the voice of the normally strong woman, whose throat became thick with tears. "I did have a child, a daughter, who I was unable to take care of, and the courts took her away from me. She was the joy of my life and was so beautiful. I remember I used to sing her this song when she couldn't sleep, the same song my mother used to sing to me when I was little. *'Trouble in my way, I have to cry sometime, so much trouble, I have to cry sometime, but I know that Jesus, He will fix it after while.'*"

Desire raised her head slowly as the familiar voice resounded loudly in her head. It was the exact song, the exact voice that she'd played thousands of times on an old cassette recorder.

"Mama?" was the only word Desire could muster, and she watched Mrs. Avery nod her head, tears streaming down her cheeks.

CHAPTER TWENTY-SIX

Fourteen months later, Desire graduated from the program with flying colors. When she was released, she moved in with her mother, Nika Avery. They spent every waking moment together, trying to make up for lost time.

One evening, they both were home, snuggled up on the couch, watching a movie.

"Hi, I'm Susan Hagan. Welcome to MTV's NewsFlash. It is reported that NBA superstar Sterling Rivers and R&B diva Annette Burwell have announced their engagement to wed this summer."

Desire immediately shut off the television and went to bed.

~ ~ ~

It was a Tuesday evening, and when Mrs. Avery arrived home from work, she called out for desire. She looked in Desire's bedroom, but she wasn't there. When she approached the bathroom, she could hear Desire coughing and throwing up. She rushed into the bathroom. She saw her daughter's frail and sickly body collapsed on the floor. Mrs. Avery helped Desire to her feet. She led her to the bedroom.

"Listen, baby, you need to get some medicine," a concerned Mrs. Avery said. "We are going to get dressed and go down to my doctor right now."

As Desire dressed, she asked her mother if she could call Carvelas to see if he would meet them at the doctor's office.

At the office, Mrs. Avery and Carvelas waited patiently. Finally, Desire limped toward them, the doctor by her side. There was nothing much else they could do, he told them, until the blood results came back. After her HIV status was confirmed, she would instantly qualify for Medicaid to get the costly medicine. The doctor then told them to come back in three business days for the results and he would give them a letter to expedite Desire's case. They thanked the doctor and headed home.

When they arrived at the doctor's office Friday evening, they told the receptionist they were there to see the doctor for test results. After waiting twenty minutes, they were called into the doctor's office.

"Her blood tests came back negative. All she had was a bad case of salmonella poisoning."

"But my daughter was told, she tested positive for HIV!" Mrs. Avery exclaimed. "Are you sure?"

"We're very thorough here, Mrs. Avery. Desire tested negative for HIV."

Mrs. Avery didn't want Desire to get false hope. "Listen, Desire, what we have to do is get ourselves another opinion."

Desire shook her head, still too shocked to speak.

"Wait. Desire, when you entered the program, you were supposed to take an HIV test. Did you take one?"

"Yes, but I never bothered to look at the results," Desire said.

When they got to Visions, Desire signed a release form to receive her medical papers. She was shaking so badly that her mother had to assist her in opening the folder. They flipped through each page until they got to the one they were looking for, and it was there in black and white: NEGATIVE FOR ALL HIV ANTIBODIES. Mother and daughter embraced, crying in each other's arms.

"Think backwards." Mrs. Avery folded her arms. "Desire, who was the doctor who conducted the blood tests?"

Desire called Dr. Wiggins's office, but got the runaround. She and Nika decided to pay the doctor a visit. They arrived at the doctor's office Monday morning. Since they did not have an appointment, the receptionist suggested that they make one and come back then. Desire decided to take the situation in her own hands and went straight toward the back of the offices. When Desire busted through the doctor's door, she saw him sitting at the his desk, counseling another patient.

The doctor stood up, and asked in a defiant manner, "What the hell is going on?"

Breathing heavily, Desire held the door open and ordered the patient to leave. "Get the fuck out of here."

The patient, a middle-aged white woman, looked into Desire's flaming red eyes and knew better than to challenge her order. She scurried out the door. The doctor stared at his patient's back as she ran out of the office without question.

"Now, Doctor," Desire said through gritted teeth, "Sterling Rivers was my fiancé, and we took our blood tests here over two years ago, and mine came back positive for HIV. Yesterday I found out my test results were negative. Can you explain this to me?"

The doctor's face turned red.

He adjusted his tie and lied, "I haven't a clue as to what you're talking about."

Desire's patience grew thin. "Well, maybe this will make you remember." Desire reached into her bag and pulled out a small gun. She reached over, grabbed the portly doctor's tie, and stuck the weapon in his face.

"Now, I ain't gonna repeat myself. Sterling Rivers was my fiancé, and we took our blood test here two years ago. Mine came back positive for HIV. Now today I find out that I was never HIV positive." Desire jerked his tie again, but this time she put the weapon in his mouth.

Nika stared at her daughter in horror and pleaded, "Desire, don't do it. Not like this, baby."

Desire wasn't backing down. "No, I'm sorry, Ma. My life got fucked up, and I almost died. I know Whip was behind all this shit."

The doctor nearly soiled his pants at the mention of Whip's name and began to whimper.

Desire pushed the weapon deeper down his throat and continued, "So either this motherfucker tells me something, or I'm blowing his fucking brains out right now!"

The doctor's eyes lit up, and he tried to speak. Barely audible with the steel in his mouth, he pleaded, "Okay, I'll tell you, I'll tell you!"

Desire pulled the gun from his mouth and he fell to the ground.

"It was Whip, Whip Daniels . . . he made me do it! He threatened me with violence; what was I to do? What was I to do?" he repeated.

Desire stared at him with disgust. He and Whip equally made her suffer in an unimaginable way all for the sake of revenge and money.

Desire felt her mother's hand on her shoulder. "Come on, it's over, baby."

Just as they were about to exit the room, the doctor blurted out, "Whip wasn't alone when he paid me to falsify the records." Desire and her mother stopped in their tracks and turned toward the doctor. "Sterling was with him; he was in on it too."

᠅ ᠅ ᠅

Tiah, Chanel, and Carvelas all met up at Desire's mother's house later that evening. Desire's friends were appalled by the doctor's story. They each recommended violent ways to get back at Whip.

"Why don't you simply go to the police?" suggested Nika.

They all looked at her like she was an alien.

"Mrs. Avery," Chanel said, "in the entertainment world, they call him Mr. Untouchable because every time he is charged with a crime, the charges are mysteriously dropped or he is found not guilty."

Suddenly, Desire had an idea.

≈   ≈   ≈

Desire and Tiah got to Junior's Restaurant in Brooklyn at about four thirty that evening. They walked to the rear of the restaurant and spotted the Camera Man.

"You got the money?" he asked.

Desire nodded. Tiah looked in her purse and pulled out an envelope.

"You got the tape?" Desire asked.

He reached inside his overcoat and tossed them a large, folded manila envelope. Desire attempted to grab the envelope, but the Camera Man grabbed her.

"That there is like opening Pandora's box. You sure you know what you're doing? You ain't fuckin' with no busboy. You make enemies with a person like Whip, and you got an enemy for life. If you fuck this up, and it gets back to me, you fucking with my life."

≈   ≈   ≈

Annette Burwell sat inside the sauna of an upscale salon and spa located in SoHo, when Tiah and Nika walked in.

"So what is it you do again?" asked Tiah, in the most pretentious voice she could conjure.

"Well," said Nika, "I'm the choir director of the VRC Mass Choir."

"Oh, yes, I've heard of you," Tiah said. "Your choir sings at all those celebrity weddings."

Annette lifted her towel off her head and peeked at the two women.

"So at whose wedding are you guys scheduled next?" asked Tiah.

The older woman blushed and said, "Well, I'm not at liberty to discuss my clients' business."

"Aw, come on, this is just between us two. I won't say anything."

Annette immediately pulled the towel back over her head to feign disinterest.

"Well, let's see," Mrs. Avery said as she lowered her voice. "I have Donald and his new bride in September; Russell and Kimora plan to renew their vows in October; and you won't believe this one . . ."

Annette snatched the towel off her head and introduced herself.

✿　✿　✿

Hundreds of cameras and media personalities from MTV were on hand to cover one of the biggest prewedding extravaganzas in the history of the sporting and entertainment world.

Never one to miss out on a dollar, Whip negotiated a deal with a television network to make the events leading up to the wedding and the ceremony itself into a reality show. The contract entailed exclusive, unlimited filming rights. They hinted to Whip that the more cinematic drama involved in the show, the higher the ratings. This suited Whip Daniels just fine, as he had something in store for the bitch of a bride who had been complaining about her deal with his record company.

The guests were having a good time at the gala. It was difficult for the waitstaff to get them seated for their five-course meal. When everyone was finally in their proper place, Whip stood and tapped his champagne glass. The room grew quiet and attentive as the guests turned their attention toward the long table where the bride, groom and their parents sat.

"At this moment, I'd like to propose a toast to the lovely bride and groom. I hold these two people dear in my heart. They are the most loving and perfect couple that I have ever had the privilege to meet. They are truly meant to be." Whip hugged his wife, who stood next to him. "May their marriage have the same love and happiness that I've enjoyed for eighteen years now."

Everyone in the audience melted as he and his wife kissed each other tenderly. Whip pulled a handkerchief from his pocket and wiped a crocodile tear from his eye.

"I'm also happy to announce that I and the staff at Central Booking Records have put together a video collage for the couple, from their climb to prominence to their journey into marital bliss. Of course, none of this could have been possible or more interesting without the help of their parents, who provided us with some never-before-seen and magnificent footage of when they both were preschoolers."

Carvelas's company was providing the technical support for the event. They were busy rigging up the lighting and sound systems. Carvelas himself was inside the technical booth, working feverishly to ensure that every wire, switch, and computer feed was operating properly.

After dinner, everyone anticipated the grand finale as the choir made their way to the stage. Above them hung a giant fifty-foot television monitor. Nika raised her hands slowly. The heavenly voices from the sopranos led, followed by the altos and tenors. The gospel hymns blended perfectly, and suddenly a powerful lead voice filtered through the speakers. As the unseen vocalist continued to sing, everyone clapped and nodded their pleasure at the divine angel's voice. A spotlight suddenly came on as the lead singer walked onto the stage. She wore a gown that resembled a Buddhist monk's, with a hood that hung completely over her face. She stopped directly in front of the bride and groom's table just as she completed the song. The crowd gave her a standing ovation. There was an eerie silence before the vocalist raised the microphone to her mouth and sang in a capella, *"God, don't like ugly, He's gonna make you pay, for what you have done to me, can't you see . . ."* In unison, the rest of the choir joined in the song. One by one, they walked off the stage, leaving behind the robed singer, who began to preach.

"Matthew 5:39 states, for your greatest enemies turn thy cheek. That was my grandmother Hattie Mae's favorite passage. But my favorite passage in the Bible is Romans 12:19, which states, 'Avenge not yourselves, beloved, but give place unto the wrath of God: for it is written, Vengeance belongeth unto me. Do not be overcome by evil but overcome evil with good.'" That was Carvelas's cue.

The mammoth television monitor came on, to the start of Annette's music video. *"In life, the dirt you dish out to others has a funny way of coming back to you . . . It's called KARMA!"*

Carvelas hit another switch and the video was replaced with a picture of Desire. The words underneath the photo read: "But when you mess with me, it's called *you done fucked up!*"

Desire lifted the hood off her head. Whip and Sterling stared at her in horror. However, their eyes were stolen away by the images on the large monitor before them. Whip's eyes lit up like a Christmas tree as he stared at himself on the screen in his underwear with a bedsheet tied around his neck. He was jumping on the bed yelling, "I'm Batman, I'm Batman."

"Turn it off," Whip screamed as he pointed at the screen.

The homemade movie continued. "Robin, where are you? Robin I want you to go in my bat hole!" Sterling Rivers came out of the bathroom wearing a supertight pair of red hot pants and high heels. "I think I can fill that order, Batman." They chased each other around the room, giggling and groping each other.

Sterling sat in his seat, defeated. His fiancée began crying and hitting him. Several cameramen took close up shots as reporters closed in for the inside scoop.

CHAPTER TWENTY-SEVEN

One year later, life was just beginning to get back to normal when Desire started receiving threatening phone calls. At first Desire and her mother paid them no mind, until two New York City detectives showed up at their door.

"What is this about?" Desire asked, worried that some long-forgotten part of her past had come back to haunt her.

One of the detectives, a tall, gruff-looking man, responded, "I'm Detective McCarthy and this is my partner, Detective Byrnes. Mrs. Evans, have you come in contact with one Lucious Jackson?"

Desire froze at the mention of the name.

Seeing the fear in her daughter's eyes, Mrs. Avery asked, "Desire, what's wrong? Who's Lucious Jackson?"

Detective Byrnes interrupted, "Ms. Evans, we understand you were a victim of Mr. Jackson on an attempted murder charge several years ago. You may know him by his street name—Lyfe?"

Hearing his name sent chills down Desire's spine. He was the one person that she ever feared because he got into her mind. Desire looked into the detective's eyes and nodded slowly.

"Mr. Jackson was paroled two weeks ago," Detective McCarthy said. He was silent for a moment before he continued. "Three days ago his codefendant who had signed a statement implicating him in your case was found murdered. We found evidence at the scene implicating Mr. Jackson and got a warrant for his arrest. We went to his last known address and found a picture of you with the words 'DIE BITCH' written across it."

Desire's heart started beating wildly. She knew what Lyfe was capable of.

"We also found a piece of paper in one of his coat pockets with your telephone number and address written on it. We can't locate him, but what we can do is take you downtown where you can fill out an order of protection."

"That won't stop him," Desire said, resigned to her fate.

"That's the best we can do."

"I'll have to think about it, detectives. I'm not sure what I'm going to do."

"Look, here are our cards," Detective Byrnes said, holding out the cards. Desire simply stood there, while her mother reached out and took them. "Call us if you hear anything."

⌐ ⌐ ⌐

Desire and her mother called the detectives daily to find out if Lyfe had been apprehended, but each time were told that there wasn't any progress on the case. After several weeks, Desire's anxiety faded and life once again returned to normal.

One evening, on her way home from a Narcotics Anonymous meeting, Desire called Tiah on her cell phone. "Where you at, Tiah? You were supposed to meet me at the meeting so we could look at my new apartment in Brooklyn."

"I know," said Tiah, but I got caught in rush-hour traffic. I'm ten minutes away. Get dressed so that when I get there we can bounce."

Desire sucked her teeth and teased her sister. "Now you rushing me?"

"Naw, I'm just tired, so meet me in front of your building in ten minutes, aiight?"

Desire smiled and said, "Aiight."

Inside her mother's building, Desire got off the elevator and fished through her purse for her keys. When she got to the apartment door she noticed it was ajar. Her first reaction was to run back to the elevator to get help, but all she could think of was her mother in the apartment. She slowly opened the door, peeked in, and called out to her mother. She eased slowly into the apartment, paused, and listened for any signs of movement. Hearing none, she proceeded to her mother's bedroom and opened the door. When she looked around the bedroom she noticed her mother's pocketbook and keys lying on the dresser. She suddenly heard the toilet flush.

Desire closed her eyes in relief. She walked out the bedroom, stood by the bathroom door and shouted, "Ma, why you didn't answer me when I called out? You scared me to death!" Desire tapped on the door and repeated, "Ma, you hear me?"

The toilet flushed again.

Fearing something wasn't right, she opened the door. Her heart skipped a beat when she saw her mother gagged and bound sitting on the toilet. Desire froze as she stared in her mother's terror-filled eyes. Nika mumbled through the masking tape that secured her mouth, snapping Desire out of her momentary paralysis. Desire's hands trembled as she removed the gag from her mother's mouth.

Nika took in a deep breath of air as she gasped, "He was here, Desire, and he said he's coming back for you."

Desire rapidly pulled off the remaining tape and rope as her mother continued.

"He kept saying over and over again how he's gonna get you back for fucking him over and for ruining his life."

They ran out the bathroom and Desire yelled to her mother to call the police.

She ran to the front door and secured all the locks before running back to her bedroom to get the pistol out of her purse. Desire wanted to get back to normal, but after the detectives' visit she decided she wasn't taking any chances and rarely left home without her gun.

Her mother yelled from the bedroom, "The phone's not working. I'm not getting any dial tone."

Desire ran to get her cell phone when they heard a knock at the door. Both mother and daughter froze as they stared at the front door unsure of what to do next. Desire looked at the pistol in her hand and at the cell phone in the other and slowly walked toward the door. Her mother ran to the kitchen and got a large knife and stood ready to do battle as Desire gingerly put her eye to the peep hole. Relief overcame her when she saw the profile of Tiah's face.

"It's Tiah, Ma."

As soon as Desire unlocked the door, Tiah's body was pushed into the apartment, knocking Desire to the ground, causing her to drop her pistol and cell phone.

Nika watched as the man who tied her up earlier brutally kicked her daughter in the face. With an eerie yell, Nika gritted her teeth, sprang into action, and charged her attacker. Nika caught the intruder off guard as she moved quickly. "You motherfucker!" she shrieked as she raised the knife high into the air.

But she was no match for the bullet that ripped through her shoulder.

Horrified, Desire watched it all go down as if it was a demented dream and stared at her mother writhing on the ground in pain, clutching her shoulder. Desire tried to shake herself out of her daze and looked around for the pistol but not before the intruder walked toward her and kicked it out of her reach. As the man hovered over her, Desire looked over at her mother, then at Tiah whose unconscious body lay next to hers, then she slowly turned her gaze toward the man who was about to take her life. Terror, fear, and shock coursed through her all at once as she stared into the eyes of an old acquaintance from her past—Lil Dollar.

He bent down and stared at her with a triumphant smile before he raised his gun and knocked her out cold.

When Desire finally came to, she felt a sharp pain in her head. She attempted to touch the bruise, but realized her hands were tied behind her back and she sat in a chair. She looked down and saw that her feet were also wrapped heavily with tape. As she gained her equilibrium, she looked around the living room and saw Tiah staring at her from across the room. Tiah was also bound and gagged and signaled with her eyes toward the corner of the room. Desire turned and saw her mother lying on the floor moaning and bleeding profusely. Everything rushed back to her as she looked back at Tiah and read the fear in her eyes. In a panic she tried to rip the tape off, but then she heard footsteps coming in their direction and ceased her fruitless struggle.

Lil Dollar walked in carrying a five-gallon can of gasoline. He smiled when he saw Desire had regained consciousness. "Miss Sleepy Head has finally awakened."

Desire watched helplessly as he unscrewed the cap on the gasoline can. Desire knew he was going to kill them, but she didn't know why, so she thought the best thing to do was speak to him calmly and reason with him.

"Dollar," she asked as he poured gasoline across the floor and furniture, "what are you doing, baby? Why you got us tied up like this?"

Amused, he continued to pour and replied, "Oh, I'm your baby now? I wasn't your fuckin baby when you dissed me for that bitch-ass NBA nigga."

"Dollar, I know this isn't about that nigga. You bigger than that."

He looked up at her and snarled, "You fuckin' right I'm bigger than that! I'm big enough to finish what the fuck you started." He approached her and got on his knees beside her and asked, "Did you know how much I loved you? I gave you everything you ever wanted and how do you repay me? By using me like a chump, by sabotaging my shine on the biggest night of my career so you and that bitch sister of yours could get ahead. That's right. Old Dollar ain't as stupid as you thought I was. I had a lot of time to put it together."

He paced around the room and began talking to himself as if he was fighting demons in his head. He then suddenly ran up to Desire and said, "Do you know how it feels to be a washed-up rapper? Niggas dissin you left and right, callin you a bum. You can't even go out anymore because everywhere you go niggas be tryin you, testin your manhood. The little jewelry a nigga had left he had to pawn or them young Brooklyn thundercats whipped my ass and took it." He chuckled and said, "Shit, I was the one doing that same shit to niggas when I was wildin. I had no more money, no more cars or jewelry."

He stared at Desire and said, "When you was with me, I spent thousands on you and when my shit ran out you jumped ship and went to the next nigga. Believe it or not, I dealt with you going to that nigga, but when my shit got salty and I tried to holla at a sister to let you know I'm the type that knows he fucked up and need to hold something, you ain't even tried to hear a nigga. I had to get a messenger job 'cause I'm broke and stinkin. Get mad stares from people because I'm riding the train just like them. It got so bad that I stopped coming outside anymore and became a prisoner in my grandmother's house, smoking weed and drinking Henny twenty-four-seven."

Desire tried to reason with him. "Listen, Dollar, I'm sorry for real. I was dead wrong. But check this out—I found out that

Whip has been cheating his artists for years and I started a class-action lawsuit against him and his company to get the money owed to us. We are talking millions of dollars."

Lil Dollar continued to shake out the gasoline, not paying her any mind and then dropped the can and began checking his pockets.

"Dollar," Desire shouted, "did you hear me? You may be getting back all the money he cheated you for!"

Lil Dollar had a sadistic and crazed look on his face as he shook his head and chuckled. "Ain't nobody getting no money."

Desire attempted to explain further, but he put his finger to her lips and said, "Shhh, don't talk. I took care of Whip and his boy, Sterling. Whip's not going to be doing much of anything ever again. Let's just say they met a similar fate as the one you're about to."

Confused, Desire looked at Tiah, who now had tears falling from her eyes. Desire began to beg for her life. "Dollar, please don't do this! I'm sorry for what I did to you. I'll make it up and give you anything you want, but don't do this to me. To them . . ." she pleaded, motioning toward her mother and sister.

He scowled at her and said, "You don't fuckin' get it! You dead and that's that."

Lil Dollar shook his head. "It's a shame you got to die 'cause even to this day, I never had a bitch sex me like you." He paused and smiled. He snapped out of it and searched his pockets for his lighter and then cursed when he couldn't find it. Without saying a word he walked out of the living room.

Desire knew he was going to the kitchen for matches and

began to work quickly. She took a deep breath and began to raise both her arms from behind her back. Her shoulder bones began to crack loudly as she gritted her teeth. At one time her double-jointed limbs earned her a lot of money; today they would save her life. She flipped both arms to her lap. Sweating and nervous, she looked toward the kitchen and began to work the tape off her arms and then her legs. Free, she stood up quickly and looked around the room for the pistol but when she heard Lil Dollar coming down the hall she quickly sat back down and put her arms back around the chair.

Lil Dollar entered the living room holding a fresh pack of matches. He smiled and said, "Aiight, bitch, get ready to die slow." His smile disappeared when he noticed unraveled tape behind Desire's chair.

Desire saw by the look in his eyes that she was busted and sprang into action. Lil Dollar quickly reached for his weapon in his waistband and pointed at her before she could reach him. Desire couldn't breathe as she stared down the barrel of the gun. Lil Dollar smirked at Desire, who threw her hands in the air, frightened for her life. "You think you could get over on a nigga like me, bitch? Just for that"—he grabbed her by the throat—"I'm gonna let you watch your mother and sister die before your eyes."

Desire shook her head and pleaded, "Please, Dollar, don't do this. They ain't got anything to do with—"

Lil Dollar slapped her across her cheekbone with the gun and said, "Shut the fuck up and watch your mama die first!"

He grabbed her by the hair and turned around, and when he did, a pistol was pointed directly in his face. Lil Dollar's eyes widened as he attempted to raise his gun, but Nika was quicker and squeezed off a round hitting him in the stomach, which gave Desire enough time to knock the weapon out of his hand. Stunned, Lil Dollar rushed Nika as she squeezed off two more rounds, missing him with both shots. Lil Dollar grabbed her wrist and they both fell to the ground, struggling for the weapon. Desire reached down quickly and grabbed his gun. She put it to his head and cocked the trigger, and with ice in her voice, threatened, "Move one more motherfuckin time and I'll blow your fuckin head off."

Lil Dollar complied as he removed his hands from Nika. Desire delivered a brutal blow across the back of his skull, which knocked him out. Breathing rapidly, she stood and spit on him, saying, "That's for shooting my mother, bitch!"

When Lil Dollar came to he found himself tied to a chair with all three women standing over him and Desire still pointing the gun at him.

He laughed. "I let three stick-ass bitches get the best of me." He chuckled again and said to Desire, "Why don't you pull that shit, bitch? I ain't afraid to die."

Desire aimed the gun at him and said, "I don't think so. That would be too easy. I'd rather see your ass rot in jail."

He smiled. "So that's your plan? Bitch, I was raised in prison. I can eat years like Chinese people eat rice."

"True, but did you ever do time as a washed-up rapper? If you think those young cats ain't feeling you on the streets, imagine how they gonna feel about you up north."

Lil Dollar looked at her as if she were insane. "Bitch, you think

I'm worried about them lil niggas? I'm an O.G., original gangsta. Shit, even if them niggas want to get it on, I got my Brooklyn Jamaican posse to hold me down and they straight killers."

Desire smirked and looked at Tiah. The two women began to laugh.

Curious, Lil Dollar asked, "Fuck is so funny?"

"You ever heard of the Denton Posse?" Desire asked.

Lil Dollar shook his head proudly. "Do I know them? Dems my niggas from Flatbush. Straight gangstas. Got the entire weed connect in Brooklyn on lock."

Desire looked him straight in the eye. "Did you know that Tiah is from Jamaica?"

Lil Dollar shrugged. "So?"

"Tiah, what's your full name?" Desire asked her.

"Juahtiah Denton," Tiah replied with a smile. She then walked over to her purse and pulled out her wallet. She pulled out a photo and showed it to Lil Dollar. His jaw tightened when he saw a picture of four men dressed in state-issued greens at a state correctional facility striking a jailhouse pose. He recognized each one as a member of the Denton Posse. Beads of sweat started to form on his forehead.

"Now do you think it's gonna be a party in prison when Tiah puts the word out that you tried to kill the Denton Posse's baby sister?"

They laughed at him chillingly. "Ma, go next door and call the police and tell them to pick up this piece of shit," Desire said.

Lil Dollar stared at them with dread, but he still had one more trick up his sleeve.

"I still remember what Hattie Mae said just before she died," he said slowly.

Everyone stopped moving when he said her name and stared at him.

Lil Dollar smiled wickedly as he continued in a southern accent. "She said, 'Please make sho' you tell my babies I'm sorry I didn't get ta say good-bye ta them before I left to see my Jesus.'" His eyes beamed as he watched them hang their heads in shame.

After a few moments, Desire, still uneasy, told her mother, "Ma, go make that call so we can get this nigga out of here."

As Nika proceeded to exit through the front door, Dollar blurted loudly, "I say again, that was the last thing she said"—his eyes narrowed—"right before I put the pillow over her face and smothered the life out of her old ass."

It was as if the world came to a halt. Nika closed the door without a word and turned around slowly. The three women looked at one another and knew exactly what needed to be done. There were some lessons from the streets that couldn't be forgotten.

Nika turned and locked each lock and walked into the living room and began to help the two girls move furniture out of the way. Lil Dollar looked at them confused but continued to enjoy every moment of their pain. Then they began taking off all their jewelry and putting it on the mantle. Desire walked to the kitchen and came back out with a sharp knife.

"Yeah, that's right, bitch. Cut my throat. Cut that shit deep," Lil Dollar said.

Desire put the knife to his throat, bent down, and whispered in his ear. "Naw, I'm not going to cut you just yet, but you do, however, got to answer to Hattie Mae."

Desire cut the tape from off Lil Dollar's wrists and legs and said, "Now it's time to get your back dirty, bitch!"

Desire showed him both guns and tossed them out the window. All three women began to swarm around him and told him to get up.

He ripped off the remaining tape and smiled at the women. "Showdown at the Ho-Kay Corral, huh?"

The smile was wiped off his face when Desire hit him in the eye with a straight right. When he felt his eye to see if she had drawn blood, he was hit by another right, this time from Tiah. When he turned toward her, Nika hit him from behind causing his eardrum to ring. They were relentless in their assault and pounced on him like killer bees, hitting and stinging him from all directions. Even when he caught one of them with his own blow, they took every one of his punches like troopers.

"You killed my grandmother, bitch?" *Whap!* "Take that!"

"How does it feel now, motherfucker?" *Whap!*

"Don't bleed now, nigga! Fight back!" *Whap! Whap!*

"You done fucked with the wrong bitches!" *Whap! Whap! Whap!*

"What now, nigga? What?" *Whap!*

They beat Lil Dollar without mercy for nearly forty minutes. Tiah and Nika looked at Desire and gestured for her to end it all. Desire centered herself in front of Lil Dollar, pulled back her right arm, and gave him a crushing blow to his face with her elbow. He fell back, his head thudding loudly against the floor.

Desire looked down at Lil Dollar's still body, then at the blood on the floor and on her fists, and suddenly began to get emotional. "It was all my fault she died," Desire moaned. "If I had been there when she wanted me to be, she would still be here."

Her mother approached her and lifted Desire's chin until she was looking into her eyes. "Desire, it's not your fault. Hattie Mae told me a long time ago that before you came into her life, she had no reason to live because she had nothing. But when you came along"—Nika smiled as she gently touched the wounds on her daughter's face—"she felt that God gave her a purpose to live again."

Nika grabbed Tiah's hand. "And I bet that when you came back into her life, and brought Tiah along, you girls added even more years to her life." Nika looked at both girls and smiled. "If there was one thing Hattie Mae would have wanted, what would it have been?"

The girls didn't have to think long as they said in unison, "For us to be a family."

Desire knew her mother was right as she closed her eyes and felt the warm embrace of the two people she loved the most and realized that, at last, she finally had a complete family.

Desire snuggled in their arms, never wanting the moment to end.

Seconds later, from the corner of her eye, Desire saw a movement, then a rising shadow. As if it was a slow-moving nightmare, she watched in horror as Lil Dollar rose to his feet, sneering at the three women. Neither Tiah nor Nika saw him stand up. Desire got in front of her mother and sister and yelled, "Stay behind me. I got this."

Desire and Dollar stood face-to-face. With his chest heaving heavily and a vengeful look on his face, Dollar spat clots from his bloodied mouth. Then Desire watched the movement of his jaw and the probing of his mouth. She knew and expected what came next. In a flash, Desire saw a thin piece of metal fly from his mouth and into his hand. Fear was no longer an option. She reacted with equal speed and precision, spitting a razor from her mouth as well. Razors in hand, they went on the attack, raising the lethal blades high in the air, almost simultaneously. Desire was lightning quick, delivering a lethal gash across Lil Dollar's throat.

CHAPTER TWENTY-EIGHT

It was four years later, and Desire was now a college graduate and a caseworker for ACS. Her relationship with her sister, Tiah, was back on track and she and Chanel had even become friends. She and Carvelas were even growing closer again, and though she now realized that she loved him more than life itself, he was still afraid to make any long-term commitment because of their erratic past. She was okay with his indecision and didn't blame him. She was just extremely happy to have him in her life. On the surface, everything seemed perfect but for some reason something deep within her made her feel that something was missing.

Desire was on the A train on her way to work that morning when she suddenly began to think of Hattie Mae and something she had told her years ago. "You got to remember Desire; you are a prophet, a godsend, a miracle, which was put on this earth for a purpose. God anointed you with a gift to spread His good word through gospel to save souls high and low. You got to allow God to use you or you will forever be going against the grain and will never feel complete." Suddenly everything began to make perfect sense. Desire was so involved in her thoughts that she nearly missed her stop and rushed out just as the door closed. When she got to work, she walked straight into her supervisor's office and turned in her resignation with a smile. Desire immediately placed a three-way call to both Tiah and Chanel. When she explained to them that she just quit her job, they both called her crazy. But then she told them what Hattie Mae had said to her years ago and what she planned. To her surprise, they supported her decision and said they would join her. After that, Desire began to contact old connections she still knew from her heydays and started putting her plan into action.

Desire, Cream, and Dream was no longer an appropriate name for their new direction so they decided to call themselves the DCD Gospel singers. DCD was an instant sensation, and the buzz about them was so great that they went on a thirty-one city national Gospel Fest tour, performing with some of the biggest names in the industry.

After three months on the road, DCD was scheduled to end the tour with a sold-out performance in their hometown at Madison Square Garden. Desire invited everyone including her mother, former coworkers, and every single staff and client from Visions Rehabilitation Center. Desire also invited Carvelas and gave him tickets for his parents.

The night of the performance, Carvelas was anxious to spend time with Desire, whom he hadn't seen in months. While Desire was on tour, they spoke on the telephone several times a day. The passion and romance between them had been rekindled and they vowed to make the relationship work this time around. After Carvelas and his parents found their seats, he decided to go and visit Desire in her dressing room. Since Carvelas's union was working the show that night, he had no trouble gaining access back stage. He wanted to surprise her by proposing and asking for her hand in marriage. He walked toward her dressing room, beaming as he felt the tiny velvet box in his pocket. As he approached her room, he stopped in his tracks when he noticed a very tall and handsome man holding Desire's hand while they spoke by her dressing room. Desire appeared to be rubbing his hand and fingers affectionately. Peering at them from a distance, Carvelas was stunned.

The stage manager walked toward Desire and told her, "Ten minutes till stage time, Ms. Evans." Carvelas went numb and eyed the floor, unsure of what to do next. When he finally looked up, he saw the man look around and place something in Desire's hand. She looked at the contents in her hand and nodded to him. Carvelas felt his heart break all over again and cursed himself for once again being a fool. This was the last time he was going to let Desire play him for a sucker. Carvelas reached into his pocket and pulled out the ring box, tossing it in the garbage can.

Desire, Tiah, and Chanel had the entire crowd on their feet as they sang their first hit gospel single entitled "Hattie Mae's Song," which had been written and arranged by Nika. Carvelas sat through the concert for his parents' sake but planned to leave as soon as they finished the performance. He vowed never to see Desire again.

After DCD finished the song, the lights went down to a blue hue and Desire asked the audience if she could take time to give them a testimony. In unison, the crowd expressed their approval by shouting and clapping loudly. Chanel and Tiah took to the background and began to sing in a soothing harmony as Desire took center stage.

"Tonight, ladies and gentlemen, I want to talk to you about love." Everyone suddenly began to whoop and clap. "And I ain't talking about the kinda love that you can see, I'm talking 'bout the kinda love that you can feel in your heart, feel in your soul, feel in your spirit!" The crowd clapped loudly. "But tell me this, y'all. What happens if all your life you were so shallow that you couldn't feel it in your heart because you were heartless, couldn't feel it in your soul because you were soulless, or feel it in your spirit because you were spiritless? I'm talking about myself. I didn't know how to love, y'all.

"I know this may sound cliché, but all my life I've looked for love in all the wrong places. I looked for love in fame and fortune and all I found was pain and sorrow. I looked for love in the flesh and when it as all over, I found pain and sorrow. And then I looked for love in drugs and alcohol and all I found was pain and sorrow to the tenth degree. The Devil is busy, y'all, because where there's no God, there is no peace. Amen."

There was a thunderous applause.

"The truth of the matter was I didn't love myself, and if I didn't love myself how the hell could I say I love God, who made me? No God, no peace. Amen."

Everyone repeated, "No God, no peace. Amen."

"It wasn't until I fell to my knees and claimed the blood of Jesus and begged God to deliver me from looking for love in all the wrong places, deliver me from the lust of the flesh, Amen, deliver me from the drugs, the alcohol, oh Lord and deliver unto You oh, Lord, so I can know You, Lord, so I can know You, Jesus, so I can walk the path that's right. Oh Lord! So I can know what true love is." Desire worked the crowd to a frenzy of tears and praise were shouted throughout the arena. Desire herself was in tears as she said, "But ladies and gentlemen, I would like you to know one thing." The arena went silent as they hung on to her every word. "Because of His grace . . ." A huge sign lowered from above, which said:

"I K-N-O-W GOD AND I NOW K-N-O-W PEACE!"

The entire arena was on their feet applauding, yelling, crying, and praising God. Desire paused for several minutes until she was able to continue. "Not until I was in my dressing room talking to a beautiful, beautiful friend of mine did I realize what real love was about and what I had to do." Carvelas shifted around in his seat. He grew uneasy and decided to skip the rest of the performance. He whispered to his parents that he had some emergency work to do for his job and he would call them later. He stood up to leave.

Desire continued, "It's funny how in life you can search your whole life over to find love and happiness and everything that you ever needed was right there in front of you all the time." Desire suddenly searched the crowd and blurted out to the audience,

"Carvelas Vera, where are you?" Carvelas had just reached the aisle when he heard his name and turned around.

Carvelas's father stood up proudly and pointed. "Carvelas is right there."

Desire searched the audience and asked, "Carvelas, is that you? Oh, there he is." A spotlight fell on Carvelas as he stood there frozen. Desire began to walk off the stage toward him and said, "Ladies and gentlemen, this is Carvelas Vera." There was a loud applause. "And we've known each other since we were eleven years old. I remember the first time this beautiful man came to my rescue—it was at a high school prom." She turned toward the stage and said, "You remember that, Tiah and Chanel." They both chuckled as they nodded their heads. "Well, back then I considered myself an ugly duckling and the only person who wanted to take a person like me was Carvelas." The women in the crowd melted.

"See, Carvelas saw the beauty in me when nobody, including myself, saw it in me. He spent a lot of money on the prom that night and all he wanted in return was the last dance to a song by Lenny Williams, the same song his parents danced to when they fell in love with each other. I agreed. Anyway, the strangest thing happened the night of the prom: I got dressed up for the first time in my life and I no longer looked like that ugly duckling I thought I was, and all the boys at the prom thought so too. All the boys were suddenly showing me all this attention that night, including the most popular boy in the school, who asked me for a dance. I danced with him the rest of the night until it ended, never giving Carvelas his dance." Desire took Carvelas by the hand and led him toward the stage when the song by Lenny

Williams came on. When they got on stage Desire embraced Carvelas as they danced slowly to the song.

"Even after that he stood behind me through everything you can imagine." Carvelas was uncomfortable at the thousands upon thousand of eyes that were upon him. Desire continued, "And all the while I didn't do nothing but take advantage of him when he showed me love because I was always on my high horse." Desire and Carvelas were face-to-face as she took him by the hand and said, "I used to think that you had to get to the highest mountain in order to see the truth." Desire slowly got on her knees, never losing eye contact with Carvelas, and said, "but people like me, we have to get to our lowest of lows."

Desire pulled out a small velvet box and opened it and said, "Carvelas Vera, you stood by me time and time again. You believed in me when I didn't believe in myself. You loved me even when I didn't love myself. And I promise that I will spend the rest of my life giving you all the love you deserve. Carvelas Vera, will you marry me?"

On stage, Chanel and Tiah hugged each other and smiled through their tears. They, along with everyone else in the arena, held their breath as they awaited Carvelas's answer, which seemed to be taking a long time.

Carvelas looked down at Desire, caressed her face, and got down on one knee to look her directly in the eye.

"I thought you'd never ask."

CHAPTER TWENTY-NINE

One year later, Desire and Carvelas were on their way home to Harlem from a weeklong honeymoon in Cancun, Mexico. They were in a cab and Desire was talking about how happy she was to be home when she noticed that Carvelas's attention was elsewhere as he stared at someone or something on the street.

Desire turned to where he was looking and tapped him and said jokingly, "You better not be looking at another woman because you're a married man now." She held up her ring finger.

Out of his fog, Carvelas smiled and said, "Naw, I ain't looking at no woman; you are my only eye candy." He looked back once again, put on a faint smile, and said, "But listen, I got something real important I got to do and it ain't gonna take but a minute." He looked at the driver and yelled, "Cabbie, let me out on the corner here."

Desire was surprised by his abrupt need to exit the cab and questioned him. "Carvelas, what's wrong? You want me to come with you?"

"Listen, I got something to take care of real quick." He reached in his pocket, gave Desire cab fare, and said, "Just tell the driver to take out the luggage and wait for me in front of the building." He caressed her face, gave her a light kiss, opened the cab door, and walked quickly down the block. Desire watched him from the window as he walked through traffic.

Carvelas stood silently in the doorway of a building for nearly twenty minutes as he watched from across the street while two men completed a drug transaction. Both men then went their separate ways. That's when Carvelas stared into the face of a man he hadn't seen in years—Lyfe. At that moment Lyfe looked around cautiously and made his way to his building up the block, oblivious to the fact that he was being hunted. When he got half way up the block Carvelas made his move as he followed him to the building with a two-by-four behind his back.

ACKNOWLEDGMENTS

To God, who continues to carry me from internal darkness and into the everlasting light. Continue to use me as you see fit, and I will continue to warn others of the consequences of their actions.

To my four beautiful children, Steven (the handsome baller), Treasure (America's next top model), Trevor (the pretty boy genius), and Justice (the future heartbreaker). Thank you for being the motivation in my life and giving me the strength to do what I do. Daddy loves you!

To my sisters and brother, what can I say? I guess I'm never going to live up to your high expectations.

To the entire Sellers family in Maryland and D.C., y'all might as well change my name to Treasure E. Sellers the way you guys took care of me and accepted me in your family. Carvelas, I gained another brother in you and I will forever—forever, black man—be fiercely loyal to you and your family through hell and high water. Dolly, in that brief time we had together you gave me a mother's love, something that I hadn't had in years. I could never repay you for what your family so freely gave me. My sister Tiah, we have the perfect brother-and-sister relationship; we yell and scream at each other one day, love each other the next. Thank you for not being a punk, and for telling me the truth about myself when necessary. Love you.

To Liza, you are the sweetest person I know and you prove this to me over and over again with your actions. You have always been there for me whenever I needed you, and would ride or die for me if I asked you to. You are truly the best girl I never had. Love you.

To the mothers of my children: Nichele Gadson, Kimberly George, and Sandra Vera, I know we haven't always seen eye to eye, and I'm sure I caused you plenty of hardship and pain. I have no excuses. I can, however, assure you that I'm no longer the cold-hearted person I once was and have suffered a great deal to get where I am today. The change is very evident in this open statement, admitting my wrongs for all to see. Once upon a time you fine ladies loved me unconditionally, but I was unable to love you back the same way and it's my loss. You all did a tremendous job raising my children to become the fine individuals they are today and I'm truly thankful. I'm not asking for a sudden change of heart, but with my deeds and actions, I pray that in time you'll find it in your hearts to forgive a wretch like me.

To Ms. Nakea Murray, you know you had to be among the first. Thank you for absolutely everything. There are not enough words in the English language for me to say what I really feel about you. But the closest words I can conjure are "A TRUE FRIEND," and I thank God that I have a person like you in my life who doesn't want anything from me but success. I said it before and I'll say it again: All you Pretty Ricky's and all you Gooches better beware, 'cause she got too many brothers! Passion, stay beautiful.

To all the people at Random House who showed me it's not always all about business, but personal growth and understanding: Jane von Mehren, Kim Hovey, Lisa Barnes, Brian McLendon, Crystal Velasquez, and Thomas Wengelewski.

I would especially like to thank the beautiful Ms. Melody Guy. It still amazes me to know that there are people like you who can understand and trust in someone even though he couldn't trust himself. When I felt down and out, your gentle, kind words gave me the strength to get up and plod on. I can't thank you enough for being not just my senior editor, but a proven friend. I thank you. To Danielle Durkin, thanks for all the little notes of encouragement. They meant a lot. I would also like to thank Dreu Pennington-McNeil for reading my mind and giving me such a perfect cover.

To my agent, the unstoppable Ms. Tracy Sherrod, a smile is on my face right now as I think of your wonderful smile and your contagious laugh. But I'm not fooled by your cute face and smile because I know you are a strong business woman. You shared things with me in confidence that made a world of difference to my understanding of not only this business, but life. Thanks for being strong and assuring and unafraid to tell me how it really is. Thank you, Ms. Sherrod.

This section is for my closest friends in this book industry. Thanks for the many conversations we had and I look forward to politicking with you all soon.

To Hickson, my Harlem homedude, and one of the closest and realest cats that I know. Thanks for the countless discussions we had, both business and personal, but most of all thank you for allowing me to be me—good, bad, or indifferent. To Brandon McCalla, now, you already know what it is. Yo, me and you rode together in this business and have been down ever since. We saw each other through all our women drama, business drama, and every other drama in between, and continue to do so. You are the single most underrated writer I know, but your time is coming real soon, trust me!

To Kashuan, you are my baby, for real. You also stood by me no matter what and checked me hard when I needed it. I want you in my life forever because you truly got my back no matter what! Peace to your beautiful family; to your sister, Queen Pen; your mother; and your cousin in North Carolina, Carol, who showed me love.

To Ms. Teri Woods, I'm honored to be your friend and even more honored to know a down-to-earth person like yourself. You were right about everything you told me regarding this business. Thank you for showing me how to absorb this sometimes overwhelming industry. Forever loyal!

To Tu-Shonda Whitaker and my homegirl Danielle Santiago, I'm proud to be part of your world and happy to know two of the literary geniuses of our generation. Brother James, in N.C., thanks, baby! Brother Zaire in Philly, peace!

To Deshuan Taylor, the ultimate hustler, you know I had to put you in a class by yourself. You are one of only two people I met who can hustle hard like ya boy! See you in the Millionaire Boys Club.

To the other person in this business who can keep up with my hustle, Richard Jenty. Congratulations on your baby girl; I'm proud of you. To my homedude Kwan, yo, you my dude for real and thanks for always keeping it gangsta and grimey, just the way we do it. To Anthony Whyte, Mark Anthony, Eric Gray, Shannon Holmes, Leondrei Prince, Al-Sidiq Banks, Therone Shellman, K. Elliot, and JoJo, certified hustlers in this game, make money!

To my mentors, Ms. Nikki Turner and Ms. Ebony Stroman, thank you both for inspiring me and showing me that I could become an author. I can't thank you enough. Kiki Swinson, when you gonna stop playing around and come on and become Mrs. KiKi Blue? To Anna J., if I ever want to know the truth about something or myself all I gotta do is call you because you would tell me just that—the truth, even if it hurts. Kashamba Williams, the female Trump. Dwayne Murray, I'm so proud of you and your beautiful wife, Angela. T.N. Baker, Kavan Brown, Azarel, T. Styles, Lady Sha, my protégée Jasmine—Harlem here! The female hustler Yazmine, keep doing the do!

To Patrice and Turtle, the Bonnie and Clyde of Brooklyn. Thanks for being the good people you are and staying my friends. Give your beautiful girls a kiss for me. Love y'all always. Lil Dollar, you about to blow up!

To Norma (I know you smiling). Thanks for everything and showing me love from the very beginning when I entered into this business. Good luck in your promo business and tell The Whispers

Treasure said whud up! Adrianne from Newark, you think I forgot you, boo? Thanks for the constant unwavering love you have shown me over the years. I love you for that and I'll never forget you. See you soon.

To the Marsh family, also in Newark. Thank you for accepting me and showing me love with all the home-cooked dinners and cookouts. Andrea, you still got my heart on lock and I'll always will be there when you need me.

To Mother Montrose, Ms. Hemmingway, Ms. Adorno, and Mr. Shaw, thanks for all the good work you do for so many soldiers. It doesn't go unnoticed. Larry, Glennsy, Michelle, Yvonne, Ms. Shirley, and Anthony, thank you all for the many conversations you endured. To Ms. Wright, thanks for being understanding of my plight; I learned a lot from you. To Benny and all the staff in the PTSD unit, thanks for screwing my head back on. To my dude Omar Muhammad, thanks for saying out loud what most people are too afraid to say. Stay real.

To my good friend Rodney Williams from Yonkers, thanks and I look forward to us hooking up in the future. To Joe Prelli, my buddy from the beginning. We went through a lot and are still standing. Thanks. To John Wiggins from Jersey City, holla at ya boy. Big Chalae, it ain't over. Big Keith and Chris. Big T, thought I forgot?

To *Don Diva* magazine for informing the street on what it really is. Thank you for supporting me.

To Black Star Videos, you brothers are pioneers and about your business. When you were at your other spot uptown, you were the first people who took my book, and many other people's products for that matter, and gave us a chance. Continue to build your empire and I will always be there to support you.

To the staff at Hue-Man Bookstore & Cafe, my home base, all I can say is thank you for everything you do for me. And finally, thanks to Karibu Books for always supporting me and having signings in your store.

ABOUT THE AUTHOR

TREASURE E. BLUE was born and raised in Harlem. He formerly worked with the New York Fire Department as a supervising fire inspector in the Bronx. He now devotes himself full-time to writing and promoting his novels.